THE UNPICKING

DONNA MOORE

First published October 2023 by Fly on the Wall Press
Published in the UK by
Fly on the Wall Press
56 High Lea Rd
New Mills
Derbyshire
SK22 3DP

www.flyonthewallpress.co.uk
ISBN: 9781915789051
Copyright Donna Moore © 2023

A CIP Catalogue record for this book is available from the British Library.

To my mum, Joyce, and my grandmothers,
Floss and Betsy.

THE BIRDCAGE

PROLOGUE

It has been months since my last entry, dear Journal. I am ashamed by my lack of industry, but I have had much on my mind. The death of my dear parents affected me greatly and I did not have the strength to write. Aunt Evelina's insistence that I close up Eastdene Manor and move in with her in Clifton was something I did not welcome. Bristol is such a short distance away from Eastdene in miles but...oh...the dust and the crowds and the noise and the bustle. It was so utterly overwhelming and I spent goodness knows how many weeks and months in my room, unable to do anything for myself.

Aunt Evelina was so kind. She decorated the room in my favourite colours and with all my precious things from home and offered to take me out in the carriage on visits here and there, but I simply couldn't. She even tried to tempt me out of my room with sweetmeats and other treats, as though I were her shy pet rabbit. I must have worried her terribly.

In the end, I am glad I did not have the strength to resist Aunt Evelina. Bristol brought me something so wonderful that I still cannot believe it! I am married! Even saying the words makes my heart flutter so. And you, dear Journal – although it is doubtless silly of me to refer to an inanimate object like that – are the first I have even whispered that sentence to out loud. Yes, the thoughtless, carefree child that was Lillias Gilfillan is no more. She has been replaced by Mrs Lillias Strang – mistress of a home, possessor of a set of keys so enormous it is a chore to lift them, and cherished wife and helpmeet of the kindest of men. But, I get ahead of myself and must tell this properly.

I am so happy that I let Aunt Evelina persuade me to attend Lady Summerscale's ball – my very first one, in fact. I had not wanted to go, and almost…almost…pleaded a sick headache, but I could tell that Aunt Evelina was beginning to despair of my recovery and, after chiding myself for my ungraciousness, I pulled myself together and called for the maid to help me dress.

A steady stream of broughams and landaus was arriving at Summerscale Hall at the same time as ours and we were conducted upstairs with a flurry of other ladies to the dressing room set aside for us, where a smiling maid helped me to rearrange my dress and added a pin or two to my hair. As we made our way back down the grand staircase, with its balustrades festooned with evergreens, flowers and swathes of gauze, Aunt Evelina and I headed for the refreshments room. Tea, lemonade, bonbons, iced sherbet, lavender biscuits, Florentines, ginger buns and brandy snaps were beautifully displayed. For the first time in a long while I felt hungry and I'm sure that pleased Aunt Evelina. Then we headed for the ballroom. Yes! Lady Clara Summerscale has her very own ballroom. Not for her the need to draw a cloth over the carpets and remove the furniture in the drawing room. Instead, the polished floor, smelling faintly of warm honey, reflected the light from the flickering globes hung at frequent intervals on the pale-yellow walls. The drapes, too, were yellow and the overall result was warm and welcoming, despite the large size of the room. At the top of the room, the musicians – a piano, a violin, a cornet and a violoncello – entertained the assembled throng. Aunt Evelina led me to a quiet corner where we sat on a cane bench and gazed about us.

Elegant crowds ebbed and flowed around us, dancing, laughing, conversing. The ladies were dressed in dazzling shades of crimson, cerulean, magenta and emerald and I felt like an insubstantial wraith in my grey half-mourning, and then immediately felt guilty for the thought.

My heart had no sooner calmed itself when Lady Clara came over and bent her head to mine. "My dear Miss Gilfillan," she said, "Please allow me to introduce Mr Arthur Strang, a very fine gentleman of my acquaintance." I'm sure that I blushed as he bowed low over my hand and then turned to Aunt Evelina. As the band struck up a quadrille, Lady Clara took my dance card and filled in Mr Strang's name. I shook my head in mortification, but Lady Clara insisted. I looked at Aunt Evelina who frowned and seemed about to say no, but even she found it impossible to resist Lady Clara. And, oh, I'm so glad she did!

The quadrille is a sociable dance and, as the demands of the dance separated and then returned us to each other, we positively bubbled with conversation. We discovered a shared love of nature, poetry and art. By the end of the dance, it was as though we had known each other for months instead of mere minutes. As Arthur returned me to my seat, Lady Clara laughingly snatched my dance card from me and filled every space with Arthur's name, despite my protestations. "It is *my* ball, and so *I* will say what is and isn't proper." I could tell that Aunt Evelina was not happy, but what was she to do?

So Arthur and I advanced and promenaded and turned and chassezed our way through two waltzes, a polka, a mazurka, another quadrille, a Caledonian and a jovial and energetic Virginia Reel that left me breathless and, doubtless, pink-cheeked. At the supper intermission Lady Clara spirited Aunt Evelina away to meet an elderly widow of her acquaintance and Arthur and I continued to share our hopes and dreams over tiny morsels of tongue and guinea fowl, trifle and tipsy-cake. Oh, dear Journal, after the death of my parents I feared that I would never be happy again, and here I was, having the happiest evening of my life.

I don't know what I would have done without Arthur. He put it so poetically, saying that mother's death, coming so soon after father's, had left me like a little boat that had lost its oars and was drifting on a stormy sea. I told him that he could be a rival to Lord Byron, but he simply laughed, in that self-effacing way of his, and lifted my hand to his lips, saying that he wanted to be my oars. He said it so shyly that I think I must have fallen in love with him there and then.

Aunt Evelina was not pleased. She felt that our courtship was too rushed, and I too young, and a target for men who are in pursuit of my inheritance. As a result, she took against Arthur with no just cause. Arthur persuaded me that many girls get married even before they are sixteen. He told me I am my own person and that my inheritance is mine alone — I have the right to do with it as I wish, and that Aunt Evelina is a bitter old spinster. I laughed a little at that and then immediately felt guilty. She has been so kind to me, after all.

Arthur wanted us to marry straight away, since he had to return to business in Scotland and couldn't bear to be parted from me. He is so romantic, hiring a carriage and spiriting me away like that. We married en route — a small ceremony, but Arthur says we will have a big celebration on our first anniversary and invite all our friends. But no Aunt Evelina, he says!

Yes, Ardellen House is now our very own home. Luckily, Arthur knew it was for sale but wanted to wait until some money that he is expecting was released, but I insisted and Arthur finally laughed at my stubbornness and gave in. I was so happy to give him the money. I haven't seen the house yet, of course, since we are spending a few days here in Gretna, but Arthur says it is a beautiful home and that I will be happy there. He says I am still too sad, sometimes, dwelling on the loss of my parents, and that I have him now, and must be happy. And he is right! How could I be lonely and sad, when I have him?

Speaking of Arthur, here is the dear man now. We are soon to set off for our new home, dear Journal, and I will write more there.

Ardellen House, Stirlingshire, 29th September 1877

"Are we nearly there, Arthur?" Lillias was tired but excited. The last few weeks had been exhausting and stressful, secretly and feverishly planning the elopement with the assistance of Lady Clara, lying to Aunt Evelina and dealing, for the first time, with her own finances. Added to which, they had been travelling from Gretna for the last two days and her bones ached from the constant bumping and rattling of the carriage on the rough country lanes. She wanted to get to her new home – a home which had cost them a vast sum of money and which she had not yet seen. Lady Clara had advised her that living in lodgings wasn't the way for a young couple to start married life.

Arthur smiled at her lovingly and rested his gloved hand on her own. "Not long now, my little goldfinch. You will love it and, once we're settled in, we'll have a big dinner party to celebrate our wedding."

"We haven't seen any other house for miles. I do hope I won't be lonely."

Arthur kissed the top of her head, smoothing her hair. "I told you, you'll soon make friends, you'll see. And we'll invite Lady Clara as our guest of honour to thank her for bringing us together, so you'll have a good friend there."

"And Aunt Evelina?"

Arthur glanced out of the window as the horses slowed. "Look, we're almost home." They turned into a sweeping driveway, curving to the right. After another half mile, the silvery-white trunks of the birch trees opened out to reveal the house, square and solid and as though it knew its place in the world. Trees and house alike were sparkling in the midday frost and the sun shone off the windows, rendering them an impenetrable gold. The house would be even more splendid in a couple of months, when the birches were covered in their brown winter catkins. Each season would dress the house in new garb.

"Oh! It's beautiful!" Lillias almost couldn't breathe, so strong was the joy that overtook her.

"There, I told you, goldfinch." Arthur opened the door of the carriage and breathed in deeply. "Ah, that air smells so crisp and fresh. It was dreadfully cramped in Bristol; it feels good to have space to breathe." He put out a hand to help her out of the carriage, lifting her slight frame and twirling her in the air before placing her gently back on the ground. "We're surrounded by magnificent countryside. You need fresh air and good, long walks to bring some colour into your cheeks."

"Just like yours?" Lillias laughed and gently pushed him away. "It's not fashionable for a young lady to be brown as a nut and ruddy-cheeked, although I wish I could be as free and energetic and vital as you." She took off one of her grey kid gloves and reached up to smooth his unruly light-brown hair, which was fast becoming a tangle of curls in the brisk Scottish wind. She lifted her fingers to her nose and inhaled the scents of sage and orange left by his pomade.

He swept her into his arms and strode towards the door. "Come along, Mrs Strang, let's investigate our new domain, like the lord and lady of the manor that we are." He kicked open the door and deposited her in the hallway, holding her shoulders and turning her slowly in a circle. Gas lamps lit the space, flickering on the warm, dark wood of the doors and staircase. The tiles under their feet were a hypnotic geometric design in shades of blue, terracotta and white.

The decoration in the house was dark and gloomy and Lillias excitedly voiced her plans to make it lighter and brighter as Arthur flung open the doors of room after room. "Arthur, we're going to rattle around in this place!"

"I doubt we'll be alone for long, my dear." He grinned as a blush spread across her face. "After all, I'm sure you'll want a cook, a butler, a housemaid or two..."

She flapped a hand at him. "Don't tease, Arthur!"

"A nurserymaid..."

Lillias' face was mottled with pink, and she turned away from him, shyly. "Look at this grand room! This must be the drawing room. A calming sky blue and white in here, I think. These two windows are so glorious, looking out onto that lovely little formal garden at the side and the heather-covered hills crested with snow in the distance." She spun on one foot, taking everything in at a glance, her usual timidity forgotten. "I want curtains of deep, Prussian blue velvet, to frame the scene. And the dining room shall be a striking vermillion and rich amber for walls, upholstery and drapes, with an enormous mahogany dining table in the middle. Such rich colours; the gas lamps and candles will cast a warming glow to make dinner parties so cosy and comfortable."

She continued with her plans in every room of the house, dragging Arthur behind her, protesting good-naturedly. "And where do we get the money for all this from, my dear? You know the situation with my business at present."

"Then we will use *my* money. Oh, just look at this little guest bedroom! This will be a veritable feast of nature. The delicate blue-green of a thrush's egg, the violet of larkspur and vibrant marigold."

Arthur's face darkened. "I can't take any more of your money, goldfinch. It was bad enough having to borrow from you to buy this house."

"Nonsense, Arthur. We're married. It's your money too." Before he could speak, she flung open the next door. "And this must be our bedroom. Oh, Arthur, I'm so glad you insisted on having furniture for this room ready for us. Look at this beautiful brass bed." She ran her fingers over the smooth, shining walnut of the dressing table. "The walls will be that delightful fern green, sprigged with red and yellow flowers that Lady Clara has in her own bedroom." She paused and became serious for a moment. "Are you sure you won't countenance separate rooms for us? Lady Clara said that most married couples have separate rooms."

"You're my wife and must share my bed. You'll get used to it, I promise you. And what is this little room to be, do you think?"

"Oh, look at that view! We've saved the best until last. If you have no objections, I would love to have this for a little withdrawing room; a pretty little primrose-coloured bower where I can read, and sew, and watch out of the window for your carriage. Oh, I have the most delightful life!"

Ardellen House, Stirlingshire, 25th October, 1877

"Overnight? At your Club? But…Arthur…we haven't been apart overnight since we married." Lillias sank down onto the little embroidered stool at Arthur's feet and looked up at him.

Arthur took his wife's dimpled chin in his hand. "Then all the more reason why we should, my dear. After all, I don't want you getting bored of me. And, sometimes, you can be a little cold to me. Perhaps a night apart every now and then is a good thing."

Lillias' face registered her distress. "Oh, Arthur, no! As if I could ever be cold to you. It's just…" She didn't fully understand her own thoughts and feelings on this aspect of marriage yet, so came back to the thing that most immediately troubled her. Her bottom lip wobbled slightly. "It makes me fret so, being here on my own after the women from the village have left, waiting for you to come home. I don't want to stay here alone at night."

Arthur laughed. "Is that it, my little goldfinch? Surely you're not scared of the dark?" She pursed her lips and looked at him, eyes brimming with tears. Even the use of the pet name didn't appease her. "See here, my dear, you mustn't become hysterical." He smoothed a stray tendril of her hair. "There's no need for concern. I wouldn't leave you entirely alone overnight. I've asked Mrs McLuckie to stay, and Ambrose and Nimmo will be here, of course."

"Nimmo?" her voice was suddenly sharp.

Arthur tutted and shook his head. "Really, Lillias, I don't know what you have against Nimmo. He's a good man, and very useful to me. And until my funds have been released, we can't even think about hiring more staff."

"What *is* the problem with your funds, Arthur?"

He took her chin in his fingers once more and kissed her lightly on the forehead. "It's a business matter, my dear, very complicated. And I'm sorry if it means that you'll have to wait for a maidservant, and a second cook, and housemaids, and an under-butler and footmen and whatever else and whoever else it is you want, but there it is."

Lillias drew back and raised a finger to touch the two deep lines that always appeared at the sides of his nose when he frowned. "I can help. Let me give you the money to do that."

He stood, suddenly, almost dislodging her from the footstool and caught her arm with a mutter of apology. "I can't simply hold out my hand to you for a sovereign here and ten shillings there; it isn't right."

"Then don't. I'll speak to my banker and get him to send you whatever you need so that you can deal with...all these things that need doing."

"Oh, I couldn't possibly do that..." He turned away and walked to the window, hands in pockets. "Although...it *would* make sense. And I'll ensure that you are paid back every penny once my business is completed." He turned back to her and Lillias snorted and fluttered a jewelled hand at him. He held his own hand up in turn. "No, no, I'll draw up a document immediately." He strode to the desk for paper and pen and sat down to write.

Lillias skipped after him, carefree once more. She placed a hand on his shoulder and planted a kiss on the top of his head. "And some paper for me, too, if you will."

He laughed. "Paper for you, goldfinch? And why would that be?"

"Well, if we're finally going to have a staff, we can have that dinner party you mentioned." He laughed again and handed her some paper. "Besides, I thought I might invite Aunt Evelina to stay for a while. Now, don't look so glum. She has my best interests at heart; she just needs to spend time with you and get to know you as I do."

"By all means, my dear. Do write to her. I'll take your letter when I leave." He continued to write for a moment, before handing her the document he had been working on. "Here you are. You need to sign it at the bottom."

She smiled brightly at him and waved her own letter. "Excellent. I'll read it while you read this letter to Aunt Evelina."

"No need, my dear. I'm sure you've given her my best wishes." He plucked the letter out of her hand and folded it into the envelope she had prepared. "Now, if you would just sign that, I'll be on my way."

"Very well." Lillias signed her name boldly across the bottom of the document Arthur held out for her, shifting his gloved hand from where it rested on the paper, to give herself room. As soon as she lifted her pen from the last flourish, he took the paper and waved it in the air to let the ink dry, before tucking it into his breast pocket. He then kissed her lightly on the lips and left the room.

Lillias hurried over to the large bay window and pushed the heavy velvet drapes aside. She watched him as he strode down the wide driveway, donning his coat in one fluid movement and stepping up into the carriage with a final word to Nimmo. She ran the gold tassel tying the curtain open across the palm of her hand, enjoying the soft feel of it, and watched the coach until it rounded the first bend of the drive. Then she turned away and surveyed Arthur's office, tapping the tips of her fingers together thoughtfully, her mind already on how to make the room lighter and more welcoming for her husband.

Ardellen House, Stirlingshire, 14ᵗʰ December, 1877

Lillias paced her little primrose withdrawing room, her face set in a frown. It was the one place in the house where she felt as if she could be herself and that no one was monitoring her every move and judging her for it. Less than two months ago she had been looking forward to hiring a staff – a jolly, rosy-cheeked cook smelling of ginger and warm apples; an avuncular butler who would be at her side at dinner parties, gently and unobtrusively guiding her on matters of etiquette; a cheery and obliging ladies' maid who would brush her hair and share her little secrets. Instead, Arthur had taken it upon himself to hire the dourest, most unfriendly household that he could possibly have found. Nimmo was bad enough, always looking at her with that sneer on his face, but at least he spent most of his time outdoors and she didn't have to see him every day.

Lillias had not wanted to seem ungrateful – Arthur wanted to take the burden off her fair shoulders, he had said; but she felt unhappy and alone. To make matters worse, she had now written to Aunt Evelina three times, and had not received the courtesy of even the shortest of replies. Lillias knew that her aunt had been displeased by the way she had left Bristol without telling her they were getting married, but she thought that an invitation to spend Christmas with them would have appeased her aunt a little. Perhaps she needed to be more apologetic. She would try once more. It might be too late now – Christmas was only eleven days away, after all – but she would write one more letter, full of love and gratitude. Yes, that was the thing to do. She would do it right now.

Arthur was out, so she went downstairs, let herself into his study and took a piece of the fine creamy paper with their address at the top. She took a pen from the stand and scored out Arthur's name on the letterhead. She would get Ambrose to get one of the men take her down to the village and send it off to the post. And while she was in the village, she would enquire about hiring a girl she could train up as her lady's maid, so that she would at least have one friendly face to look at. Ambrose would glower at her – as he always did – but this time, she decided, she didn't care one ounce. After all, he might be the butler but *she* was the lady of the house and should at least be able to choose her own maid.

Ardellen House, Stirlingshire, 24th December, 1877

Lillias put down her spoon and stared at Arthur. His flushed face was even redder in the light from the candelabra reflecting off the shining mahogany dining table. He was drinking too much port and she wanted to chide him on that, but his moods had been fierce lately, and she thought it best to keep her counsel. She weighed her words carefully now, but his most recent statement couldn't be left without comment. "You're going hunting tomorrow? But it's Christmas Day. I thought…"

"You thought what, Lillias?"

His voice was sharp, and she flinched. When she spoke, it was in conciliatory and soothing tones. "I…I thought we could go to Church and then come home and spend a cosy day, just us, in front of the fire. You said we wouldn't invite anyone so that we could spend our first Christmas together…And Mrs McLuckie is preparing pheasant and goose and an enormous plum pudding."

"Oh, for heaven's sake. It's tradition, the Christmas Hunt. Besides, I promised McAllister I would be there; you know how important he is to my business success. I shall be out before you even get up and back in time for Mrs McLuckie's feast."

McAllister. Another reason she didn't want Arthur to go, but she couldn't tell him that, for a reason she was unsure of, she didn't like this seemingly charming friend who held so much sway over her husband. Arthur appeared to prefer spending time with McAllister to spending time with her. Perhaps she was just jealous. She didn't want to cry, but the tears came anyway and with them came another thing that had been upsetting her. "And the tree. You haven't said anything about the tree."

"The tree?"

"The tree in the hall. You haven't said anything about it, and I spent so long today, decorating it while you were out. I'm sorry, Arthur. I don't *mean* to be hysterical. I'm trying not to be, I promise. It's just…" It was cold in the dining room and she rubbed miserably at the goose-flesh on her forearms.

He stood up from the table and came around to her side, laughing, his mood undergoing a sudden transformation. "Come, come, goldfinch. Don't cry so; you know I detest it when you're sad. I'm sorry I didn't say anything about the tree. It's just that I've so much on my mind; things that you won't understand, my dear."

"Business things, you mean. Oh, you know I don't want you to worry about all that."

He stroked her shining hair and kissed the top of her head. "I know, goldfinch, and I have another paper for you to sign later. Now, come and show me this marvellous tree." He led her out to the hall. "I was in such a hurry to see *you*, my dear, that I didn't even glance at it." He laughed. "Although I have no idea how I could have missed such a monstrous twinkling thing."

The tree was enormous. "Ambrose helped." Arthur raised his eyebrows. "I know, but I think he rather enjoyed it in the end. He decorated the top half of the tree and, look, he even made those little decorations with the holly berries. And Mary Grace and I wrapped all the bonbons and sugared almonds and tied them on with ribbon."

Arthur's face darkened at the mention of Mary Grace. "I still can't believe you went behind my back and hired that pudding-faced creature. The girl doesn't even know how to answer the door properly."

"She's bright and she'll learn." She squeezed his arm. "Please let's not argue. I want our first Christmas together to be perfect; that's why I got upset about the Hunt and you not noticing the tree. I'm sorry for being silly. Look! Don't the candles on the tree twinkle so?"

Lillias held her breath until Arthur's furrowed brow cleared. "It's a delightful tree, dearest. And I promise I'll be home early tomorrow evening. We'll enjoy your tree, and I will claim a kiss under the mistletoe that I see over by the staircase."

Lillias blushed and started to speak, but her response was cut off by the sound of carriage wheels on the driveway.

Arthur frowned. "Who the devil's this?" He strode to the door and flung it open.

No devil stood outside, but, instead, Lillias' Aunt Evelina Gilfillan.

Ardellen House, Stirlingshire, 25th December, 1877

"Dante, Dorcas, come here." Arthur's voice was sharp and the whip cracked. They turned abruptly and came obediently to him, one on each side. Arthur leaned down to each in turn, scratching Dorcas's smooth head and clapping Dante on the flank.

Arthur refused to look back at the house. He knew Lillias would be watching from the window, wanting him to turn and wave as he always did, to send the dogs bounding towards the house to roll in the grass and make her laugh. He enjoyed that too, seeing Lillias' fair curls bouncing as she tilted her head backwards, laughing; her pretty little face rosy and round. But he would not turn. Not this time. Not with that aunt of hers no doubt hovering at her shoulder and casting her coldness around the room. What right did she have to interfere where she wasn't wanted? And what had Lillias been thinking to go behind his back and invite her?

He cracked the whip against his boot and the dogs looked up at him, alert for sport, their breath steaming in the cold air. "Are we taking the carriage, sir?" Nimmo's voice was hopeful. He had the guns and the supplies, and the moor was a fair walk. But Arthur wanted to burn off his frustration.

"No. We'll take the short cut over the brae and meet the rest of them by the stream." Arthur could almost feel Nimmo's disappointment. "One of the party will offer to bring us home, I'm sure. I need the exercise, Nimmo. Don't you feel it, cooped up in there?" Nimmo didn't respond and Arthur hadn't really expected him to; he was a man who kept his words close and his thoughts closer. It was one of the reasons Arthur employed him.

They strode silently up the slope and through the wood of Douglas firs, their breath condensing into wispy clouds with the exertion. The sounds of their footsteps and the panting of the dogs at their side were absorbed into the eerie silence of the snow that covered everything. The heavy canopy of trees protected them from the snow which started to fall again as they left the house, but the echoing crack of a branch breaking off occasionally under the weight of snow accompanied their passage through the trees. Arthur could feel his heart beating faster in anticipation of the shoot and, as always, it took his mind off his troubles.

"How many are expected today?"

"Six pairs of guns, sir, I understand."

Arthur nodded. McAllister would be among them, he knew. Lillias didn't understand that these hunts were not simply sport but also a good opportunity to make contacts and transact business. McAllister was from a powerful family, well-connected in both society and business, and had his fingers in several pies, despite being roughly the same age as Arthur. He'd been good enough to let Arthur in on a superb investment opportunity – shares in the new Caledonian and Northern Railway. It was a certainty and his discount-house in Glasgow was pushing it heavily, he'd told Arthur. Shares in railway companies were a sound investment and could only increase in value as the railways expanded. McAllister had put several hundred pounds of his own money into this ambitious new venture and had persuaded Arthur to do the same, even loaning him money until he could come up with it.

It wasn't the first time Arthur had borrowed from him, but this was a substantial sum. Lillias' inheritance was a god-send. He hadn't told her what the money was for because she didn't understand business and would worry that he'd over-extended himself. He needed to get her to release more funds so that he could pay McAllister back. She would reap the rewards: he imagined himself showering her with gold coins and telling her to decorate the house with all the frills and furbelows she wanted. He smiled to himself at the thought, before bringing his mind back to the hunt. "And good shooting expected?"

"Yes, sir. McDade over at Kellburn Hall tells me we can expect a few hinds."

Arthur smiled. "Mrs McLuckie will be happy if we bag one of those."

"Aye, sir, she will indeed. But she won't thank us if we haul it home while she's preparing her Christmas feast."

The anticipatory excitement of the hunt ebbed slightly as the mention of Christmas dinner reminded him of what awaited him on his return. He knew he would be able to talk Lillias around, but her aunt was a different matter. Damnable woman. He flicked his whip and it caught Nimmo's boot. Nimmo glanced at him but said nothing and Arthur didn't bother to apologise.

As they emerged from the stand of trees, they were rewarded by the sight of a grouse, flying fast and low, the red flash over its eye still visible despite the early morning fog pressing down on the snow-covered moorland. The bird's distinctive call was rather muffled, but the "*goback, goback, goback*" still caused the dogs to halt, pointing. However, the guns remained open in Nimmo's hands and there was no urgency in their master's step, so they relaxed and continued heading in the direction of the stream. Grouse was not the prey for today; wildfowl was for Boxing Day. Arthur could just make out a group of dark specks. They made their way over and the dogs sniffed and nuzzled each other as the men shook hands – master with master, servant with servant.

As they set off across the moor the fog started to lift and Arthur's spirits along with it. His luck was changing; of that, he was certain. His sweet Lillias had plenty of money and would be happy to give it to him. After all, he was her husband and knew what was best for them. And her shrew of an aunt would surely depart soon. Yes, today was set fair to be a good day.

McAllister offered Arthur a ride home in his carriage, hinting that there was a business matter he wanted to discuss. "You had some luck today, Strang. Not a bad day's hunting at all."

Arthur laughed and clapped him on the back. "Not as good as yours. That hind is magnificent." McAllister always seemed to have the luck of the devil; another reason Arthur was drawn to him.

"Ah, a lucky shot." McAllister gestured for Arthur to climb into the carriage ahead of him. Nimmo sat up front with McAllister's man and the dogs ran on ahead, still bursting with energy even after the day's hunting.

Arthur settled into the carriage and took out his timepiece – a handsome gold half-hunter that had been a gift from Lillias. He was later than he had promised, but a talk with McAllister would be worth it. He settled back into the seat.

McAllister wasted no time in getting straight to the point. "I'm glad we have this chance for a talk. I'm afraid I have some bad news." Arthur could feel his gut tightening. "That investment opportunity I put you in the way of turned out to be a bad business."

"Damn it, Douglas. I thought you said those shares were a certainty?"

"Well, it looks as though I was misled on that front."

Arthur slumped in the seat. "Worth waiting until they recover?" McAllister shook his head, briefly. "Then I suppose I'll just have to sell them and cut my losses."

McAllister shook his head once more. "I'm afraid not. They're not worth a farthing."

"Nothing? Dear God...I..."

McAllister's eyes were hard. "It's not just you, I was heavily invested myself, as you know. I'm going to need my money back by the end of January."

"January? How am I supposed to get my hands on—"

"That's not my concern."

"But—"

"The end of January, Strang. The interest we agreed, too."

Despite the blazing fire in the grate and the candelabras on the dining table, the atmosphere was frosty. Lillias picked miserably at the cod in oyster sauce. This was not how she had imagined her first Christmas dinner in her new home. She had imagined chatter and laughter, smiling, flushed faces all around the long table, music and dancing and fun until the small hours. Instead, the three of them sat silently at one end of the table, not even looking at each other, let alone talking. Evelina's back was rigid against the back of the chair, her lips were pursed, and she picked at her cod as though out of duty, rather than pleasure.

Arthur pushed his plate to one side and called for the goose to be brought in. His voice was slurred, and Evelina looked at him a moment, before turning to Lillias. "Have you thought any more about what I said earlier?"

Lillias stole a quick glance at Arthur. "No, I...I haven't had a chance to discuss it with Arthur, as yet."

Arthur reached for the carafe of red wine, filling his glass and taking a large slug. "Discuss what with me?"

Lillias looked pleadingly at her aunt, but Evelina patted her mouth with the serviette, folded it neatly and placed it in front of her. "I have suggested to Lillias that she should employ the services of my lawyer and financier to handle her affairs."

Arthur put his glass rather heavily back down on the table. Lillias watched as the red liquid slopped over top, made its way down the side of the glass and pooled on the polished mahogany. "We do have bankers and financiers in Scotland, you know. It's not the heathen country some of you English seem to consider it."

"I am perfectly aware of that, Mr Strang." Evelina, it seemed, could not bring herself to call him Arthur. "I simply feel that it would be in my niece's best interests for someone to assist her with her finances. Her inheritance was not inconsiderable. I'm sure that, had my brother thought that he and his wife would pass on so soon, he would have made provisions."

Lillias could feel her eyes prickling and she screwed up her napkin tightly in her hand.

Arthur picked his wine glass up again, swirling the wine around and holding the glass up to the candlelight. The wine had not been decanted properly and small flecks of sediment circled as he brought the glass to his lips. "Are you saying, Miss Gilfillan, that I do not have my own wife's best interests at heart? And that she needs to be protected from me by a banker some four hundred miles away?"

Evelina's back straightened further. "Indeed I am not. However, Lillias let slip this morning that she has invested certain sums of money in your…business…and that these sums are increasing and becoming more frequent…"

She broke off as the serving staff brought in the roast goose and placed it on the table with a flourish, together with a roast pheasant covered in bacon, its jaunty tail feather sticking up as decoration. Plates of steaming boiled beetroot and onions, glazed carrots, braised cabbage and mounds of potato croquettes followed.

Arthur picked up the carving knife. "My business affairs are precisely that: *my* affairs. And Lillias is my wife. I will thank you not to interfere." With that, he plunged the carving knife into the breast of the pheasant. Grease oozed out and the head and neck, wired and placed on the dish for decoration, sprang up as if alive, before falling back onto the serving dish. Lillias covered her mouth and pushed her chair back, before rushing out of the room, sobbing.

Ardellen House, Stirlingshire, 2nd January, 1878

Lillias perched on the edge of her aunt's bed as Evelina Gilfillan watched her maid pack her things. "Do you really have to go so soon?"

Evelina sighed. "I must, my dear. Your husband doesn't want me here, it's clear, and I don't want to make things worse for you." She looked at the pale face in front of her. "You know, Lillias, you've grown to look more and more like your mother since I last saw you."

"I miss her so much."

24

Evelina sank onto the bed next to her and took Lillias' hand. "I know. So do I." She smiled. "I remember when John first brought her home to introduce her to the family. I knew then that my little brother had made the right choice. She was such a sweet, innocent thing and she radiated warmth and kindness." She laughed. "Why, I remember John's dog changed his allegiance and used to follow her around all day once they were married. I believe we all felt a little like that."

Lillias dropped her head onto her aunt's shoulder. "She always said you were like a real sister to her."

"That's how I felt about her, too. And she loved you more than anything in the world, you know."

They were silent a moment.

"She would have liked Arthur, I'm sure." Lillias' eyes were pleading, and Evelina looked away. "Arthur loves me."

"I'm sure he does, my dear." She wasn't sure at all, not one bit, but she knew it would do no good to say so right now. All she could do was look after Lillias' interests as best she could. And that was one reason why she needed to go home. She also needed to investigate this McAllister who seemed to have altogether too much influence over her niece's husband. Besides, she knew that she wouldn't be able to restrain herself from telling Arthur exactly what she thought of him if she had to be around him for much longer; and that would just not do. Even though Evelina had been named in her brother's will as Lillias' guardian, that role had been snatched from her the day Lillias had married Arthur. Evelina felt that Arthur was, at the very least, weak and unprincipled, but she had absolutely no legal say in her niece's affairs anymore. She would need to be circumspect. And she needed to get on with her nephew-in-law. However, there was absolutely no way that she could do that when she was under his roof, that was clear. At least she had arranged her own affairs in such a way that Arthur would not be able to touch the substantial capital amount, only the income, when the time came.

She took Lillias' face in her hands. "You're looking quite peaky, my dear. I haven't seen the pink in your cheeks since I arrived. Are you sure you're quite well?"

"Just a little tired." Lillias tucked a stray curl behind her ear. "Everything's so new and different. I'm just getting used to things, that's all."

Evelina was not convinced. "I'm not sure that Scotland in the winter agrees with you. Perhaps Arthur will let you spend some time in Bristol with me."

Lillias made a face. "Perhaps in a few months." Evelina wasn't convinced of that, either.

Ardellen House, Stirlingshire, 5th January 1878

Arthur stood in front of the window, his hands behind his back, rocking on his heels. Lillias paused in her embroidery to enjoy the sight of him. The low winter sun was strong and picked out the glints of red in his curls, giving the impression of a decorative and jaunty halo. She threaded the needle back through the white silk of the antimacassar she was embroidering with tiny blue speedwells. "You've been very quiet, recently. Is everything alright?"

Arthur strode over and perched on the edge of the chair next to her. "I do have something I need to speak to you about, goldfinch."

Lillias carefully laid the needle down on her lap and placed a hand on his. "What is it?"

He laughed and patted the hand that now caressed his. "Well, my dear, I'm afraid that you've been a little too willing to spend money, recently."

Lillias drew back, slightly, leaving her hand trapped between his. "Have I? But…"

"Hiring that waif and stray from the village, for a start. The girl is always lurking uselessly underfoot. She spilled some of my best brandy yesterday."

"You scared her when you barked at her. Mary Grace is still learning. Besides, she's cheerful and she makes me feel…" Lillias trailed off before the words could spill out and anger him. He would be unhappy if she said that a servant girl could make her feel less lonely, purposeful…present, even. Sometimes as she moved around the house, she wanted to scream and shout, just to prove that she was there. But, of course, she didn't.

"And your insistence on all those presents and decorations and food, Boxing Day gifts for the servants, that new dress of yours." He laughed at her stricken face. She had only done all those things to please him. "And you looked beautiful in it, my dear. But I don't think you realise how much all these things cost."

"Oh! I'm sorry! You should have told me!" She made a move to stand up. "I have ten pounds upstairs in my withdrawing room. Let me go and get it for you."

Arthur held tightly onto her hand, leaving her standing awkwardly, one hand clutched in his, the other clasping her embroidery.

"Ten pounds, goldfinch? I'm afraid I need slightly more than that. I need you to sign another paper for me."

Lillias gripped the embroidery tighter, ignoring the sharp jab of pain as the needle pierced her finger. "I…Aunt Evelina told me I mustn't sign any more papers. She said…"

Arthur pulled her towards him and sat her roughly on his knee. "Aunt Evelina said what, goldfinch?" His breath was sour with drink and she wrinkled her nose, squirming in his lap.

"She said…she said that her lawyer is coming up next week to meet with me. She wrote to him before she left and arranged it all."

"Oh, she did, did she?" Arthur stood up abruptly, tumbling Lillias to the floor, where she sat looking up at him. "And what right did she have to do that? You are my wife. Your money belongs to me." Lillias' eyes filled with tears and she struggled to get up, hampered by her skirt. Arthur bent down towards her. "*You* belong to me."

Lillias drew away from him. Arthur had a temper, but she had never seen his face like this before. His dark brown eyes looked almost black, and his face was red and perspiring freely. The smell of his sweat, mixed with the sage and orange of his hair pomade, made her feel nauseous. She turned her face away and started to sob.

"Oh, stop this hysterical nonsense, Lillias. These outbursts of yours are getting simply too much. It doesn't become you." His voice was weary. He reached out and struck her face with his open hand and she was so shocked that she stopped crying at once and lifted her hand to her stinging cheek. What had she done? Arthur was looking at his hand, as if horrified.

She reached out and laid a hand on his arm. "Forgive me, Arthur."

Ardellen House, Stirlingshire, 7th January 1878

Mary Grace cleared away the tea things, slopping tea from the delicate china cup onto the wooden floor. Mrs Strang hadn't noticed. She was sitting absently looking out of the window, her sewing abandoned on her lap. A bracelet of bruises encircled her wrist, like purplish-blue pearls. Mary Grace cleared her throat. "Mrs Strang?"

Her mistress started. "Oh! Yes, Mary Grace. What is it?"

"D'you want anythin' else, Mrs Strang?"

"Will there be anything else?"

"Aye. Will there be anything else, Mrs Strang?"

"No, that's all." Mrs Strang turned to face her now and Mary Grace saw that one side of her chin was the same purplish-blue as her wrist. Mary Grace bobbed her head and picked up the tray to leave the room. "Oh, yes, there is something, Mary Grace. Could you please tell Mrs McLuckie that Mr Strang will be away overnight and I won't be requiring dinner. If she could just send up some arrowroot pudding to my withdrawing room, I'll eat there this evening."

"Aye, Mrs Strang." Mary Grace bobbed her version of a curtsy once again and nudged the door with her hip to open it, looking back to see Mrs Strang bent over her sewing once more. Mary Grace shook her head and left the room, descending the stairs with great care. The china tinkled on the tray but didn't topple or fall and she reached the kitchen with everything intact for once.

She placed the tray on the big wooden table in the centre of the room. Mrs McLuckie chewed slowly on a mouthful of boiled ham, her currant-like eyes watching Mary Grace with an unblinking stare. Mary Grace loftily imparted the message about dinner.

Mrs McLuckie snorted. "Arrowroot pudding for her ladyship, as though she's some poor invalid who's taken to her bed."

"Aye, well, she didnae look well." Mary Grace started to unload the tray and carry the dirty crockery over to the sink.

Mrs McLuckie snorted again. "No' well, indeed."

Not ill, perhaps, but even though Mary Grace had only been at Ardellen House for a few weeks, she could tell that *something* was not well here. She wished that Mrs Strang's aunt had not left, and she wished that there was something she could do.

"Did you see..." Mary Grace's hand fluttered to her neck.

The currant eyes narrowed. "Naw. And neither did you, if you know what's good for you, lassie. Now, get me that nutmeg grater for this pudding."

Beau Rivage Private Asylum, 8th January 1878

Doctor Carruthers-Browne leaned back in his chair and watched as his visitor continued to pace on the other side of the desk. The man looked as though he hadn't slept for days and kept putting a hand to his temple and pressing his fingers along his eyebrows as if trying to push them into his skull.

"Do please sit down, Mr Strang," he gestured towards the comfortable chair he kept for paying clients. "I have worked with lunatics who were calmer than you." He smiled to show that it was a joke designed to put his visitor at his ease, but Strang continued to pace.

"Can you help me, Doctor?"

Carruthers-Browne steepled his forefingers and brought them to his mouth, furrowing his brow and pursing his lips as though he was giving the matter serious consideration. It was a well-practised gesture, and one which was replicated in the life-size painting of himself which hung behind him on the wall of his office. Truth be told, he was giving the matter no serious consideration at all. There was no doubt that he would help. The only thing Carruthers-Browne was considering was whether he could increase the sum he had mentioned. No matter. There were always extras which could be easily justified.

"Of course." His voice was just the right combination of authoritative and soothing; again, carefully cultivated to impress and reassure. "I can assure you that I have dealt with many such cases at my previous institution down in Surrey." He hurried on before Strang could ask him the reason for his move up to Scotland. That wasn't something he was prepared to go into. "Yes, very sad cases indeed, and many of them ladies of the highest quality. I can assure you that many families sought me out as an expert on hysteria and its symptoms and consequences." However, it was clear that Mr Strang was not interested.

"And having her committed as a lunatic would enable me to...take control of her affairs for a time? Until she's better?"

A-ha. Here was the crux of the matter. Carruthers-Browne now understood the situation. This was the best of all reasons in his book. A man who wanted rid of his wife due to an affair of the heart often changed his mind when the new fancy turned out to be imperfect. And a man whose concern about his wife's health was genuine would ask whether she would be treated kindly, or how often she would get out into the garden or some other such nonsense. Men who were driven by financial reasons – whether through greed or desperation made no difference – were by far the easiest to convince. "Yes, indeed. Now, I will come down and assess your wife myself, of course. Do you have another physician who would be willing to certify?"

Strang stopped his pacing and shook his head. "What do you mean?"

Carruthers-Browne resumed his steeple-fingered pose now that he had his visitor's attention. "Two doctors are required to certify in cases of insanity. I assumed that your local doctor..." He let the sentence politely drift off.

"No!"

The loudness of the response startled Carruthers-Browne and he leaned forward in his chair. "I'm terribly sorry, I didn't mean to upset you."

"I'm sorry. It's just that...well...I don't want any of the local men involved. Or my wife's family. It would...upset them too much."

"Ah. Of course, of course. Completely understandable. As it happens, I do know a man who has helped me out on many occasions. There would, of course, be an additional fee..." Carruthers-Browne was beginning to get an inkling of the sort of case this was, and his fingers tingled with anticipation at the additional services he could sell. He picked up a pen and made a note in neat, cramped handwriting. "Now, would a week tomorrow be a good day to come and visit your dear wife for a formal assessment?"

Strang started pacing once more. "No! That's no good. It needs to be soon. Tomorrow, preferably. The day after at the latest."

Carruthers-Browne feigned a look of shock. Yes, this was indeed just the sort of case he imagined it to be. "An assessment in absentia, so to speak," he mused as if to himself. "Well, it can be done, of course, but it will cost slightly more, I'm afraid."

"I don't care."

Carruthers-Browne blinked. "Certainly, certainly." He made another note in the large, leather-bound book in front of him. Perhaps this was a good time to test how far Strang would go. "Now, this is rather a delicate matter, but...when Mrs Strang is feeling better and returns, have you thought about how you will relinquish the reins on her finances?" This was none of his business, but he wanted to sew the seed in Strang's mind.

"What do you mean?"

"Well," Carruthers-Browne waved his hand vaguely. "In my experience, some gentlemen I have dealt with have experienced tremendous problems once the lady has returned home." He had no idea if this was true. Anyone who left his care was immediately forgotten about since there were no more fees to be collected.

Arthur shook his head, confused. "I thought...I want..."

"Of course, you want Mrs Strang home as soon as possible. I completely understand. But... if you *did* desire her to remain here indefinitely, I want to assure you that that would be an option which many gentlemen have gratefully accepted."

He watched as Strang chewed this over. "Well, I don't know..."

Carruthers-Browne was satisfied. He would let that simmer a while. He was a good judge of character – particularly weak ones like Strang – and was certain that the old adage 'out of sight is out of mind' would apply here. He was quite convinced that there would be many years of fees forthcoming in this case. "Now, will you be bringing Mrs Strang to us yourself, or would you like me to send a carriage?"

"A carriage?" Strang let out a tense laugh. "You make it sound like a jaunt."

"Well, we do like to make the trip as pleasant as possible for our charges, but she would be accompanied by either myself or one of my men and a nurse at all times. Discreetly, of course. That's, as I say, assuming you don't want to bring her yourself..."

Strang's face was pale, and his hands were trembling. "I've... I've told her that I'm arranging for her to go away for a month or so on a rest cure. I'd rather you came to collect her. She wants her idiot maid with her. I assume that won't be an issue?"

"We do have plenty of our own idiot maids, Mr Strang." He smiled once more to show that this was another joke. "But no, it won't be a problem. Several of our more refined inmates bring their own maids and manservants. I find that they can be quite...useful."

Strang nodded. "My wife has given her maid a few days to finish up some household tasks and take her leave from her family." His face clouded. "You won't...she won't...be harmed in any way, will she?"

The doctor was confused. "The idiot maid?"

"Of course not. My wife, I mean."

Carruthers-Browne composed his face into the one he generally reserved for bereaved friends and relatives. Perhaps he had misjudged this Strang. "Not at all; she will be most comfortable here. And, as soon as she's well again, she will be returned to you whole, healthy and happy." He hoped it wasn't *too* soon, paying patients of this quality were getting harder to come by. Strang's next words reassured him, however.

"No, perhaps you're right. It might best if she doesn't come back for a while, Doctor."

Ardellen House, Stirlingshire, 9th January 1878

"A spa, Arthur?"

"Yes, goldfinch. It will do you good. Your cheeks are so pale, these days and your lack of appetite is worrying. And you must admit, my dear that these hysterical outbursts of yours are increasing. A short break, recuperating in the best care, will do you the world of good."

Lillias raised her hands and pressed them against her cheeks as if not only willing them to turn pink, but also to try and hold back what Arthur called her 'outbursts'. "But I don't want to, Arthur. I promise I will eat, I promise. And a few walks in the fresh air, here, just like you said. Mary Grace can come with me. She can——"

Arthur shook his head, firmly and held up a hand. "This is what I mean, Lillias. You are overwrought and need some peace and quiet."

"But, Arthur, it's so quiet *here*. Can't I stay with you?"

"I've made up my mind, my dear. Dr Carruthers-Browne is coming to collect you tomorrow."

"Tomorrow?" Lillias could sense her voice rising. She needed to be calmer, to make Arthur see that she wasn't hysterical. "But if I am to go, I shall need to pack, to…"

"It is all organised, my dear. I've asked Mary Grace to prepare a trunk for you to take with you, with everything you might need."

"For how long?" Lillias couldn't keep the fretful note from her voice.

"For as long as required, Lillias. Until you are fully recuperated and I don't need to worry about your health. You will enjoy it, you'll see. After all, didn't you tell me that your trip to Bath Spa after your parents' death was beneficial to your health?"

"Well yes, but——"

"And didn't you trust your Aunt Evelina to know what was best for you on that occasion?"

"I did, Arthur, but——"

"Then please, goldfinch, do me the courtesy of trusting the same of me, as your husband."

Ardellen House, Stirlingshire, 10th January 1878

"But aren't you coming with me?"

Arthur turned away from her as one of the horses snorted and reared its head impatiently. "No, I'm afraid I can't. I'm sorry, goldfinch, but we've already discussed this; you know how my business affairs are at present."

Lillias saw nothing but distress in his face and felt a huge wave of love for him. Things *had* been difficult these last weeks and she knew that she had only made them worse with her hysterics, her fretting and constantly feeling ill. Poor Arthur was having to bear the brunt of her childishness. And he was doubtless right. She had been feeling unwell of late and off her food. Perhaps a change of scenery *would* be good for her. She needed to be brave now, and she forced a smile. "Of course you can't. I'll be fine with Dr Carruthers-Browne and Nurse Rintoul. And you'll send Mary Grace in a week or so. We will get on splendidly." Her voice wavered slightly, but she attempted to keep her smile bright and relaxed.

Arthur strode over and hugged her to him. His breath warmed the top of her head. "Goodbye, Lillias, goodbye. Don't…It…I…"

He trailed off and she drew away from him, placing her gloved hands on either side of his face. "Tears? Oh, no, that will never do! I'll write to you every day and I will be back in a month. And I'll be your chirpy little goldfinch again, I promise you."

He nodded, without saying anything further. He turned to Carruthers-Browne. "You *will* take care of her, won't you, Doctor?"

Carruthers-Browne helped Lillias into the carriage. "Of course, Mr Strang. Your wife will have rest and nourishment and the banishment of all cares and worries while she's with us...however long that takes."

Lillias stayed the doctor's arm as he was closing the door. "A month, Arthur. I will be back in a month, I promise you."

The gatehouse was small and unimposing, almost hidden in the trees at the end of the driveway. In the neat garden heartsease and pansies, still vibrant and plentiful even at this time of year, carpeted the beds. The carriage stopped at the gates. Nurse Rintoul, who had been entirely silent and almost motionless for the last six hours, opened the door of the carriage to speak to the gatekeeper. Lillias leant forward to catch the faint, sweet smell of the early daphne growing up the side of the iron railings.

Carruthers-Browne smiled. "Ah, you like the flowers, Mrs Strang?" He didn't wait for her to answer. "Then you'll be delighted when you see the grounds. We have the most beautiful gardens, with many varieties of rose and, my favourites, the rhododendrons. You'll enjoy strolling there in late April when they start to flower, I'm sure." Lillias opened her mouth to remind him that she wouldn't be there in April, but he continued. "And we have the most charming glasshouse. Many of our patients gain great benefits working in the grounds — gardening is such a boon for the unquiet mind."

The carriage set off up the driveway, which curved up and round. Lillias had not considered the others who might be here. Arthur and the doctor had stressed the tranquillity of Beau Rivage, and how she would be able to recuperate and rest, and she had somehow not thought about other patients. How foolish.

She felt her lips twitch and Carruthers-Browne appeared to take that as encouragement to continue to extol the virtues of Beau Rivage. "But, of course, it's not just about beauty. We are quite self-sufficient here. We grow wheat, oats, barley, vegetables of all descriptions. We have an apple orchard and a walled garden where we also have variety of other fruit trees. And," he gestured towards the slope down to the river, "we have four wells. Four! Can you imagine?"

The house finally came into sight, topping the rise. It was an imposing four storey building, with a stone staircase leading to a sturdy oak door set into the square, battlemented tower that was the centre of the façade. The two front corners were marked by smaller towers and Lillias could see two more such towers further back, behind the sloping roof.

"Isn't it magnificent? Beau Rivage Asylum sits on around a hundred acres. The Lunacy Commission in England recommends one acre of land for every four patients. *We* have one whole acre per patient." He sighed happily and sat back, still smiling and nodding.

Not a spa – an Asylum. Lunacy. Is that what he thought she was? A lunatic? She must be.

One hundred lunatics.

Beau Rivage Asylum, 11th January, 1878

Nurse Rintoul stopped short as she stepped out onto the patio of the sheltered courtyard and looked at the bowed head of the woman sitting on the lawn. The woman's back was straight and still, her figure well-proportioned and her abundant grey hair was coiled and braided and expertly swept up on top of her head, kept in place with a shining tortoiseshell comb. Her dress, although clearly two decades out of fashion, and faded through frequent wear, was well-made and neat. Nurse Rintoul scowled and moved towards the seated woman. Damnable thing that she was. The nurse's lip curled into a sneer. "Binnie." The word was snapped out, but the seated woman did not look up. She simply continued with the task that kept her eyes and hands busy. "Henrietta Binnie, why are you not in the laundry?"

No response. The hands were industrious and moved fluidly and smoothly without registering the interruption in any way. "Don't just ignore me, Binnie. It's eight o'clock. You should be at work in the laundry rather than fiddle-faddling around in the weeds."

Again, no response. The hands continued to twine and twist as the delicate chain of violas gained in length. Nurse Rintoul glanced at her pocketwatch. She was due in the receiving room in ten minutes to assist Doctor Carruthers-Browne in formally admitting the new inmate. She kicked out at the small feet in their scuffed black boots that pointed skywards as the woman worked. "I refuse, Binnie, I refuse, I tell you." The nurse placed her fists on her hips, knuckles white with hardly repressed anger. "I will not call you by that ridiculous name. I will not humour you as some of these other ninny nurses do. Now, get up and into that laundry before I am forced to drag you there."

Henrietta Binnie twisted and threaded another viola onto the stem of the previous one, holding up the chain and surveying it from every angle. Purple, yellow, white, violet. There was a pattern there for anyone who cared to look for it. Nurse Rintoul didn't care to look for it. The violas were plentiful here, always sheltered in the courtyard from the snow and the worst of the frost. Henrietta Binnie's thumb nail sliced a precise half-moon into the stem of a new viola as a low growl started in Nurse Rintoul's throat.

The doors to the patio grated open once more. "Ah, Henrietta; here you are. I believe you're on laundry duty this morning."

"I think you'll find that I have this under control, Nurse Welsh."

38

"I'm sorry, Nurse Rintoul, I didn't realise you were already here. I thought you were on admissions this morning. Perhaps I can walk Lady Bermondsey to the laundry."

"Lady Bermondsey, indeed. Why do you *insist* on humouring these pathetic delusions? I swear the idiot woman looks down on us, just because she used to be a nurse herself once. Well, she came to us from the poorhouse and if she ever gets out of here it will be *back* to the poorhouse."

Nurse Welsh smiled pleasantly. "To you, Nurse Rintoul, it's a delusion. To Lady Bermondsey here, it's just a matter of fact." She turned to Henrietta, who was now linking one end of the chain of violas to the other. "Shall we go, your Ladyship? I believe the sheets and aprons are awaiting your expert attention." She held out a hand and Henrietta took it, smoothing out her dress as she stood. The frost on the grass had transferred itself to the back of her skirt, turning it a shade darker, but the cold and damp didn't appear to bother her.

As Nurse Welsh placed a guiding hand on her elbow and gestured that the older woman should move ahead of her, Henrietta Binnie delicately placed the necklace of violas over the head of the smiling nurse and stepped past Nurse Rintoul, casting not one glance her way. She strode regally off towards the laundry.

Dr Carruthers-Browne and Nurse Rintoul looked up from the sheaf of papers when Lillias was shown into what the young nurse who accompanied her had informed her, in a breathlessly awestruck voice, was the office. The nurse had volunteered little other information, almost pushing Lillias into the room before scurrying off.

Carruthers-Browne stood up and advanced towards her, smiling. "Ah, Mrs Strang. Do sit down." He gestured to an armchair on the other side of the desk. "And how are you this morning? I trust that you found your rooms to your satisfaction? I put you in our choicest quarters, well away from the general wards and the dormitories for the pauper patients. You slept well?"

Lillias nodded. She *had* slept well, despite the strangeness of her new quarters and the presence of the young nurse throughout the entire night. Her bedroom was small but pleasant, decorated plainly and simply; and she had been pleased to discover that she had a separate sitting room with a cosy fireplace and two comfortable chairs. She had been assured that a cot would be brought in for Mary Grace when she arrived. "Yes, Doctor, although…I was surprised that the nurse stayed with me. Was that really necessary?"

Dr Carruthers-Browne waved a hand in dismissal. "Simply a precaution, that's all. We lock the doors of patients' rooms at night. However, I felt that might discomfit you on your first night here, so placed Nurse Duthie there instead."

Locked doors? Lillias started to protest, but Carruthers-Browne grabbed her wrist. "Now, Mrs Strang, paperwork, paperwork." He took her pulse and Lillias looked about her, surveying the cabinets of bottles and boxes behind the desk, the shelves of books and an array of bound files. Nurse Rintoul was holding a similar file, her pen poised for Carruthers-Browne's pronouncements. As he made Lillias put out her tongue, checked inside her ears, pulled up her eyelids, and got her to stand on a contraption that measured her height and her weight simultaneously, he kept up a steady stream of questions: What did she think of Disraeli's foreign policy? Had she heard about the terrible mining disaster in Blantyre? Had she read Mr Hardy's *The Hand of Ethelberta*? To which her answers were that she thought Mr Disraeli was doing a good job both at home and abroad; no, but how dreadful; and yes – her aunt had subscribed to the Cornhill Magazine where the story had been serialised.

He measured every area of her face with a curved set of callipers, barking out words and numbers: biparietal, fronto-occipital, bitemporal, antero-posterior, seven and four-fifths, thirteen and three-quarters; which Nurse Rintoul scribbled down, frowning. Finally, as Lillias was about to protest that she felt like a racehorse he was thinking of buying, he beamed at her. "There we are, all done. I'll get Nurse Rintoul to call Nurse Duthie and she can show you around before luncheon. Do ask her to show you the bowling green, the chapel and the ballroom in particular. I believe you will be particularly impressed with those."

As Nurse Rintoul left the room, Lillias patted her hair, which had become disarrayed by the callipers. "Your Nurse Duthie offered to unpack my things last night, but I told her to wait. My husband seems to have asked Mary Grace to pack rather a lot and she's bringing more when she joins me in a few days. Although it seems such a shame to drag her away from her parents and her family and friends—" Lillias broke off, suddenly aware that she was blabbering away, discomfited by being left alone with the doctor. "Anyway, I'm sure I won't need all those clothes. Can you...can you tell me how long I'll be staying? I *will* be home within a month, won't I? I promised Arthur I would."

"Well, we shall see, Lillias, we shall see."

Ardellen House, 13th January, 1878

Mary Grace was on her hands and knees behind the table in the dining room, blacking the grate, when Mr Strang and his friend Mr McAllister came in. She wasn't supposed to be there; she had promised Mrs McLuckie she would do the blacking last night, but she had been so tired, and then she'd slept in this morning, so she was trying to catch up. When she heard the men's footsteps, she crept underneath the dining table. She held her hand over her mouth, hoping they wouldn't hear her breathing, or the sound of her blood pounding so loudly in her ears. She didn't want to lose this job, just as she was about to be sent to Mrs Strang. Nobody was kind, here, not now that her mistress had gone away, but at least they didn't beat her like they did at home. She would *never* go back home. Hopefully the two men wouldn't remain there long, just long enough to make a hasty breakfast of the kedgeree from the serving dish on the sideboard, and a dram of whisky to warm themselves up before heading out to hunt.

The delicious scent of smoked haddock made her stomach rumble so loudly that she thought they would hear that, too, but they wolfed down the food, talking about the hunt and some business involving the railway, and how Mr Strang was a lucky devil. "You have the perfect marriage," McAllister said and they both laughed.

Mary Grace stayed as still as she could, even though her right leg had gone into a cramp. Her heart sank when she heard the glasses being refilled.

"May all our wives be mad and rich, Strang." Glasses clinked and the two men left the room. Mary Grace continued to crouch under the table for a few moments more, contemplating what she'd heard. This wasn't right. Mrs Strang wasn't mad. She might be ill, but she wasn't mad.

Finally, she stretched her cramped legs, hauled herself out from under the table and retrieved her cleaning things from the hearth. On her way out of the room she quietly lifted the lid of the silver salver and helped herself to an enormous spoonful of the creamy, spicy kedgeree.

Beau Rivage Asylum, 16th January 1878

Lillias walked along the corridor, her eyes nipping with the burning tang of vinegar that three patients in brown linsey dresses were using to clean the floor further down the hallway.

She raised a hand to her mouth, an acid taste rising in her throat. This place gave her a feeling of nausea that never seemed to abate. One of the patients ahead of her swiped a mop rhythmically from side to side. As she did, she repeated a refrain from a ballad Lillias recognised: "The tempest rolled, and the waves did roar. And the valiant smugglers were driven far from shore." With every repetition of 'roar' the mop plunged into the bucket and with every 'shore' the woman gave the bucket a sharp kick to edge it forward. The white cloth shoes the woman was wearing suffered every time the vinegar-water slopped over the edge, but she didn't seem to care. Behind her crawled the two other patients on their hands and knees, using cloths to dry the sodden floor. One of them was wearing the hat padded with straw that marked her out as an epileptic patient.

Lillias edged past the women, her eyes stinging even more as she passed the bucket. The women ignored her and went about their business and the tuneless falsetto followed her down the corridor, getting fainter as she descended the stone stairs. She knocked on the door of Carruthers-Browne's office, opening it when she heard a muffled "Enter."

Carruthers-Browne sat behind his desk, a neat pile of files the only thing spoiling its smoothness. "Ah, Lillias." He looked behind her, but she shut the door. His brow folded in on itself. "Did one of the attendants not accompany you?"

"No. Is that customary?"

He fluttered his fingers and sat back. "Well, it's certainly not customary for patients to wander the corridors unaccompanied."

"I'm sorry. I didn't realise I was wandering. I just wanted to consult you."

He leaned forward and smiled, fingers steepled in front of his tiny rosebud mouth. "Of course, dear lady. What can I do for you?"

"Is there still no word from my husband?"

Carruthers-Browne shook his head indulgently. "It's been

less than a week, Lillias!"

"But I've sent him three letters and haven't heard from him in return. I presume my letters *were* sent? I posted them in the letter box in the dayroom."

The doctor looked taken aback. "Why do you ask that?"

"One of the women told me that patients' letters are monitored, and that some are never sent."

The little mouth pursed still further. "Only if there is cause not to send them." He waved a hand vaguely. "Fantasies, delusions, etcetera. Sometimes it's better for families not to be troubled by their loved ones' ramblings. Your husband is a busy man, my dear. You ladies never seem to understand men's lives."

Lillias nodded. "I was also wondering if I could have a fork, Doctor Carruthers-Browne."

"A fork?"

"Yes, at meals. I'm not used to eating everything with a spoon. I find it...distressing."

"Distressing? Ah, well, I think you might find it even more distressing to have your fork taken from you by one of the chronic lunatics and used against you, wouldn't you?"

"Well, I..."

"Of course you would. Now," he stood up and held out a hand towards the door. "I won't detain you any further. But you mustn't worry yourself about news from the outside world. You're here to get better, my dear. Fresh air; restful sleep; good, plain, nourishing food; and a quiet mind. That's what you need."

Lillias curled her fingers on the arms of the chair. It was taking her all her courage to stand her ground, faced with his smug self-confidence and authority. "I would quite like some books, Doctor."

"Books?"

Why did he have to repeat everything in that disdainful voice? "Yes, my eyes tire with sewing all day. I'd like some reading materials."

"Ah, and have you found the little shelf in the dayroom? It should be adequately stocked with suitable materials."

"Yes, I have." She didn't mean for her reply to come out so sharply, but the Bible and various prayer and hymn books weren't what she meant by reading materials.

Carruthers-Browne thought for a moment. "Well, I'm sure we can arrange for the Chaplain to give you access to the Asylum library. I do believe he's recently acquired a new copy of Miss Yonge's most excellent *The Heir of Redclyffe*. A very worthy book."

Lillias sighed. She'd read it. It was unbelievably dull.

Ardellen House, 17th January, 1878

Mary Grace felt underneath the thin mattress. Her hand went directly to the letters and she pulled them out and looked at them in the dawn light that edged its way in through the tiny window in her room. She hadn't tried to read them, that wouldn't have been correct, but her ma had taught her to read, and she didn't need to get up and light the candle to know that they were addressed to Mrs Strang and were postmarked Bristol.

She had retrieved the first one from the hearth, where she had found it, covered in soot, the day Mrs Strang had left. She didn't think it had been burned by accident, and she didn't think Mrs Strang had even read it. The seal was still intact, although it was only half a letter, really. The other one she had found in the wickerwork basket full of scraps of paper and slivers of wood next to the fireplace the previous evening.

Mary Grace assumed that the letters were from Mrs Strang's aunt. She had been very kind to Mary Grace when she visited at Christmas, just like Mrs Strang was very kind to Mary Grace. Mary Grace felt the lack of kindness keenly. She missed Mrs Strang, even though she had only been gone a week, and she was worried about her. She wanted to tell her about the letters. But

Mrs Strang wasn't here, and it was almost as though she'd *never* been here, the way Mr Strang was behaving.

Mary Grace had been told by Mr Ambrose that she was being sent to join Mrs Strang with more of her mistress' belongings in the next week. She didn't know exactly where she was going – nobody seemed to know or, at least, they weren't telling *her*. Perhaps it was just an excuse to get rid of her, too. Well, as long as she didn't have to go back home, she would be happy. And the further away from home she was, the happier she would feel. She turned the letters over in her hand. She knew what she had to do.

Ardellen House, 21ˢᵗ January, 1878

Mary Grace stood in front of him, head bowed. She was such a pathetic chit; he was glad to be rid of her, moping uselessly around the house like an orphaned calf. He had intended to fire her, but he'd been persuaded otherwise. Arthur handed her a letter. "This is to be delivered to Dr Carruthers-Browne on your arrival."

She took the letter and nodded. "Yes, sir."

"You are not to open it." She simply looked at him blankly.

"Don't fret, Arthur, the girl probably can't even read."

Arthur glanced over at his friend. It was McAllister who had suggested using Mary Grace as additional insurance against interference from Evelina Gilfillan. As a spy in the camp, so to speak, she could be useful. It was irksome that he was having to pay for her keep, even though Carruthers-Browne would be getting an additional maidservant. Still, McAllister was right; it was worth it for the peace of mind. Besides, Carruthers-Browne would doubtless regret agreeing to the transaction when he discovered how useless the girl was. "And, if you want your mistress to get better you are to ensure that she receives no correspondence from outside the Asylum. You understand?"

The girl nodded. "Nothing. No gifts, no notes. Nothing. Is that clear?" The girl nodded again, biting her nails.

Arthur glanced over at McAllister, who smiled slightly. "I shall find out, you know, if you disobey my orders. And you'll be out of a job and back in the village in disgrace without a reference if you don't keep your mouth shut." The girl blinked, as though she hadn't understood a word.

Beau Rivage Asylum, 23rd January, 1878

Dr Carruthers-Browne tapped the envelope on the desk and glared at Mary Grace. She felt quite aggrieved. She hadn't done or said anything to deserve the glare. She hadn't done or said anything at all, in fact. She'd been shown into the office, curtsyed as instructed, and now stood with her hands neatly folded in front of her. "You are to join my staff, do you understand?" She nodded. "You will report to Nurse Rintoul and ask her to provide you with a uniform. Your main duty will be to look after Mrs Strang, but if you should be needed to help with anything else, you will do so."

He was obviously expecting an answer. "Yes, sir."

"I am generously providing you with board, lodging and training and you will work as and when required, if you wish to remain here." He looked at her. "I presume you *do* wish to remain here?"

"Yes, sir." She most definitely did wish to remain there. Living in a madhouse would be preferable to the terror of life back with her father and brothers. She also knew the doctor was lying. She had carefully unsealed the letter in the inn they had stopped in the night before and read its contents before sealing it back up with the one candle she had been permitted to light in her tiny room in the inn's attic. Dr Carruthers-Browne was *not* paying for her board and lodging, Mr Strang was. There had also been no mention of Mrs Strang's return, quite the opposite in fact. She wasn't quite sure what to make of it all, and some of the letter she hadn't fully understood. However, she was there to look after Mrs Strang and that she most definitely could, and would, do. All of the things she had seen and heard at Ardellen House, and the injustice of Mrs Strang's situation weighed heavily on her, but she would keep these things to herself for now, until she had worked out the lie of the land in this strange place.

Beau Rivage Asylum, 2nd February, 1878

Lillias sighed and put down her sewing. She glanced over at Henrietta, her companion in the dayroom – friend, as she had come to think of her in the short time she had been there, even though Henrietta had never spoken. Nor, in fact, did it seem as though she even listened when Lillias spoke. Lillias smiled to herself. Perhaps that was why she liked her; she could ramble away and not be interrupted or judged or told she was ill or making things up. The only other occupants of the dayroom were a snoozing attendant, sitting on a birch sofa at the other end of the room, and a bird in a cage, fluffing up its feathers in the chill air. All the other patients had been shoo-ed out to take a turn in the airing court.

Henrietta's nimble fingers were making light work of the constant mending that had to be done. Lillias, of course, was not tasked with mending. She was a private patient and her own sewing was purely for pleasure. Pleasure. She derived absolutely no pleasure from the Bible verses and endless 'Home Sweet Home's she had sewn onto samplers in the short time she'd been here. She would have been glad to have done some proper sewing, something with a purpose, but, of course, that wasn't allowed. Her mind was not to be troubled. She jabbed her needle into the sampler. As if her mind would be troubled by mending a hole in a pair of linen drawers.

"Your stitches are so neat, Henrietta. One would almost think that those chemises hadn't been mended at all." Henrietta carried on sewing. "Did you hear the commotion last night? Margaret Steel's singing kept me awake, until they eventually gave her opiates, but it seemed after that that nobody could settle. I'll have to ask Nurse Duthie about it when she comes to take me back to my rooms for lunch." She sighed again. "I wish they'd let you take your lunch with me. It's quite lonely eating on my own. Mary Grace is a dear little soul, but she refuses to sit with me for meals. Says it's not proper. And the attendants tell me off for pushing the food around my plate. My stomach feels so bloated and sore; I don't think the food here agrees with me. Bland and starchy and a uniform grey, so as not to over-excite the patients, I assume." Lillias snorted. "As though we're all going to start dancing about hysterically at the sight of a plate of salmagundy." She stood up and went to the window that looked out onto the women's courtyard. "I keep telling the nurses and that young medical officer who visits us every week that I feel unwell, but he just mumbles and prescribes castor oil, which is very unpleasant."

She rubbed at the condensation on the window and looked out. Apart from those who were too ill, too mad, too lazy, or too stubborn for the attendants to deal with, most of the women patients were shuffling around the courtyard. The majority wore the asylum dresses in dark brown or blue linsey, hemmed in that unfashionable way above the ankle so that they didn't drag through the mud. Some of the dresses were trimmed with the crocheted lace the patients had worked on. Some patients, like Lillias, wore their own dresses. Lillias knew that the men – fewer of them and in a small wing towards the back of the asylum – had their own accommodation and those who were fit enough would probably be out seeing to the grounds at this time.

"I see that Charlotte Cunningham isn't out with them. That's the third time in a week. According to Mary Grace, she tore her blankets to shreds and spilled the opiate they gave her. Very violent and destructive, Mary Grace said. Did you know, she almost killed the goldfish in the middle gallery by letting out all the water last week. Charlotte, of course, not Mary Grace. But then that's obvious, isn't it? Did anybody ask Charlotte, I wonder, why she did it?" She picked up her sewing from the chair she had been sitting in before dropping it on the floor. She would need to unpick the last few stitches, but not now. "And Mary Grace says that young Lizzie Mackie is in trouble yet again for moving all the furniture around in the conservatory and rearranging items on the whatnot. Really, why don't they just let her get on with it? Mary Grace said it looked much nicer after Lizzie had finished." She laughed to herself. "Honestly, Mary Grace has only been here just over a week and already she knows all the gossip there is to know. I don't know how she does it."

Lillias threw herself back into her chair again, kicking her embroidery to one side. "They don't say it, but they think I'm mad. Well, I wasn't mad when I came in, but I swear I *shall* go mad if I have to stay here much longer. What can Arthur be thinking, insisting that I stay here? Dr Carruthers-Browne tells me that he's been sending him reports of my progress and that Arthur is happy that I should stay just another week, just another week, just another interminable week...I've nearly been here a month already and the Doctor said yesterday he thinks it would be wise for me to stay another. I can't bear it. And if Arthur's been in contact with *him*, why doesn't he answer *my* letters?"

Henrietta held up her sewing and bit down on the thread, snapping it neatly and precisely. She folded the drawers she had mended and put them on the pile beside her, before picking up another chemise.

Ardellen House, 5th February, 1878

"Where is my niece?"

Arthur could feel his face flushing. "Please, Miss Gilfillan. Come into the drawing room and sit down. I'll get some tea brought in."

Evelina Gilfillan pulled off her soft leather gloves and slapped them across one palm. "I do not want tea; I want to see my niece. I have written and written and have had no word from her. Where is she?"

Arthur looked over at McAllister. His friend was lounging against the bannister of the staircase, swirling the last dregs of brandy around in the glass he was holding and looking amused.

"At least come in and take a seat. We'll be more comfortable in here."

Evelina Gilfillan allowed herself to be shown into the drawing room but refused to be ushered to the green and gold brocade settee. Instead, she perched on the edge of a straight-backed chair and folded her hands in her lap. "Where is my niece?"

Arthur could feel his underarms prickling with sweat and ran a hand across his brow. "I'm afraid she's indisposed." He glanced once again at McAllister, who had followed them into the room and was now standing proprietorially in front of the fireplace.

"Indisposed?"

McAllister cleared his throat. "She's unwell, Miss Gilfillan."

Evelina Gilfillan turned her sharp gaze on him as if noticing him for the first time. Arthur was glad of the temporary reprieve from the glare which he felt could strip his flesh from his bones.

"And who, may I ask, are you?"

McAllister gave a half smile and bowed, rather mockingly, Arthur thought. "My name is McAllister. I am Mr Strang's... business partner. And friend."

51

"Ah, McAllister. I assumed as much. Well, as I thought, you have nothing of interest to tell me about my niece." Evelina Gilfillan stood up in one swift movement. "I will go up to my niece's room. I presume it is the same one as when I was here before?"

McAllister moved from the fireplace and stood in front of Lillias' aunt. "I'm afraid that your niece has been removed to an asylum for her own safety and for the safety of those around her."

Miss Gilfillan rocked back on her heels, as if McAllister's words had physically struck her but her voice, when it came, was as flinty as ever. "Is that so? And when was this?"

Arthur looked down at the elaborate swirls and loops on the settee, and let McAllister take control of the situation once more. McAllister waved his glass and answered as though the question was a trivial passing remark about the weather and responding was a tedious chore. "Almost a month ago, I believe."

"A month? And when was my niece's husband going to tell me this, since you seem to know so much?"

McAllister laughed. "I have no idea. As her husband, he is the one who makes decisions relating to his poor wife's care and health."

"And her finances, too, I presume?"

Arthur glanced up. Evelina Gilfillan's cheeks were pale, but she stood straight and firm, looking up at McAllister who was now toying with the bronze statuette of a small drummer-boy which was on the fire surround.

McAllister shrugged and replaced the statuette, carefully pushing it a fraction of an inch to the left before he answered. "Again, I have no idea, but that is generally the way of things, is it not?"

Arthur stood and took a step towards her. "Miss Gilfillan, I…"

"Where is she?"

"I love her. I love my wife..."

"Where is she?"

"She...I...she is very sick. In the mind...unbalanced and hysterical, the doctors say. She——"

"Where?"

McAllister cleared his throat, as if in warning, but Arthur's heart was racing and his knees felt weak. "It's some... some distance away. Please...stay and rest." Arthur looked at McAllister for help, and his friend simply shook his head, once, his hand still resting on the drummer-boy. "I'll write the address down for you," Arthur said, meekly, glad of an excuse to leave the room for a few moments and compose himself in his study.

When he returned, Evelina Gilfillan was standing by the front door, pulling on her gloves. He held out the piece of paper. "I assure you; she's being very well cared for. I do have Lillias' best interests——"

"We shall see about that. Once I have seen my niece, I will be paying a visit to the authorities. You will never see her, or her money, again." With that, she opened the door herself and strode off towards the carriage which was waiting a little way down the drive.

Arthur rushed back into the drawing room. McAllister was now sitting on the brocade settee with a glass of whisky. "That was very foolish of you, Arthur. She's going to go up there and spoil everything."

"What could I do? What could I *do*?"

"You could have sent her off with a flea in her ear, that's what. For God's sake, what could the old woman have done? You could at least have stalled before giving her the address, so that we could make plans."

"She's going to take Lillias away from me."

"You're a damned fool. She's already away and she's not coming back."

"Perhaps we could send a letter to Carruthers-Browne? Tell

him not to let her in."

McAllister swirled the whisky in his glass, before drinking the rest of it down in a quick motion. "That will only defer the problem. Not solve it. I didn't get the impression that she's the type of woman to give up easily."

"Hell and damnation, what am I to do? I'll lose everything." Arthur collapsed onto the settee, in a vain attempt to stop his knees from shaking.

"Aye, and so will I, because of your stupidity. You're weak; a weak, pathetic excuse for a man. Look at you snivelling and shivering like a drowning cur."

"I'm sorry, I'm…What can I…?"

McAllister strode over to the settee and grabbed Arthur by the shirt front so hard that his collar came loose. McAllister threw it on the floor and picked up his hat and gloves. "I'll fix your mess for you, as always."

"What…what are you going to do?"

"I told you; I'll fix it so that dear Aunt Evelina can't interfere. You owe me, Arthur. I'll make sure you remember that."

Beau Rivage Asylum, 6th February, 1878

Lillias shivered in her undergarments at the side of the big porcelain tub, turning away from the junior attendant, not wanting the girl to laugh at her skinny thighs and bloated stomach. The attendant ran the cold water first and then stemmed the cold tap before adding hot water. She tested the temperature over and over, dipping the wooden-handled thermometer into the bath and pulling it out until it read precisely ninety-four degrees Fahrenheit. She turned the tap off and motioned to Lillias to get in. The water barely covered the bottom of the tub.

Mary Grace entered the room, carrying a jug. "I'll give Mrs Strang her bath."

The attendant folded her arms. "But Nurse Rintoul—"

"I always give Mrs Strang her bath. It's alright, I know what to do, Nurse Duthie showed me. I'm sure you've got plenty of other patients to see to." She shoo-ed the attendant out of the room and turned the taps back on. "That amount of water wouldn't bathe a kitten."

Once the tub was filled to her satisfaction, she helped Lillias into the bath. Lillias immersed herself in the tub, letting her long hair fan out into the hot water and sighing with pleasure. There were no patients being bathed in the remaining two cubicles today and Lillias lay back and enjoyed the unusual silence. Generally, her own bath was accompanied by the not unpleasant sounds of splashing, soft voices and, very often, laughter from other attendants and patients. Somehow, the water seemed to have a calming effect on even the most troubled inmate and Lillias felt safe here, even if she did, sometimes, have to share the water with the previous occupant. Not since Mary Grace's arrival, however, she realised.

She stood up and soaped her body with the cake of carbolic soap, releasing its fresh, antiseptic scent. "I can't stop thinking about those letters from my aunt. I can't think why Arthur didn't send them on... Anyway, I'm so glad you found them." Mary Grace shrugged and picked up the brush. She gently turned Lillias round and applied the brush to her shoulders and back. Lillias pulled away slightly from the coarse bristles, so Mary Grace eased off the pressure.

"I've written to both her and Arthur. Will you take my letters down to the village and post them for me tomorrow? I don't want to put them in the post box in the dayroom again. I'm sure Doctor Carruthers-Browne hasn't been allowing them to be sent because he thinks my fretting to come home will worry Arthur. So I've made sure this one is full of happy things and how much better I'm feeling." Lillias lathered up her hands and pushed them into her hair, piling it on top of her head and rubbing at it with the soap, before sitting back down to allow

Mary Grace to rinse her hair with the rosemary-steeped water from the jug. "And Aunt Evelina needs to know that I'm well. She'll be worried if she doesn't hear from me." She lifted her hand and watched the drops of water as they fell back into the tub. "She's probably worried anyway. Of course, Arthur may have written to her already." Of course he would have. She hoped he had.

"Are you sure they'll let me out to post them, Miss?"

Lillias laughed. "Don't be silly, of course they will. Unlike me, you're free to come and go any time." Nausea rose in her throat. "Goodness, I wish I were you. I'd be out of here so fast..."

Mary Grace looked horrified. "Wish you were me? No, Miss, of course you don't." She scoffed, as if at the thought of it. "Why would anyone wish they were me?"

She sounded so aggrieved that Lillias immediately felt bad. "I meant..." She stopped, realising that she didn't actually know *what* she meant.

Mary Grace set the jug aside and held out a hand to help Lillias out of the bath.

"I'm sorry, Mary Grace. You know *everything* about my life, and I've just realised that I know *nothing* about yours."

She shivered and dripped on the thin rug. "No, Miss, an' nor should you. You wouldn't..." Mary Grace picked up the towel and began to rub her dry.

"Oh, but I should, I...ouch! Can you stop rubbing *quite* so hard? My skin will come off."

"Sorry, Miss. But it's not right. It's not..." She sighed. "Anyway, yon doctor told me that I'm now an asylum employee and will be held to the highest standards and must do what I'm told. Perhaps I won't be allowed out into the village, let alone take your letters."

"Well, all the other staff get a half day off every week; there's no reason it should be any different for you, even though you're only a temporary member of the asylum's staff and will leave when I do."

"They all get paid, too, though."

"You're not...oh, I'm so sorry. I just assumed...I'll speak to the doctor in the morning."

Mary Grace shrugged and held out Lillias' robe for her to step into. "I'd rather you didnae, Mrs Strang. I don't need anything. Now, let's get you dry before you catch a wee chill."

Beau Rivage Asylum, 7th February, 1878

Mary Grace was excited. It was the first time she would be getting out and into the village since she had arrived. Since then, she'd been wearing the same dark blue dress as the attendants, with the unbecoming starched white cap and white apron. With its feathered straps, the apron was the only part of the uniform she liked. But for a trip to the village, she was able to wear her own clothes for once, and Mrs Strang had made her a new pale green sprigged cotton dress with a lace trimmed bodice. She'd started it, she said, once she knew Mary Grace was coming. One of the attendants had to cut the pattern, of course, since no inmate – no matter how trusted – was allowed to use scissors. And Mrs Strang had promised her a pink silk dress for the next entertainment evening. Mary Grace topped the whole thing off with a jaunty hat which was also a gift from Mrs Strang and admired herself in the mirror. Her smile faded. Mrs Strang had been so kind to her, and she still hadn't told her about the letter Mr Strang had given to her for Dr Carruthers-Browne. It had been clear from the contents that this wasn't just a temporary stay. She was worried about what this would mean – both for her and her mistress – but she knew they were better off here. Neither of them would be safe at home. Mary Grace realised that although the work here was hard and she was sometimes scared of some of the patients, her life was so much easier now she was away from her family. She sighed. She felt she had the measure of this place now, and the information she had gleaned she would be able to use to help her mistress, but she still wasn't certain whether Mrs Strang was strong enough to hear what she had to tell her. And she didn't want to distress her mistress further by telling her that she had written to Miss Gilfillan herself. Mrs Strang might think that impertinent.

Still, she would worry about all that later. Right now, she had a trip down to the village to look forward to. Mrs Strang had given her some money from the meagre weekly allowance she received from Mr Strang. She was to go to the haberdashers for some silk ribbons and trimmings for Mrs Strang's sewing and some hair grips for herself, since she was always losing them. She was also to go to the chemists for some nice violet soap for Mrs Strang's baths instead of that overwhelming carbolic.

And Mrs Strang had given her a whole ten shillings for herself. She was going to see if she could get some sturdy buttoned boots for walking in the grounds, which were marshy in places. And she was going to buy a whole cake, one that she wouldn't have to share with anybody. A tipsy cake or, better still, an Albert cake with its crisp pastry base and light sponge inside, covered in sweet white icing that would make her teeth hurt. She would make sure she had money left over to buy Mrs Strang a sweetmeat too. An apricot pithivier, perhaps. She knew she liked those. She picked up the letters Mrs Strang wanted her to post and left their rooms.

She popped her head into the office of the wardress on duty and was happy to see it was Maud today. Mary Grace excitedly told her where she was going.

Maud beamed at her. "Ah, and will ye be goin' tae Gow's? Could ye get me a wee poke of barley sugars?"

"Oh! Yes! I want to get Mrs Strang some mint humbugs and aniseed twists. She doesn't seem to have a fancy for anything, so I want to see if I can tempt her with those."

"Aye, a wee peppermint might settle that belly of hers." Maud waved her off. "Now, don't you be out 'til all hours."

"I won't, I'll be straight back." Mary Grace waved a goodbye and headed out of the front door and down the driveway. It was long and sloping and you couldn't see the end of it from the house. She had never walked this far before, but recalled the gatehouse from her arrival, grand and formal. Now it seemed much smaller than she had remembered. It was surrounded by the vibrant yellow of wild gorse and blankets of delicate white snowdrops. The heavy wrought iron gates with their curlicues and spirals and fancy 'BR' were closed, of course, and she waved to the porter so that he would open the little pedestrian entrance for her, just as Maud had told her to do.

He watched her for a few moments through the window, stuffing pieces of pie into his mouth and chewing slowly, like a thoughtful bull. Finally, he filled his mouth with the last substantial piece, wiped his hands on his jacket, and came out to greet her.

"You'll be wantin' the gate open, I suppose."

Mary Grace wasn't sure if she was expected to answer, so she simply nodded. He nodded back and continued to look her up and down, picking pieces of pastry off his whiskers and popping them into his mouth.

"An' where are you aff, lassie?"

"Into the village." She frowned up at him. "It's allowed. I'm not an inmate, you know."

He laughed, but without humour. "Oh, aye, they all say that. An' then who gets intae bother when wan o' yis lunatics goes missin' eh?" Again, he didn't seem to expect an answer, so she didn't give him one. "Muggins, here, that's who. Name?"

She told him and he went back inside the gatehouse and consulted a big book, muttering to himself as he did so. He came back out, shaking his head. "Your name's not in the book, lass."

Mary Grace could feel her splendid day out slipping away

59

from her. "But...but I *am* allowed. I promise you."

He shrugged, sucking on his teeth. "I'll need tae check." He unhooked a huge set of keys from a nail on the wall and attached it to his belt before setting off up the driveway, without the slightest hint of urgency, whistling tunelessly to himself.

Mary Grace sighed and looked for somewhere to sit down and wait. There was no point in doing anything else. She knew that the gate was always locked.

Finally, she saw him reappear around the bend, his face much redder than when he had set off and he was puffing slightly. Mary Grace wasn't sure why. He'd hardly exerted himself, lumbering along as if wading through treacle. He surveyed her for a few moments and nodded. She wasn't sure what the nod signified.

"So...can I go into the village?"

"Aye. They confirmed your story."

Mary Grace felt a sense of relief and smiled happily. "Thank you." She turned to the gate.

"Not so fast, lass. What have ye got there?"

Mary Grace was confused. She lifted the moss green velvet reticule with its cheery red tassels and looked at it. "This? My mistress gave it to me."

"What's in it?"

"Money. Mrs Strang's money." She held on tightly to it. The bag contained two shiny half-sovereigns, three silver shillings, four pennies and two farthings. She knew exactly how much because she'd counted it out several times before she left. It was more money than she had ever held at one time before, and ten whole shillings of it were hers.

The porter nodded and his eyes narrowed. Mary Grace's confusion lifted. Ah! So that was what this was about. He wanted her to pay him to open the gate. But how much? Her hand rested on the top of the bag. Was a penny too little, a shilling too much?

As she debated, he continued. "And what else?" She blinked at him. "In the wee green bag. What else is in it?"

"Oh! Two letters that I'm posting for Mrs Strang."

The porter took the keys from his belt and unlocked the gate. He stood in front of it so that she couldn't get through and held out a meaty hand and smiled at her almost kindly. "I'll just take those letters, lass."

Beau Rivage Asylum, 12th February, 1878

Carruthers-Browne studied his visitor. The man's eyes were bloodshot and the shadows underneath them were heavy. "And are you sure you don't wish to tell your wife yourself?"

"Quite sure. I only came rather than writing because I felt I should tell you in person and…well. I wanted to reassure myself that she's being looked after well."

Carruthers-Browne bridled at this slight upon his care. "Of course. And I presume you wish us to continue doing so? In the same manner?"

"Yes. I want her to have the best possible care."

"And her attendant?"

"Her attendant?"

"Yes. The girl eats a substantial amount, you know. We haven't made any arrangements for her upkeep; the letter you sent with the girl seemed to assume that her keep would be covered by the payments you make for your wife. That isn't the case. She eats like a horse. And there is also the matter of her training." He pushed across a piece of paper. "I've set out some accounts."

Arthur Strang glanced down at the paper. "Yes. Of course. Yes. I'll make the necessary arrangements with my bank."

"Excellent." Carruthers-Browne thought that he could push things still further. "Now that Mrs Strang has been with us for the month's initial period, it would be wise to pay for her care in advance."

"In advance?"

"Yes, in case of eventualities such as the sad, sad circumstance you came here to tell me about today. After all, if anything similar were to happen to you…" He waved a hand delicately.

Strang barked out a humourless laugh and ran a hand down his face. "I think that's very unlikely, but if you insist."

"Excellent. If you could arrange for a year's fees for Mrs Strang and her maid, I think that would be adequate."

"A year?" Strang's face blanched.

Carruthers-Browne steepled his fingers. "Mmmmmm. After all, I'm assuming Mrs Strang has now come into a further substantial…?"

"Yes. Yes, of course." Strang stood abruptly, almost toppling the rather fine chair he had been sitting in. Carruthers-Browne frowned but said nothing. "I must go." Strang hesitated. "She won't…she's not…?"

"Wandering around?" Carruthers-Browne looked at his gold pocket watch and shook his head. "Oh no, she'll be in the dayroom or the airing court right now. I'll wait for half an hour or so and then ask an attendant to bring her to my office."

"And you'll be…kind?"

Carruthers-Browne bridled once again at this affront to his professionalism and care. "Indeed I shall, Mr Strang. Most kind."

Arthur Strang nodded once and left the doctor's office, swiping at his eyes with the back of his hand.

Carruthers-Browne yawned and rang the bell. A male attendant came scurrying in. "Ask Nurse Rintoul to bring Mrs Strang here, would you. I'd like you here, too. I have some bad news to impart to her."

The attendant nodded and left the room. Carruthers-Browne moved to the window and watched Strang's carriage as it headed off down the driveway. The man had looked quite distraught, almost haunted; he would not have thought him capable of such feeling based on their previous discussions and correspondence. Carruthers-Browne regretted not taking advantage of the situation more. Still, he was sure he could always come up with something that would require a further injection of cash in due course. The planned extension to Beau Rivage would cost a fair amount. Necessary though, if he wanted to attract a richer clientele and – the last snub still smarted – if he wanted to be accepted into society here. Damn them for their snooty, insular Scottish ways.

Nurse Rintoul and the attendant came into the room with Mrs Strang. Carruthers-Browne motioned her to sit on the low horsehair couch he kept for inmates who were unwell or in the grip of a fit and turned back to the window. He gazed out into the distance. "I'm afraid I have some bad news for you."

The woman gasped. "Arthur? Is he...?"

The Doctor turned towards her. She had remained standing, which rather annoyed him. "Don't worry. Your husband is well, Lillias. He has just taken his leave."

"Arthur's here? Has he come to take me home?"

Carruthers-Browne laughed. "I'm afraid not. You're still not well. You must understand that your husband and I know what's best for you. And what's best for you is to remain here in this place of care. No, I'm afraid the news concerns your aunt, a Miss...Gilfillan."

"Aunt Evelina?"

"Yes."

"Is she ill?"

"I'm afraid that she's dead."

"Dead." The word wasn't so much spoken as breathed.

"Mmmmm. Apparently, she was on her way here to visit you when her carriage was involved in some sort of accident. Both she and her coachman were killed."

"Dead." Again, the word was just a breath.

"Mmmmm. Broken necks, I understand." He sighed.

"Dreadful business." Something else was required, he felt. "I'm terribly sorry for your loss."

Lillias screamed and put her hands to her face, her body swaying. She made as if to rush towards the door. Nurse Rintoul and the attendant jumped to support her, pushing her over to the horsehair couch. They pulled her down until she was sitting on the couch between them. They were close in, each one holding tightly onto a wrist, which they pushed down onto her thighs. Nurse Rintoul kicked Lillias' feet apart. She and the attendant each wrapped a leg around one of Lillias'. Carruthers-Browne nodded in approval at the well-practiced move.

Lillias continued to scream and shake, her eyes wide and glassy. "Take her to her room and restrain her. Then give her a dose of chloral hydrate to calm her. Get one of the attendants to sit with her until she's in possession of her senses again — I think this calls for more than her own girl. If necessary, remove her to the padded cell." Carruthers-Browne picked up his pen and dipped it in the inkwell. "I'll write it up in her notes." He sighed. "Very unfortunate situation."

Mary Grace fussed with the flowers in her hand as she climbed the stone staircase. Her daily walk around the grounds had yielded a handful of early crocuses which had been nestling in the lee of a low stone wall down near the river. She wasn't supposed to go down there, but she had spotted the delicate lilacs and purples contrasting with the vibrant orange of the centre of the flowers. She had picked them for Mrs Strang, together with a profusion of snowdrops, and would make a lovely display out of them for Mrs Strang's bedside cabinet.

She entered their wee living room and called out a hello, but there was no answer from the bedroom. Mrs Strang must be in the dayroom with Miss Binnie. But the door was ajar and Mary Grace spotted one of the junior attendants sitting by Mrs

Strang's bed, her hands folded in her lap. Was Mrs Strang ill?

Mary Grace pushed open the door of the bedroom. Mrs Strang was lying in bed, eyes closed, her face pale, but with two livid red spots high on her cheeks. Her hair was tumbled about on the pillow and Mary Grace's fleeting thought was that she had forgotten to brush it that morning. But then she noticed something else. It wasn't the usual bedding. Instead, towels – wet towels, it looked like – had been pulled tightly around Mrs Strang, so tight that she could see the outline of her mistress' slim body. The towels were tucked into the bed frame, pinning her arms to her sides and leaving only her head visible.

Mary Grace dropped the tiny flowers, trampling the bright pollen into the rug.

Beau Rivage Asylum, 15th March, 1878

Mary Grace put down the book she had been reading and sighed. "I know Dr Carruthers-Browne said you weren't to be excited, but really, this book is dull. Look," she nodded over at Henrietta, who had fallen asleep on the other side of Lillias' bed, her sewing still in her hand, "it's too dull even for Henrietta, and she's easily pleased."

Lillias forced herself to smile. "The Chaplain recommended it as a book which would build my strength with its messages of hope and morality. His exact words, as always."

Mary Grace stood up and stretched. "When I asked him if he had that *Castle of Otranto* you told me about, he practically had apoplexy on the spot."

This time, Lillias' smile was unforced. "Really, Mary Grace, I swear you are a changed girl from the little mouse who first came to me."

Mary Grace looked stricken. "Oh! I'm sorry, Mrs Strang! My ma always did say I'd be in trouble for my cheek one day. I don't mean anything by it, really I don't."

Lillias reached out a hand and touched Mary Grace's arm. Sometimes it was as though she and Mary Grace had switched positions, which, in a way, they had – Mary Grace was in charge of her wellbeing and she had risen to the challenge admirably. Sometimes, however, they reverted to their previous relationship as mistress and servant, mostly when Mary Grace felt that she had offended in some way. Even her voice, grown strong, determined and with the precision of the other attendants since her arrival, changed back to the heavily accented hesitance of her time at Ardellen. "No, I like it. It's only…" she laughed, "Well, when I hired you from the village, I assumed that *I* would be the one helping *you*. The reality, however, is very different. I just don't know what I would have done without you."

"Well, you *did* help me, Miss. More than you could ever know. Besides, you've changed, too, Miss."

"Have I?"

"Aye. You seem older. An' you're sadder, but…you also seem happier than you were with…" She left the sentence unfinished, her face full of worry that she had said too much.

Lillias reassured her. "Perhaps you're right. Anyway, I'm very glad you're here with me."

Mary Grace beamed. "An' I'm so glad I'm here, too. I'm staying as long as you'll have me." Suddenly, her face fell again.

"What is it?"

"Nothing…it's nothing, honest."

But Lillias didn't believe her.

Beau Rivage Asylum, 25th March, 1878

Nurse Duthie had left Lillias at the top of the stairs, saying she needed to see to a patient who had been struck by a sudden attack of melancholia and needed to be watched carefully. The door to Lillias' rooms was open and Lillias saw Mary Grace over by the bed, smoothing out the white counterpane. The girl had not been her usual smiling self recently and Lillias felt that her shoulders were heavy with the weight of something other than her work.

The cocoa matting covering the wooden floor silenced Lillias' footsteps. It was only when she went over to the window to raise the sash by its permitted five inches to let some air in that Mary Grace turned from making the bed and gasped. Her eyes were red rimmed and her cheeks were blotchy.

"Oh, miss! I never heard you!"

"Whatever is it? You seem troubled."

"Aye...aw, it's nothing." But she sat down on the neatly-made bed, rumpling the smooth counterpane.

Lillias hurried over and sat down next to her, taking the large, calloused hands in her own small ones. "Nothing? You're the very definition of misery. Now, tell me what's wrong. Are you missing your family? You can...go home if you like. I'll be fine here on my own." She hoped Mary Grace didn't want to go home, as she wasn't sure how she'd cope without her, but something was bothering the girl. "Come, now, surely it can't be as bad as all that?"

Little bubbles appeared at Mary Grace's nostrils as the tears which hadn't been far away started to flow. Mary Grace lifted her hands, still clasped in Lillias' own and used her sleeve to wipe the bubbles away. "It's nothin' like that, Miss. An' I *never* want to go home. This is my home, wi' you. It's just...what I heard...an'...an'...since your aunt...what I think...An' maybe it's my fault for sending...I'm scared, Miss."

Lillias patted Mary Grace's chilled hands. "Now, my dear girl, tell me everything."

And Mary Grace did. She told her about where she'd found the letters, about the conversations between Strang and McAllister that she'd overheard, and she told her about the letter she'd written to Miss Gilfillan herself. She told her that she didn't think her aunt's death was an accident. Lillias listened, her body growing more rigid with each new revelation.

When Mary Grace's story came to a sobbing end she sat quietly for a few moments, still gripping onto her hands. "Arthur wouldn't do that, Mary Grace. Not kill my aunt. He loves me, I know he does." Mary Grace opened her mouth to speak. "I believe you. I believe you heard all those things and that he's in trouble and about my money. I believe you and I want you to know that. But…" she shook her head. "Not *that*, he wouldn't do *that*."

"Oh, Miss." Mary Grace's voice was almost pitying, but with an undertone of bitterness. "You don't know what they can do. My da….You don't know how it is, Miss. An' now I'm worried about you even more, now you're…in that condition."

"Condition?" Lillias was disappointed that even Mary Grace thought she was mad. "But I'm not a lunatic. You know that."

Mary Grace shook her head. "You're not a lunatic, Miss. No. No, it's because he'll take it away when he finds out. He'll take it away."

Lillias was exasperated. "You're not making sense."

"The baby. He'll take the baby. *Your* baby."

"*My* baby? But I…I…I'm not…"

Mary Grace's eyes widened and her tears stopped. "Oh, Mrs Strang! Surely you know you're going to have a baby? The sickness, your belly getting bigger?"

Lillias put a hand to her stomach. "A baby? But how would I know? Nobody's ever talked about…"

Beau Rivage Asylum, 4th April, 1878

A crocodile of women wound their way around the grounds. Now that the weather was more clement, Dr Carruthers-Browne insisted that all inmates who weren't dangerous, confined to bed, locked in the padded cell or isolated due to fever in the Hospital Ward, should take a daily constitutional in the grounds: Mondays, Wednesdays and Fridays for the men, Tuesdays, Thursdays and Saturdays for the women. Sundays, of course, was a rest day, for religious contemplation.

After a turn around the perimeter of the house, those who could be trusted on their own were allowed to wander freely and enjoy a game of croquet, or lawn bowls for the very energetic, with attendants posted at judicious points to foil attempts at either escape or suicide. The remaining inmates were shepherded into the walled garden, where they could roam safely, under the watchful eyes of staff. Lillias and Mary Grace sat on a bench facing the distant hills. The low sun had turned the slopes shades of gold and pink. Henrietta sat on the grass at their feet, making daisy chains and humming tunelessly to herself.

Lillias took the shawl from her shoulders and leaned towards her friend. "Henrietta, dear, that grass must be damp. Here, take this to sit on or you'll catch a chill." She encouraged Henrietta up by taking her hand and laid the shawl out on the grass where her friend had been sitting. Henrietta sank back down and continued with her chains.

"So, what are we to do, Mary Grace?"

Mary Grace shrugged. "One of the attendants commented yesterday that she thinks I'm stealing sweetmeats from the kitchen for you. She says you're putting on weight, even though you only pick at your food at mealtimes. We shan't be able to keep it a secret for much longer."

Lillias sighed. "It may be time to tell Doctor Carruthers-Browne."

"Ye'll no' want to do that, yet awhile." Lillias and Mary Grace stared at Henrietta. She tucked one stem into another, then laid the chain in her lap and looked up at them. "Ye'll want to keep it quiet until your sixth month at least. Then it'll be too late to move you." She let out a peal of melodic laughter. "Ye'll be doubly confined, as it were. They'll no' notice. Maist o' they so-called nurses widnae recognise an expectant woman if she delivered triplets in front o' them."

"Henrietta!" Lillias clapped her hands in delight, worries temporarily forgotten. "You *can* speak!"

Henrietta continued as if Lillias hadn't said anything. "Mind you, thon footpad Carruthers-Browne would happily snatch the Queen's Bounty out of their wee fingers if *that* was the case. Ye'd better hope it's *no'* triplets." The sing-song laugh pealed out once more.

Lillias was paying more attention to the fact that Henrietta had spoken at all, rather than to what she was saying. All she could do was repeat her previous words. "You can speak!"

"Aye, that I can. I just choose not tae. Makes my life a damned sight easier, so I'll thank you to no' let on, if ye'll be so kind." She plucked another daisy from the lawn and slid it carefully into the stem of the one before. "No. Keep news o' the bairn to yersel'. You're nothin' but a wee skelf. Ye'll no' show properly until six months, at least." Lillias put her hands protectively to her stomach. "An' ye'll no' want to do that, lass."

"But they'll take it away. They won't let me keep it."

"There are other children here. Babbies, too." Lillias knew this to be true. There was an eight-year-old girl on the General Ward who was incapable of speech and a woman who was admitted from the workhouse shortly after Lillias arrived had given birth in the padded room, where she'd been taken to be restrained to prevent her from harming either herself or her unborn child. Lillias saw them sometimes. And there were children of the staff who lived on the grounds who played around, and even with, some of the inmates with touching unconcern.

"What about Arthur?"

Henrietta snorted. "Ye think he'll want to be burdened wi' a bairn?"

"Miss Binnie's right, Miss. Mr Strang won't want a baby around."

Lillias sighed heavily. She realised now that none of this had in fact been a mistake. Arthur would not be returned to her as the man she had first met and that they wouldn't live the life she had longed for. She was a different person now. She was on her own and had a baby coming; a baby that she would love and was determined to keep from harm. "I hope you're both right."

Henrietta held up the finished daisy chain and admired it. "An' ye need to tread carefully wi' thon ither matter. Ye cannae go accusin' people of murder, ye know. Especially rich men fae hereabouts."

"What if Mary Grace is right? Dr Carruthers-Browne—"

"An' what exactly do ye think would happen if ye tellt that gillie-wet-foot that your dear husband murdered your aunt?"

"She's right, Miss."

Lillias looked away from her two friends. "I'm never going to get out of here, am I?"

Ardellen House, Stirlingshire, 14th June, 1878

"What do you think it's all about?"

McAllister handed the letter back to Arthur with a shrug. "Who can tell from that? You've been paying the fees, I assume?"

"Of course. I paid a year in advance back in February."

"Probably another ruse by the cheating quack to get some more money out of you. He'll be wanting to build a new summerhouse for the lunatics or something."

"Goddamn it. He'd better not be. I seem to be sending good money after bad with these investments of yours."

McAllister raised one eyebrow. "You know you can buy yourself out at any time. I'm not stopping you."

"God...no...I didn't mean..."

"Any news of the inheritance from the aunt?"

Arthur pinched the bridge of his nose. "Still tied up in probate. That damned clause in her will; the old harridan."

McAllister sneered. "She didn't think much of you, did she? If we'd only got to her sooner, you wouldn't be in this mess."

Arthur hurriedly went to shut his study door. "Good Christ, man. Watch your words."

"So, what's to be done about it?"

"I'm not sure there's anything *to* be done. The codicil states that I'm to have no access to Lillias' aunt's money; that the capital is not to be touched and that the income is to be strictly for the benefit of Lillias. Overseen by Trustees, goddammit. It will take years to sort that out in court. Lillias can't touch it either, of course, because she's in the madhouse where I put her. Well, the income can damn well pay for her to stay there. Luckily, her own fortune wasn't insubstantial, but at this rate, it's not going to last forever. Damn it, don't let me gamble my investments like that again."

McAllister bowed mockingly and gestured at the letter. "And the good doctor? What of him?"

Arthur let out a sigh. "I suppose I'll have to take a trip up there to see what he wants."

Beau Rivage Asylum, 14th June, 1878

"Lillias! Calm down!"

How could she. They were going to steal her baby from her when it was born. That's what he'd said.

"She's struggling too much to give her the chloral hydrate, Doctor."

She didn't want it. It smelled of rotten fruit and it wouldn't be good for the baby, she was sure of that.

"Pin her arms to the bed."

They were hurting her; her wrists and ankles felt as though they were caught in a vice. A drip of liquid forced its way between her lips, bitter and unwanted. She spat it out and pressed her lips together, twisting her head to one side.

"If she continues thrashing around in this way, she'll hurt herself and the baby."

She would never hurt her baby. They were the ones who were going to hurt her baby. A weight bore down on her as though someone was kneeling on her and the pungent fruit smell rose again. Pears. Black and rotting and crawling with flies.

"Mrs Strang. In your condition you *must* remain calm. There is no point in succumbing to hysteria. It's your husband's child, and I have no doubt he will look after it while you're here. Dammit, I wish I had said nothing until he got here, but I thought it best to prepare her."

Calm? She could never be calm again. She tried to move the parts of her body that were still hers. The hands — how many of them were there? — gripped and pinched even more tightly.

"Get the straitjacket."

"The straitjacket? But…"

"She needs to be restrained. Get her in the straitjacket and then put her in the padded cell to calm down. Damnation."

Beau Rivage Asylum, 15th June, 1878

Lillias turned her cheek away from whatever it was that had irritated her into consciousness. Horsehair stuffing poked out of a hole in one of the leather pouches that covered the walls and floor of the room, perhaps where a previous inmate had worried away at a weak patch until they had ripped a hole. She blinked and glanced around her. She was curled up on the floor of the cell, head resting in the bottom corner. The grey painted leather smelled of sweat and piss and disinfectant and pain and fear.

As they began to focus, her eyes traced the path of a wide crack in the leather before it feathered into a multitude of tiny lines and cracks that seemed to cover the entirety of the tiny cell. She wasn't sure if it was her chloral hydrate-befuddled brain, or whether the leather was, in fact, covered with cracks. It seemed important, but she knew it really wasn't. She closed her eyes once more, a dull ache rippling through her shoulders. Her arms were crossed in front of her, kept in place by the strange, long sleeves of the blue and white checked straitjacket, wrapped tightly around her and tied behind her back. Her nose itched and she rubbed it on the rough leather.

It had taken three of them to get her into the jacket, she recalled now, after they had dragged her out of the room. Carruthers-Browne's smug face when he told her he had written to Arthur to tell him about her condition, coming on top of the death of her aunt had been too much. She had come here entirely sane, and they had sent her mad. What sort of a place was this?

A fractured strip of light came in through the small viewing window in the door and Lillias traced it with her foot, round and round. At intervals, the patch of light darkened, as one of the attendants peered through the glass on her hourly rounds. Lillias counted eighteen such darkenings before she fell back to sleep.

Beau Rivage Asylum, 19th June, 1878

"Mrs Strang?" Mary Grace was worried. Her mistress hadn't spoken since they had brought her back up from the padded cell two hours ago. She lay, pale and unmoving, on her bed. Mary Grace was trying to rub warmth and movement back into her hands. "Please, Mrs Strang. You're scaring me."

Her mistress' eyes fluttered open and Mary Grace felt a gentle squeeze on her fingers.

"Oh, thank God! I thought..." She tailed off. She didn't want to say what she had thought.

"My child?" Mary Grace had to bend over the bed to hear the words properly.

"The babby's fine. It's you I'm worried about. I came back from my walk the day they put you in that...room, and they told me you'd been put there for your own safety. In *your* condition, too! But then they wouldn't tell me anything else. What happened?"

"Arthur..."

"Mr Strang?" Mary Grace looked around, even though she knew that was silly. "What about him?"

"He's ... going to...take the baby."

"Take the baby? What do you mean?"

Mrs Strang's eyes closed again. "He'll come. The doctor said. He'll come. To take the baby..."

Beau Rivage Asylum, 24th June, 1878

Henrietta had mopped the hall every day since Lillias had told them that her husband was coming and today she had seen the coach coming up the driveway. From Mary Grace's description of the coach and the man, she knew that the visitor must be Lillias' husband. She continued to mop the same patch of floor over and over, her head bent to the door of the doctor's office. She couldn't hear everything, but she was hearing enough to get the gist of the conversation.

"...we think some time at the end of August," Carruthers-Browne was saying.

"And you'll let me know immediately?"

"Of course. I would prefer to leave the baby with her for a little while to allow her to nurse it."

"What do you mean?"

"Well, before you take it away, Mr Strang."

"Take it away? Why would I do that?"

Carruthers-Browne sounded confused. "Well, I...do you not wish to have your child with you?"

"I...yes...of course, at some point. But I have too much business to attend to and a child would be an inconvenience. It will be far better with its mother, I am sure."

"In a *lunatic* asylum?"

"Is my wife too mad to take care of it?"

"Oh, no. She's coming along very well here."

"Are you saying that the child would be unsafe in your care?"

"Well, I...no, of course not." Carruthers-Browne sounded quite indignant, and Henrietta smiled to herself.

"Then what is the problem?"

"Well, it's just that it is rather...untoward."

"But not unheard of?"

"No, indeed not. There are generally one or two children here. But..."

"I will not be expecting you to board and feed the child without being compensated, if that's your concern, Doctor."

The voices lowered and Henrietta struggled to hear much of the next part of the conversation, even with her ear firmly pressed against the door. It was only a minute or so later that the sound of chairs scraping on the wooden floor sent her scurrying backwards with the mop and bucket. As the door opened Lillias' husband spoke again. "So, let me know once the child is born to enable me to make arrangements. If it should be a boy, I will send for him on his fifth birthday. It would not do for a boy to grow up here. If it should be a girl, then she can come to me when she is thirteen or fourteen, closer to when she is of age. Is that clear?"

"Perfectly clear." Henrietta wished she could wipe the simpering smirk off the doctor's face. She busied herself with the mop around them, dragging it across the front of Lillias' husband's feet as she did.

"Dear God, watch out, woman!"

"Binnie! What do you think you're doing? I'm terribly sorry, the woman is quite demented." Henrietta calmly put her mop back into the bucket to get it nice and wet once more, before determinedly mopping the space where Carruthers-Browne stood, soaking not only his shoes but the bottom of his trouser legs.

Beau Rivage Asylum, 26th July, 1878

Mrs Strang had been confined to her rooms, and Mary Grace with her to take care of her. It would not be seemly, according to Carruthers-Browne, for a patient to be out in public in such a condition. *In public.* As though her mistress had suggested visiting the neighbours and leaving her card. She watched as Mrs Strang put her hand on her rounded belly. She could tell that her mistress' mind was returning to the thoughts which had been occupying her since Miss Binnie had told them what she had heard.

"Do you think he meant it? That he won't take the baby?"

Mary Grace lifted her mistress' feet onto the little padded footstool. "I'm sure he did, Miss. Miss Binnie heard him say he didn't want to be bothered with a child."

"Do you think he's cruel, Mary Grace?" Mary Grace was silent. "I can't work it out. He was so happy and loving. I can't believe he would be deliberately cruel. I'm sure he loves me."

Mary Grace folded blankets, determined not to look at her mistress. They had had many conversations like this in the last month. "I think...it's a cruel thing to send someone to be locked up in a place like this, if that's what you mean."

"Do you think he would toy with me like that, though? Do you think he means to take the baby after all?"

A snort behind them made them both turn around. "I tell ye, the man'll no' want a bairn around. An' definitely no' a squalling infant."

"But what if he does? And *when* he does?"

Mary Grace tucked a blanket around her mistress. "Well, we'll just deal with that when it happens, won't we, Miss?"

Beau Rivage Asylum, 23rd August, 1878

Lillias let the letter flutter to the floor and clasped Clementina closely to her breast. Her first letter from Arthur since she'd been here, and it was as stiff and formal as if she were a distant business acquaintance. Beau Rivage was the best place for her, he said. She could keep the baby with her until she was grown. He hadn't used Clementina's name: 'the child', 'it', he'd called her. He hadn't told Lillias he loved her, or that he missed her. He hadn't called her his goldfinch. It was an 'unfortunate situation', as though one of the dogs had got into the vegetable garden. She could almost hear the coldness in his tone. Lillias realised that she didn't care any longer. She looked over at Mary Grace, sweeping the hearth and Henrietta quietly knitting in the corner, her needles clacking rhythmically, the stitches as swift and neat as ever. Henrietta had promised to teach her, so that she could knit a shawl for the baby, although Lillias knew she could never make something as beautiful as Henrietta could. She already had the wool, which Mary Grace had bought for her in the village, a delightful blue, the colour of a flax flower. Lillias bent her nose to Clementina's head. "You belong to all of us, now, Clemmie. Everyone I love is here."

THE LOCK

Glasgow – January, 1894

The sound of the heavy outside door slamming was unmistakeable. And, at this time of the morning when everyone – even the night staff – was asleep, that sound could only mean one thing. Clementina gathered up the bottom of her rough woollen nightgown and ran. Her bare feet slapped on the stone floors as she ran back along the corridor she had tiptoed through not five minutes before, back up the staircases that became narrower the higher she climbed, back into the smallest of the attic dormitories.

Thanks to the moonlight forcing its icy fingers through the narrow windows, Clementina could move sure-footedly between the eight straw pallets which lay close together, each with a small table beside it. Each table held a bible positioned in the top right corner and a ribbon, neatly folded, top left. Seven of the eight beds contained a figure huddled under a thin blanket. The eighth bed was Clementina's own, its blanket roughly thrown off when she went for her nightly roam in search of her wee edge. Sometimes, her wee edge was extra food, sometimes it was something to wear, sometimes it was information – and that was often the best wee edge of all. Tonight, however, all her roam had brought her was a forewarning of danger.

Clementina hesitated. She should jump into bed and pretend to be asleep, just screw up her eyes and breathe deeply, as she had done so many times before in the last two years. She would probably be safe, after all. She paused at the sight of a red ribbon on the table next to the new girl's bed. The rest of the ribbons were brown, the same dull brown as the blankets, and made of the same thin material. The girl – she didn't know her name – could only have been eight, nine at most, even younger than Clementina had been when she had arrived in Glasgow. Something about the stubborn set of her mouth and her obvious determination not to cry when she was brought in had reminded Clementina of her own arrival at the home for wayward girls, and the shining waterfall of corn-coloured hair reminded Clementina of her mother. After a few moments' hesitation, she moved to the side of the new girl's bed. Reaching out a hand, she slapped it over the girl's mouth, at the same time grabbing her by the arm and forcing her up out of bed. The girl, half asleep and struggling, looked at her with frightened brown eyes. Clementina shook her head and pulled the girl fully up out of bed. But the girl kicked and fought, hitting out at Clementina with her free arm and catching her roundly with a smart punch to the ear which brought tears to her eyes. Clementina scooped the smaller girl off the ground and, her hand still clapped over the girl's mouth, firmly grabbed her around the waist, her fingers pinching through the thin cloth of the girl's nightgown. She immediately felt ashamed of the pinch – the girl was scared, after all – but there was no time now to stop and apologise.

Clementina carried the girl out of the room. She would be bruised from the small feet kicking into her back and the elbow jabbing at her side, but she would worry about that later. The corridor was dark, but she knew the way without needing to see, and she could just about make out the door frame of the press at the end. She put the girl down, still keeping a tight hold on her head and mouth and the girl immediately started to squirm. "Shush, now, I'm not going to hurt you." She opened the door and thrust the girl inside, still holding the girl's mouth and whispering into her ear. "You need to stay here, just for a wee while, you understand?" The girl glared back at her, her body rigid. "I'm going to take my hand away from your mouth; promise me you won't make a noise?" The girl paused, then nodded once and Clementina released the pressure.

The girl sharply drew her head back and bit down on the withdrawing hand. "Ow, you wee..." Clementina replaced her already throbbing hand over the girl's mouth. "Look, I've not got the time to explain, you need to trust me. Please. I promise you I'll explain later, when it's safe."

Something in Clementina's face or her desperate whispers must have convinced the girl. Her tense body relaxed and she nodded. Clementina took her hand away slowly and the girl stood there, lips trembling and eyes full of tears which she blinked away angrily. "I'm sorry, hen." Clementina reached out a hand to touch the girl's arm, but it was jerked away. "Look, I cannae stop and explain why, but you have to stay here quietly, in this press, until I come back and get you."

The girl was shivering. Clementina hesitated and then pulled off her own thin nightgown, suddenly feeling awkward in this familiar place. "Here, have this." She pushed the girl gently into the press and closed the door, opening it again just a crack, to whisper, "What's your name?"

The girl glared at her and pressed her lips together so hard that they disappeared. When no reply came, Clementina made to close the door, but the girl held out a hand to stop her. "Jeannie. Jeannie Jack."

Clementina touched the thin hand. "Clementina. My friends call me Clemmie. Now, you sit tight. I'll be back soon." She took hold of the door handle again.

"Can ye...can ye leave it open a wee bit?" The eyes which looked hopefully at Clemmie were full of tears again and the older girl nodded and pushed the door to, leaving the tiniest crack. She could sympathise with Jeannie; she knew how it felt to be shut in and, even at the age of fifteen, it still frightened her. Just a wee bit, mind. And it was far, far better than the alternative.

Clemmie shivered. She would have to get one of her spare gowns out of its wee hidey hole before she went back to bed. If she was found naked she would be in for a whipping. Clemmie ran along the corridor. She would be in for a whipping anyway, likely enough. After all, she was supposed to be in charge of the room and there was now an empty bed where there should have been a girl. As she prised up the loose floorboard and felt in the space beneath that held her treasures, Clemmie heard the murmur of voices and the tread of at least two pairs of feet on the winding wooden staircase that led up to their top floor room. She quickly tugged the creased gown over her head and ran back into the dormitory on her tiptoes, pulling the door closed behind her.

Her heart was beating so loudly that she almost missed the sound of the door opening again. She hoped that the beating couldn't be heard across the room and held her breath. She heard two sets of footsteps coming into the room. One set she recognised as the Matron's – sharp, precise, like a crow pecking at corn. The other set was heavier, one step accompanied by the jingle of a coin purse or a watch chain.

"Here you are, sir." Mrs McCombe's voice was soft and low, but with a harsh edge. "The girl's in here. A good girl. Nine years old, so she is."

"And definitely a good girl?" Clemmie bit back a sob. That voice had called *her* a good girl once, too and she still heard it almost every night when she fell asleep. She'd never seen his face, or the faces of the others, but she would never forget that voice, nor the devil it belonged to. She tried to keep her body from shaking.

"Oh yes, indeed, sir. We inspect all our girls, sir, as soon as they come to the Home. Do you want to see her, sir?"

Clemmie could hear the devil's breathing, but he said nothing. Mrs McCombe made her slow way up the centre of the room, checking each bed. Clemmie knew that, like her, the

84

occupants of every bed would be awake and wary. Sleep was fitful here, when it did come, and the girls were used to keeping one ear out for danger. And this was definitely danger.

The Matron's footsteps stopped. "What in..?"

"What is it?"

"I'm...I'm sorry, sir, but the girl...doesn't appear to be here. I can't think..."

"Not there?" The devil's voice was smooth, but with a dark and lurking threat tucked inside. "You do realise that I have made promises, Mrs McCombe?"

"Yes, sir, I know you——"

"And *you* have obligations, too. Your daughter would be on the streets but for me. Your feckless son-in-law wouldn't have a job. And your grand-daughters... Well, twins are very special, aren't they?"

"Oh, sir, please...I'm sorry, sir. I'll find her, sir, so I will. An' I'll deliver her personally to you as soon as I do. An' if she's run away, sir, I'll find you another one, sir. Prettier, younger. We've three new girls expected this very week, sir." Mrs McCombe's voice managed to be both whining and sly.

"You'd best do that. And you'd best do it soon. Otherwise, it will not go well for those grand-daughters of yours." His heels rang out on the stone floor and the metallic 'chink' that accompanied every other step was a threat. He slammed the door behind him with venom. Clemmie had no doubts that the Matron would do the devil's bidding and do it gladly for a price. The girls in Mrs McCombe's care were wicked girls, girls who deserved their punishment, who must be forced into righteousness and who would atone for their sins. Mrs McCombe was doing the Lord's work. She had told them this many times and some of them even believed it now.

Clemmie waited for the inevitable. It wasn't long in coming. Mrs McCombe's strong fingers snaked under the blanket and gripped her around the forearm. The Matron's hot and stinking breath was right in her face. "Clementina Watt, get your filthy body out of this bed and tell me where the new girl is." Each word was accompanied by a tug that almost pulled her arm loose and Clemmie found herself being lifted completely off the bed and slammed down on the floor, her back hitting the small bedside table and knocking it over.

"I don't know, Mrs McCombe, I swear I don't."

"You swear you don't? How dare you?" The spit hit Clemmie in her left eye and Mrs McCombe scooped the Bible from where it had fallen and hit Clemmie on the side of the head with it. "I'll beat the very truth into you, you little slattern."

"But—"

The Matron grabbed her by the throat. "Talk back, would you?" She threw Clemmie down onto the floor. "Take that gown off and lie on your bed. You're for a beating, make no mistake. An' you'll keep quiet while I'm administering it, if you know what's good for you, so you will."

Clemmie was well used to keeping quiet; she'd had plenty of practice. As the leather tawse the Matron always carried with her rose and fell its usual dozen times, Clemmie bit her lip to keep from crying out. Mrs McCombe was not so quiet. With each rise of the tawse, she let out an oath; and each time it fell, she expelled a guttural breath. With the final, most spiteful, stroke, Clemmie bit down on her pillow as she felt the five leather fingers of the tawse digging deeply into the skin of her back. Mrs McCombe, gasping for breath, pulled Clemmie's head back and her hot, sour breath assaulted Clemmie's face. "You're lucky not to get the spray bath to follow." She drew the tawse across Clemmie's face before pushing her head back down on the bed.

Through it all – the conversation, the door slamming, the shouting, the beating – the other girls in the room remained motionless in their beds. Only once Mrs McCombe had left, panting, and the dormitory had fallen silent again, did one of them slide out of bed and creep over to comfort Clemmie.

Clemmie and Jeannie stood on the narrow window-ledge, peering out at the foggy courtyard below, their faces pressed to the sooty glass. They had gobbled down the tiny portion of tasteless oats they were given for breakfast and retired to their quiet eyrie at the top of the building, anxiously watching the clock on the tower of the chapel opposite. If they weren't back in the sewing room for eight o'clock, there would be hell to pay. Especially as this was Wednesday. Wednesday was Mrs McCombe's least favourite day of the week since she lost half a day's work to the visit from the lady child-savers. Most of the heavy work in the laundry would stop and the girls would be put to light sewing and – for the lucky ones – schooling. Not that the schooling was worth much. Mrs McCombe brought in whey-faced Agnes to teach them, and Agnes could hardly read herself. But Clemmie relished the two hours where she could sit quietly with a book, even though the books were even more dull than the ones they were allowed in the asylum. At least there her mother's maid, Mary Grace, could sometimes sneak a little more exciting reading matter in from her trips down to the village. Even so, it was a shame that the books were collected up as soon as the ladies from the Interfering Bitch Society, as Matron called them, had gone.

Truth be told, Clemmie didn't have much time for the ladies from the Society either. They swept in, a brace of Lady Bountifuls, bringing with them the sweet scents of lavender hair pomade and candied violets. On their last visit one of them – Miss Adair, Matron had called her – had waved an expansive hand around the dining room, which doubled as a school room on Wednesdays. "This would be such a lovely room for concerts," she'd said in her gentle but confident voice. "Do you think the girls would like a piano?"

A piano? What did they want with a piano? They couldn't eat a piano. A piano wouldn't do a fourteen-hour shift in the laundry for them. A piano wouldn't save them from the jingling devil and his pals. Clemmie, who was closest to where Miss Adair and the Matron were standing, had snorted scornfully, turning it into a cough as the two women had turned at the noise. Mrs McCombe's eyes were full of threat; Miss Adair's were clear and kindly, her eyebrows slightly raised. Clemmie curtsied to her. "Sorry, Ma'am, just a wee tickle in my throat from the dust on the books."

Matron had glared at her. "Clementina Watt, don't you dare open that mouth in front of Miss Adair. Come away, Miss Adair. Such a bold girl. A wicked girl. One of the worst here. I'll make sure she's punished, so I will, I promise you that."

"I'd rather you didn't, Mrs McCombe. The girl… Clementina…can hardly be blamed for a spot of dust. Now, about that piano…"

Clemmie was brought out of her reverie by coughing and talking in the courtyard below. Three young women, one only a girl and the others not much older, now stood huddled together in the centre. They were watched by the stony-faced matron who was perched on a stool with her arms crossed.

"What's happened to their hair?" Jeannie put a fearful hand to her own shining locks, which Clemmie had scraped back into two neat plaits that morning – tied, of course, with the brown ribbon, despite Jeannie's longing look at the shiny red one which poked out from underneath her thin straw mattress. Clemmie had allowed her to keep it – they all needed something beautiful in this place, after all – but had made Jeannie promise that she would never, ever wear it. A brown ribbon wouldn't keep Jeannie safe, but it would keep her from being an immediate target. To the jingling devil and his friends, the girls at the Home were of two sorts: spoiled and unspoiled. Only the unspoiled deserved a second glance. Even then, they were not individuals;

simply 'pudding-faced' or 'fresh', or 'thick-ankled' or 'innocent flower'. Mrs McCombe was another matter. However, she had been kept busy with new arrivals for the past couple of weeks and then there was the other thing. The…shock? Fear? The almost terror that had been in her voice the night of the jingling devil's visit. This was something Clemmie could use to her advantage, she was sure. She just didn't know how, yet. Clemmie was biding her time.

She turned her attention back to Jeannie. "I don't know why they shave their heads. They call them the foul patients." Jeannie looked at her, her eyes questioning. "They have the pox and Matron says they're the wickedest of wicked women and need to be kept away from everyone. They're locked in the canary ward in the basement."

"Canary ward?"

Clemmie pointed down to the three figures now shuffling around the courtyard in their heel-less slippers and rough, poorly fitting shifts the colour of jaundice. Their heads were bowed, and they looked uncomfortable and embarrassed. "The yellow dresses. They have to wear those yellow dresses. To show they're diseased, I suppose. And to keep the rest of us away from them. See the skinny one with the red hair? That's Hannah Devlin. She was in our dormitory for a wee while." She didn't tell Jeannie that Hannah had been the former resident of Jeannie's bed and that she, too, had been a good girl when she had arrived.

Jeannie rubbed at the windowpane to clear the fog caused by her breath. "What are they doing there? What are they waiting for?"

"Watch and you'll see." As they peered out of the window the big wooden door in the wall of the courtyard opened and the three girls in yellow dresses came together in a huddle once more, shoulders hunched. Two older women dressed in dark grey dresses with matching capes entered the yard, followed by three policemen. The women wore black hats, tied with black ribbons under the chin. "Nurses, maybe. Or wardresses. They look like..." Clemmie hesitated. They looked like the wardresses in the asylum. "They come most weeks. Just watch."

Mrs McCombe nodded to the newcomers and hauled herself off her stool, reaching underneath it to lift three sets of shackles and a chain, which she handed to one of the policemen. One of the nurses opened the big black book she was carrying and handed the Matron a pen. As Mrs McCombe signed the book, the three policemen shackled the ankles of the girls in yellow, enclosing each ankle in a ring of iron joined by a short chain, before roughly pulling the three scrawny figures into position so that they could be shackled together in a small, sad line.

Clemmie grabbed Jeannie by the hand. "Come on."

"Where are we goin'?"

"Just come *on*." Clemmie tugged her harder.

"But we'll be late for work."

Clemmie glanced at the clock. "We've still got ages. Come *on*, Jeannie. Look they're leaving; we need to hurry if we're going to find out where they're going."

Jeannie stopped short, horrified. "We're goin' outside?"

"Aye." Clemmie laughed. "Don't look so feart. I've been out before, plenty of times. Quickly now."

Jeannie's mouth dropped open. "You go out? And you come *back*?"

Clemmie shrugged. "Where else am I gonnae go? Now come on."

They ran down the wooden spiral staircase from the top floor, their thin shoes barely making a sound, and then leaped two stairs at a time down the stone staircase that led to the laundry. As they skidded to a halt in front of the door to the laundry, Clemmie let go of Jeannie's hand. "Just follow me and don't say anything unless it's to agree with me." She opened the door and entered the laundry, walking purposefully towards a half open door at the back, looking straight ahead and walking fast, but not *too* fast. Clemmie could hear Jeannie following her, matching her step for step. They must look like a couple of soldiers from the barracks along the road, Clemmie thought. One of the girls in the laundry turned tiredly to look at them, brushing damp hair from her face.

From a shadowy corner of the laundry came a throaty growl. "Haw, you two, whaur yiz aff tae?"

Clemmie spun round and Jeannie cannoned into her. A large, red-faced woman was glaring at them from the comfort of a well-cushioned chair over by the wall. "We've been sent to the stores, Mrs Smeaton." Clemmie gave a swift curtsy and tipped her head to Jeannie to do the same. "We've to count the chemises, see what needs mendin' and bring them back for the lassies in the sewing room."

"Aye, wull, see that yiz ur swift aboot it." And, with that, Mrs Smeaton settled herself back into her chair, her eyes already drooping sleepily.

Clemmie pulled Jeannie through the back entrance of the laundry and down a short corridor. The open door of the stores was halfway along, but Clemmie ignored it, instead lifting the bar of a small, iron door at the end of the corridor that led to a narrow passageway at the side of the courtyard. As they slipped through, she reached down and picked up a large stone, wedging it into the bottom of the frame before carefully pushing the door to behind them. Unless you looked carefully, you wouldn't know that the door wasn't quite shut.

"Now what?" Jeannie's face was flushed and Clemmie grinned as she recognised the look of excitement and fear in the younger girl's face.

Clemmie motioned to Jeannie to stay where she was and kept close to the wall of the building as she moved to the corner, peering round. The big gate was shut and there was no-one to be seen. Matron must have gone back inside. She moved back to Jeannie. "Now we go over the wall." They crept to the dark corner where the courtyard wall joined the building. The ground was slightly higher here and a pile of rubble in the corner meant that they could scramble up and over the wall. She hauled Jeannie up after her and they dropped into the close that ran alongside, separating the Home from the high sandstone walls of the timber merchant's next door. They picked their way along the clammy walls and down a flight of damp steps.

Clemmie held Jeannie back as she poked her head around the corner and peeked out. The dense, yellow fog turned the street a sickly colour, rendering everything more than a few yards distant indistinct and ghostly. A sorry cavalcade was making its way down Rottenrow. At the front were the two nurses, with their black hats bobbing. Following them, shuffling as fast and as well as the short chains would let them, were the skinny young women in the yellow dresses, heads bent, chains clanking on the cobbles. The colour of their dresses made them seem almost transparent in the fog, shadowy wraiths with hunched shoulders. Occasionally, one of them would misstep and all three would lurch forwards or sideways as the chains bit. The policemen took it in turns to haul them back up and the girls struggled to get back into step again.

Rottenrow was alive with the hum and stir of residents, passersby and hawkers, and Clemmie and Jeannie joined the throng. With the fog and the crowds, they had no trouble keeping up without being seen. They dodged between skirts and barrows, earning a curse and the sharp flick of a greasy apron from a knife-grinder as they ran into the single large wheel of his contraption, sending it tottering and shaking on its spindly legs. As they caught up with the girls in yellow and their stony-faced companions, Clemmie pulled Jeannie into the doorway of the horse dealer's. The police constable who lived at the top of the street was walking up the road towards them. He nodded briefly to the three policemen in charge of the women.

Clemmie held her breath; the raw smells of horse, hot pies and waste in the enclosed space were making her feel sick. After the policeman passed, she dragged Jeannie back out into the relative freshness of the street, spitting out the bile that had gathered in her mouth.

Several people turned their heads to look at the shackled figures but avoided their eyes. The apple seller paused and raised his napless hat to them, whether in solidarity or foolery, Clemmie couldn't tell. A few passers-by spat at the policemen who accompanied the group. A woman smoking a pipe as she lounged in the doorway of what Clemmie knew was a house of ill repute, called out as the women passed. "Ah'm just out masel, Jane. See ye in a couple of months." The oldest of the young women in yellow raised her head and paused as she acknowledged the greeting, causing all three to lose their footing once more. Clemmie and Jeannie followed behind, hugging the walls of the shops and houses. But nobody paid them any attention and they grew bolder, getting nearer to the group ahead of them.

They passed the sooty, forbidding front of the Old Men's Asylum and on down the hill, the captives' steps shorter now, as the struggle to lift the shackles and chains became harder. As they passed the Industrial School, one of the policemen broke away to chase off three jeering boys who had each picked up a handful of stones and were throwing them at either the police or the girls, or both.

The street was emptier now. Most of the shops and businesses were higher up Rottenrow or at the end of the street where it opened into High Street and Castle Street at the Barony Church, so Clemmie and Jeannie needed to be careful that they weren't seen. Clemmie led her friend across the road, away from the group, stopping as the nurses brought the trio to a halt outside a long, three-storey building, its rows of windows shuttered and barred. Over the entrance a sign read 'Treatment – Knowledge – Reformation'. There was no other sign to indicate what the place was. Clemmie read the words over the door aloud to Jeannie.

"Is it a hospital? For the pox?"

Clemmie shrugged. "It looks more like a prison than a hospital, doesn't it?"

"What does reformation mean?"

"They want to get them to change their ways, I suppose."

"What ways? Getting the pox? Is that what happens when you're bad, you get the pox?"

Clemmie couldn't find the words to explain to Jeannie that it wasn't just bad women that got the pox, so she remained silent, watching. One of the nurses knocked on the door, a thumping, dulled slightly by the layer of fog. Jeannie's questions continued. "Will I get the pox if I'm bad, or if the canary women touch me?" The sound of heavy bolts shrieking heralded the opening of the door and Jeannie fell silent. The young women in chains struggled to clamber up the small step at the threshold and the policemen shoved them into the dark interior, following on behind. The door slammed behind them and the bolts were drawn once more. Clemmie shuddered. The nearby church bell rang and Clemmie and Jeannie turned and ran back up Rottenrow.

The Home was full of the creaks and groans of a building settling down for the night. The structural groans were comforting, the human ones were not. Clemmie and Jeannie were curled up in the upstairs press where Clemmie had stashed Jeannie that first night, eating bread and mutton.

Jeannie's eyes had widened when Clemmie opened the muslin handkerchief to reveal her prize. "Where did you get that?"

"The butcher called just after dawn, with a special package for Mrs McCombe, just like every Thursday." Clemmie popped another piece of mutton in her mouth and licked her fingers. "I...got to the package first." She grinned. "Just like every Thursday."

"Dawn? Don't you *ever* sleep?"

"Not much, no."

They sat savouring the mutton in companionable silence. Clemmie pushed her last piece over to Jeannie who stared at her, eyes wide. "It's yours, don't you want it?"

Clemmie shook her head. "I don't want any more. It's too greasy."

Jeannie looked at her in astonishment. "That's just silly. Mutton can't be too greasy. It's delicious."

Perhaps it was the confined space they were in, but the smell and the grease had become unbearable to Clemmie. "I just don't want it. You have it."

Jeannie nibbled on the last bit of mutton. "My maw used to make a lovely mutton stew." Her voice was wistful.

"When did she die?"

"Last summer, typhoid. It took my two brothers, too. An' then my granny died. That's how I ended up here."

Clemmie nodded. "Aye, the fever took a few here, too." Clemmie had occasionally wished she was one of them. It would have saved her from the jingling devil, at least. "Jeannie, I need you to listen to me." She had been putting off this moment for as long as she possibly could.

"If it's about the ribbon, I'll wear the brown one, I promise I will." Jeannie reached into her pocket and pulled out the silky red ribbon and stroked it. The ribbon had snagged in several places where her fingers, dry and cracked from the laundry and sewing work, had caught and pulled at the threads. "The red one's so pretty, though."

"It's not about the ribbon. But, aye, you *must* wear the brown one. I think Mrs McCombe's been distracted, luckily for you, because of all the new girls recently." Clemmie sighed. "But you're still in danger and you must do exactly as I tell you." She gripped Jeannie around her skinny upper arm.

"Ow! Aye, Clemmie, whatever it is, I'll do it, I promise!"

"Sorry, hen." She rubbed Jeannie's arm where she had grasped it. "You must promise me that if you hear footsteps in the night, especially that jingling devil, you must come up here and hide. You might be in for a beating from Mrs McCombe the next day, but it's better than what him and his friends'll do to you."

In the dark of the press, Jeannie's eyes shone. "I know. You've told me all about that." Clemmie could see the shudder that moved her whole body. "If I hear the footsteps at night, you'll get me out of bed and you'll bring me up here and we'll sit tight until—"

"I'm not going to be here; I have to go away."

"What?" It was Jeannie's turn to grab on to Clemmie. "Where are you going? Why are you leaving me? You can't. Take me with you."

"I have to go away for a little while, and where I'm going might be even worse for you than here. Besides, I know they won't let me bring you; you're too young. I can get a job."

"I can work, too!" Jeannie's voice was indignant.

"You're only nine. It would cost more to feed you than you'd earn."

"Why do you have to go?"

Clemmie reached for Jeannie's hand and laid it on her belly. "Because of this. I'm already starting to show. And if they find out, I'm worried they'll kill it before it's born. And if they can't kill it, they'll take it from me when it is. And if it's a girl..." The tears that she had been holding back came now in full force and she wiped her nose with the back of her hand.

"A baby?" Jeannie's eyes widened. She reached out her other hand and felt Clemmie's swollen belly with both hands. "But you cannae be, you're too young."

Clemmie gave a hollow laugh. "Oh, Jeannie, I wish you weren't such a wee innocent. Plenty of lassies younger than me have babies." She took Jeannie's hands off her belly and held them tight. "Especially here."

"What happens to the girls who get caught with a bairn?"

Clemmie shrugged. "I don't know. Maybe they just throw them out on the street once they find out they're pregnant. Maybe they take them somewhere and lock them away; I just don't know. You can't have a lassie with a bairn in a home for wayward girls. After all, God would just hate that, wouldn't he?"

"Why would he? Wouldn't God want to look after them?"

"All I know is that as soon as they start to show, they disappear, just like they get rid of any lassies with the pox. Those lady child-savers would be horrified if they were met with big bellies or faces encrusted with sores on their Wednesday visits. I'm not waiting until they throw me out, or worse; I'm going by my own choice."

"But what are you gonnae do? Where are you gonnae go?"

Clemmie thought of the well-worn piece of paper in her wee hidey-hole. She whispered the name and address scrawled on it sometimes, like a prayer. It was a link to her mother, and sometimes Clemmie needed physical proof that her life had once been different. She had told Jeannie something of that life and the younger girl had been aghast that Clemmie had spent her whole life locked up with mad people; and even more astounded that Clemmie had considered it normal. She hadn't told Jeannie that the asylum was in Stirling, or that her last name wasn't really Watt, or that her own life and her mother's would likely be in danger if she was discovered. She'd told Jeannie about the gruff kindness of her mother's wardress, Maud, but she hadn't told her about the name and address Maud had scribbled on the note from her mother when she left the asylum. If the jingling devil should find out...no; it was too dangerous. "I'll be close by.

An' I'll come and see you. Watch out for me every Wednesday morning at this time, out of this window. An' if I *can* come, I will. You know how to sneak out now. We can meet just over the wall in the timber merchant's close."

Jeannie looked dubious. "But you *will* be back, won't you? Once you've had the baby. For good, I mean."

"Aye, I'll be back, of course I will." She drew Jeannie close to her. "I'll get a job – a job in a proper laundry, or as a seamstress or a maid, or at Templeton's or Lyle's. An' then I'll come and get you an' we can live together. An' you can go to school and learn to read and write better than I've showed you." As she hugged Jeannie close, she hoped the younger girl wouldn't ask how this was all going to happen, what with the baby and all.

"Books down and stand up, you little slatterns!" Chairs and benches screeched on the dusty wooden floor as the girls in the school room rushed to do Mrs McCombe's bidding. The Matron was followed into the room by a red-faced and sweating Mrs Smeaton. "All those who had laundry duty this morning, get over here, now."

Clemmie and Jeannie stepped forward, as did seven or eight other girls. They stood in a line in front of Mrs McCombe, heads bowed. The Matron walked along the line, roughly tugging a collar here, a sleeve there. When she spoke again her voice was low and threatening. "Mrs Smeaton is missing a shilling, so she is. Which one of you little thieves took it?"

The row of girls remained silent, some of them shaking their heads, the others looking down at the ground. "Wull, wan of yuz did." Mrs Smeaton's voice was aggrieved. "Ah hud it in the mornin' and noo it's gone."

Mrs McCombe walked back along the line, stopping at each girl in turn. When she stopped in front of the girl next to Clemmie, she pinched her cheek. It must have been a hard pinch because the girl flinched and Clemmie saw the mark already darkening and becoming purple. "What about you, Bonnie Patterson? I'll bet it was you, wasn't it? After all, what with your ma in the Bridewell and your ne'er-do-well father in Barlinnie, thieving runs in the family doesn't it?"

"It wisnae me, I swear it." The crying girl pulled her pockets inside out. "Look. I huvnae anythin', I swear."

Mrs McCombe flicked the ever-present tawse. "Mrs Smeaton and I are going to search every last one of you. And when we find that shilling, the girl responsible is going to get——"

The remainder of her sentence was interrupted by a series of discordant notes. Staff and inmates alike turned to watch a piano being wheeled into the room by two red-faced men in shirt sleeves. A third man wheeled in a piano bench covered in lush green velvet and Miss Adair and her friend Miss McNab followed behind with a swish of silk.

Mrs McCombe swore under her breath and gestured to the line of subdued girls. "Get back to your seats. I'll deal with you later." The girls scattered, relief on their faces from the temporary reprieve. Clemmie heard Mrs McCombe mutter, "That damned bitch and her piano," before plastering a smile on her face and striding over to greet the two visitors.

"Do be careful." Miss Adair waved a gloved hand towards the men as they wheeled the piano into position by the far wall. "You'll send it out of tune if you crash it about so." The two men ignored her and walked out of the room, followed by Mrs McCombe, fizzing with anger. "I'll play an air. Just to see if it needs tuning again." Miss Adair gathered her skirts and sat daintily on the piano stool. Clemmie returned to her book.

As Miss Adair began to play, however, Clemmie found herself looking up from her book more often than at the page; and when she did look down, she kept re-reading the same line over and over again. When Miss Adair started to sing, her voice quiet but clear, Clemmie closed the book and listened. Then came a song Clemmie knew. Clemmie stood and walked over to stand next to the piano as Miss Adair sang. "In thy dark eyes' splendour, Where the warm light loves to dwell, Weary looks yet tender, Speak their fond farewell."

Miss Adair looked up and smiled at Clemmie as she joined in with a line of the chorus. "Nita! Juanita! Lean thou on my heart."

"It's a good song, isn't it...Clementina, is that right?"

"Yes, ma'am. And yes, it is, ma'am."

"And how do you know the song, Clementina?"

"My maw used to sing it to me, ma'am." She didn't tell Miss Adair that it was on those special treat days when her mother was allowed to play the asylum piano. Miss Adair didn't need to know that.

"And did your mother have a sweet voice?"

Better than you, Clemmie wanted to say, but she restricted herself to, "Yes, ma'am."

Miss Adair opened her mouth to say something else, but Mrs McCombe returned to the room and stormed up behind them. "Clementina Watt! What do you think you're doing, bothering Miss Adair? If you don't get back to your seat right now, I shall take the tawse to you."

"Clementina is not bothering me at all, Mrs McCombe." Miss Adair raised herself from the piano stool and stood in front of Mrs McCombe looking rather put out. Clemmie was sure she could sense a 'but *you* are' in Miss Adair's tone.

"She's a disobedient girl, so she is." Mrs McCombe glared at Clemmie and stabbed a finger at her collarbone, her unerring accuracy for maximum pain honed to perfection. "Get back to your seat, girl. I'll speak to you, later."

This Miss Adair was slim, elegant and delicate-looking, but Clemmie could see a strength in her as she squared her silk-clad shoulders and glared at Mrs McCombe. "As I said, Clementina wasn't bothering me at all. There is absolutely no need to speak to her later, I can assure you. Now, it seems as though our time is up this afternoon. Come, Josephine, we should go, and leave the young ladies to their books." As Mrs McCombe stomped off towards the door, to let the two women out, Miss Adair laid a hand on Clemmie's arm. "Here." With a dainty gloved hand she placed a small bag into Clemmie's roughened red one. "Some sugarplums. I'm so sorry if I got you into trouble. I shall look out for you on my next visit and we can talk some more. I'd like to know more about you."

Clemmie tucked the bag into the pocket of her work skirt. She would share them with Jeannie, later, in the press. It would cheer Jeannie up; she had been nothing but worries and frets since Clemmie had told her she would soon have to leave her on her own.

As soon as the door closed heavily behind the two visitors, Mrs McCombe was back on the warpath. "Laundry girls, get back in line." She hadn't forgotten her promise. Instead, she seemed to have become even more incensed by the visitors and their useless gift. Clemmie stood up and got back into line. Mrs McCombe, flicking the tawse threateningly, stood in front of them, looking up and down the line. "I won't stop looking until I've found that shilling. So, if any of you have anything to tell me, you'd better tell me now, or it will go all the worse for you." Every girl in the line remained silent. Every girl in the *room* was silent. The lucky ones who remained seated were no doubt feeling thankful that they had been sent to the sewing room, or the kitchen, or set to cleaning the Home that morning, rather than being put on laundry duty. Mrs McCombe glanced sourly at each face in turn. "No? Then turn out your pockets and aprons."

Clemmie looked down the line. Several girls held out their empty hands. One held out a copper penny and a dirty handkerchief, another a slice of bread. A third pulled out half a biscuit which promptly broke into crumbs and scattered all over the floor. Clemmie, realisation dawning, took out the bag of sugarplums given to her by Miss Adair. Damn the woman for her kindness.

Mrs McCombe stood in front of Clemmie, her entire body quivering like a street cur guarding a dead rat. "Clementina Watt." She drew the name out almost lovingly. "I might have known it. Too good for the likes of us, with all your fancy airs and graces and your scorn for everyone here. But you're just a common guttersnipe like all the rest." She snatched the bag of sugarplums out of Clemmie's hand. "Here's your thief, Effie." Mrs Smeaton hauled herself forward, tutting and shaking her head. Mrs McCombe waved them triumphantly in her face. "See, she stole your shilling and sneaked out and bought herself some sweetmeats with it. A thief and greedy, an' aw. Now, what should we do with a girl like that?"

"But I didn't take Mrs Smeaton's shilling, I swear I didn't."

Mrs McCombe was nose to nose with Clemmie. "I swear I didn't," she mocked, mimicking Clemmie's voice. "Then where did you get these, you wee liar?"

Clemmie knew it was pointless trying to make her case, but she did so anyway. "Miss Adair gave them to me, just as she was leaving."

"Miss Adair?" Mrs McCombe's voice was outraged, and her sour breath was hot on Clemmie's face. "Don't you try to gammon me, you wee sneak. Why would she give any such thing to *you*?"

"I'm not lying; it's the truth. You can ask her."

The Matron had worked herself up into a hell-fired rage. She rocked back on her heels, her thin, hard-drawn mouth white and cold. "Ask her? *Ask* her? The fine lady has made her afternoon calls for the day, so she has. She'll be sitting in her withdrawing room in Blythswood Square eating oysters and congratulating herself. What, shall I send round a footman with my card on a silver salver?"

Mrs Smeaton snorted with laughter as she put one of the sugarplums into her mouth and worked at it with her toothless gums.

Clemmie took a step back and held her head up defiantly. "It's the truth. She *did* give them to me."

"Don't you back answer me, Watt. Get your clothes off."

"What?"

The back of Mrs McCombe's hand met Clemmie's face with a whack that turned her head almost halfway round. There was a concerted gasp from the other girls who, up until then, had remained totally silent.

"Get your clothes off. All of them. Chemise and bloomers too. I'm going to give you a beating you won't forget, lassie."

Clemmie was horrified. She'd had beatings before, public ones too. But if she had to take all her clothes off, her condition would be apparent to everyone. And then...she didn't want to think what might happen next. Other than the occasional sob from one of the younger girls, the noisy smacking of Mrs Smeaton's lips and Mrs McCombe's heavy, rasping breath, the room was silent. Everyone was waiting to see what would happen next. Clemmie slowly started to undo her apron, casting around in her mind for a way out.

"It was me." Jeannie stepped forward. "I took the shilling, not Clemmie."

Mrs McCombe took a swift step towards her. "What do you mean, Jeannie Jack?"

Jeannie lifted her head and looked the Matron in the eyes. "I said *I* took the shilling. I stole it from Mrs Smeaton. And then... then I sneaked out and bought sugarplums. And I put them in Clemmie's pocket because I don't have one. It was me. I'm the thief. I took it. I..." Her voice was a whisper. "I took Mrs Smeaton's shilling."

Clemmie closed her eyes as Mrs McCombe lifted her tawse.

*

Clemmie had been wandering the familiar streets for the last three hours. She knew where she needed to go but was putting off the moment. She turned into Ingram Street, passing the Union Bank and Cranston's Tea Rooms before turning down Glassford Street. She stopped at the corner where the railings on the wee island in the middle of the road led down to the public lavatories. The building reminded her of the pressure on her bladder. The sign said it would cost her a penny, which she didn't have, but some of the girls at the Home had told her that the attendant here was kindly and would probably let her in. It would save her going in one of the lanes. She hesitated before going down the steps and pushing open the door. The smell of carbolic that met her turned her stomach. Thoughts of the asylum and the Home overwhelmed her, and she let the door close again. She would do what she usually did and squat down in an alley.

Clemmie's back rested against the wall at the sheltered side of the tall monument at the highest point of the Necropolis, as she waited for her breath to return to normal after the climb. The smog wasn't quite so bad up here at the top of Glasgow's city of the dead and she took a deep breath of chilly March air. She knew the engraved words on the monument off by heart, even if she didn't really know who this Mr Knox was. He must have been important because his monument rose above all the others, grand as some of them were. She liked that he was remembered for his services to education and civil liberty, but she wasn't sure about the religion part. God was not her friend. Or her mother's.

She turned and walked the short way from the Knox monument to the tall obelisk with no name and looked towards where she thought Stirlingshire must be, lifting a hand in greeting. She wished that she could go back to the asylum, but her mother had impressed on her many times before she left that, whatever life might be like in Glasgow, if she went home, it could be dangerous for them both. Clemmie's father was a dissolute and greedy man, who planned to marry her off to his friend McAllister, she said. Her mother's money would pass to Clemmie and who knew what would happen to them both once Clemmie was under his control? Her mother had made her promise that she would not come back, would never mention the name Gilfillan and would not try to contact her. Clemmie knew that her mother had not imagined how much worse her daughter's life could actually be when she had cried and hugged her fiercely and sent her away with a new surname and talk of big houses and service and hard work. If she had known the fate that awaited her daughter, then surely she would have kept her with her? However, no matter how much she wanted to go back to her mother, even if she could find the money to travel to Stirling, she knew that she couldn't put her mother's life in danger. And she had promised.

Clemmie sank down onto the ground, feeling her knees shake and her head pound. The grass was damp in the shadow of the obelisk and she rested her forehead in its coolness, breathing in the earthy richness. No, she couldn't go back to Beau Rivage. And she couldn't go back to the Home. She only had one option now. She took the piece of paper from her pocket. It was thin and grubby, its folds almost see-through. She held it carefully by one corner and allowed it to open without touching it, even though she didn't need to see the name and address scrawled on it.

Maud, the kindly wardress who had been cautiously fond of Clemmie and her mother, had given it to Clemmie the night she had left. She had pressed it into Clemmie's hand with a whisper. "Here, a letter from your maw. And my youngest sister's address.

Tell her I sent you. But only go to her in the direst of need, if you have no other choice. It's dangerous there, in a rough part of the city, but she'll look after you as best she can."

The familiar words on the paper and in her head calmed her and she wiped the wetness from her face and stood up, brushing dirt and grass from her skirt in an automatic gesture. She placed a hand on the obelisk and traced her fingers over the words 'Beloved Mother' and around the outline of the four grieving children, before heading down the path towards the exit without a backwards glance.

At the entrance to the Necropolis, she crossed over the Bridge of Sighs and turned into High Street. It was dusk now and turning even colder. She hurried down the steep, narrow hill, dodging in and out of the mouths of the many closes. As she passed the oil merchant's and the egg and butter man and neared the Trongate, she felt more confident. She didn't draw a second glance in such a press of people.

She paused to look at the cakes in the window of Lockhart's Cocoa Rooms. A rich, glistening plum cake, with its perfect decoration of almonds and cherries, sat on a plinth in the middle of the window, surrounded by Geneva wafers, a moist and sticky-looking gingerbread sponge, delicate lavender biscuits and Shrewsbury cakes laced with caraway seeds. Clemmie could almost smell their aniseedy-goodness through the glass. The sickness of the last few weeks had gone and now she was hungry all the time. What made her mouth really water, though, were the pithiviers with their crisp and shiny puff pastry lids, filled with cherry and plum and apricot. They were her mother's favourites and a sweet remembrance of better times. Mary Grace had bought them down in the village for her mother and her from time to time.

The door of the Cocoa Rooms opened, letting out a sweet-smelling warmth along with two elegantly dressed young women, who shivered in the chill air and pulled their fur collars close around their pink faces. Clemmie reluctantly peeled herself away from the window and carried on walking down to the Cross. She paused at the Tolbooth Steeple. The junction was busy and noisy and she was buffeted from side to side as people hurried past. To her left, the Gallowgate and London Street; ahead of her, the Saltmarket and the Rag Fair; and to her right, the big statue of King William opposite the Tontine building with its fine arcade and piazza underneath. Work had finished for the day on the construction of the new railway station, with its eight sides and fancy dome. Clemmie had watched it take shape on her regular trips out from the Home, imagining that one day she would sneak through the entrance under the sign that said 'Caledonian Railway', and onto a train that would take her back to Stirling, where her mother would be on the platform waiting for her. One day.

She shook her head to clear away that picture and looked around the Cross. Here, workers and beggars mingled with the men in shiny top hats and knee-length frock coats who were gathered underneath the arches of the Tontine prior to dining or theatre-going. Shoe-blacks and street sweepers plied their trade amongst them. Pickpockets, too, Clemmie had no doubt. Sometimes she stood here and watched the milling crowd, just to see if she could spot them working, dipping their sly and clever hands into pockets and purses, but she never could. On the corner, at Nicol & Halliday, an auction was ending, and men were pouring out into the street. The awnings outside the Tontine were being drawn back and Clemmie had to step out into the street to keep from being jostled.

Her destination was hidden behind the smart frontages and thriving businesses. Clemmie had almost gone to the address on the paper many times in the two years she had been in Glasgow. She'd come as close as the door once; a week or so after the first time the jingling devil and his friends had come for her. After the initial pain had gone. But she had felt scared and ashamed and unsure of her reception, so she had gone back to the Home, returning there even before she'd been missed. And after that, well, she got used to it, they all did. Besides, she'd coped with the worst, hadn't she? Now, of course, she knew differently. Things could *always* get worse.

She left the safety of the doorway and walked a wee bit further along the Trongate, before turning out of the relative brightness of the thoroughfare into the dark narrowness of Tontine Lane. She knew from her previous visit that, even in the middle of the day, sunlight seldom penetrated here. The tenements were so close together that you could easily stand astride the stinking gutter that ran down the middle of the lane, put out your arms and touch the buildings on both sides – even with your elbows bent. Ragged clothes hung from lines that stretched back and forth across the lane, some of them spattered with waste, even though the emptying of pots was only supposed to be done out of back windows.

Clemmie pulled her thin shawl close around her and wrapped her head and the lower part of her face until only her eyes and nose could be seen. She lowered her head and hurried past the tavern, ignoring the sounds of bawling and brawling within. A man was rolling a barrel down the cobbles towards her and she had to squeeze herself up against the sooty wall of the building to allow him past. A young girl stood under the lintel of a doorway, a child tied around her in a shawl and balanced carelessly on one hip. She ignored the baby's grizzling as she watched Clemmie. Tears had left clean runnels down the child's face and little bubbles of snot pulsed at the bottom of its nose with every breath.

Clemmie continued up the lane, ignoring dark doorways and stone staircases as she passed, and striving to look as though she knew exactly where she was going. This was a dangerous place, even in the daytime. Now, with dusk falling, it was beginning to take on an air of menace.

She made her way around an abandoned hawker's barrow, which listed to one side in the absence of a wheel. The lane widened out into a courtyard where a group of women huddled together talking, outside a shop with a sign above that said 'Annan's General Store'. Outside the lodging house opposite, an elderly man sat on a rickety stool smoking a pipe. Clemmie hesitated before taking a narrow turn off to the left, raising her skirts as she stepped over a large puddle of rank-smelling liquid. The shadows closed in as she passed underneath a makeshift wooden walkway that joined the buildings on each side of the lane. She hurried on, grateful when the buildings widened out again.

It was a clear evening and the smoke of the day had stopped belching from the factory chimneys. Her way was lit by the rising of a moon that forced its way into the narrow spaces above her head. After another turn or two, she reached a dead end. At the very top, a low doorway yawned into the gloom beyond. She groped her way up a turnpike staircase, her hand flat against the clammy wall, panting as she reached the top of the third flight. Before her were two doors. Hesitating, she knocked on the left.

The man who answered the door was thin and drawn. His face had the hectic colour and large eyes of a consumptive. He held out a lantern in which a candle flickered and gazed at Clemmie. "I'm…I'm looking for Sarah Loag. Her sister Maud said I should come." The man said nothing, just turned around and shuffled back along the narrow hallway, leaving the door open behind him.

Clemmie took it as an invitation to enter and did so, shutting the heavy wooden door behind her. She followed the man into a kitchen where a fire burned in the grate, a large pot hanging over it. The room was humble, dominated by a table that looked as though it had been put together from pieces of scrap wood, but it was clean and neat and more welcoming than Clemmie had expected. Several straight-backed, wooden chairs were tucked around the table. In one of them sat a large, red-faced woman in a tartan cloak and a snowy-white cap, her breast exposed to a greedily-sucking baby. A half-naked toddler leaned into her lap, playing with the fringes of her shawl. A third child, a little boy of about five or six, was sorting a pile of rags in the corner. The man made his way to the only easy chair in the room and pulled it closer to the fire.

Sarah listened silently as Clemmie told her tale, then slowly shook her head once. "I'm sorry, lass, I know Maudie meant well, telling you to come to me, but she doesn't know how things are with us these days. I haven't seen her for years now, since she was last in Glasgow for a visit." She tipped her head in her husband's direction. "Reuben has been out of work for some time now, and what little bits of sewing and washing I can get don't keep us all fed. I've six children already. We wouldn't be able to manage to feed another mouth." She looked at Clemmie's stomach. "Let alone two."

"But...I can work. I can help you." said Clemmie, trying to make her voice firm. She didn't know what she would do if Sarah turned her away. "I'm strong and have nimble fingers. I was one of the best seamstresses in the Home. Even with the baby coming I can still do that."

Sarah shook her head. "There's just not the work round here, lass. You've seen how we're placed. People around here don't have the money to send out their washing and sewing. They do it themselves, or it doesn't get done at all."

"I can go out. I can find it. I can get you customers. Please... oh, you have to let me stay." It was all finally too much for Clemmie. She was overwhelmed by a mixture of hunger, desperation and loneliness and burst into tears.

"Now, now, lass. Don't take on, so. Look, I'll not throw you out tonight." Sarah stood up and unceremoniously thrust the plump baby onto Clemmie's lap. The toddler at her side overbalanced and crashed to the floor, looking shocked, its bottom lip quivering. Sarah moved over to the fire, picked up a wooden bowl and spooned out a ladleful from the big metal pot. She put it down in front of Clemmie and placed a hand on her shoulder, giving it a comforting squeeze. "We'll talk about it in the morning. Tonight, you can sleep with me and the youngest bairns over here." She pointed to a thin straw mattress tucked against the wall. "Reuben sleeps over there." At the sound of his name, Reuben stood up wordlessly and took himself off into the curtained-off bed recess.

Clemmie gazed into the bowl. Steam was rising from it and she breathed in the savoury scent as she raised the bowl to her lips. The liquid was thin but warming with chunks of carrot and turnip and potato chopped into it. Clemmie gulped it down, savouring the sparse, tiny slivers of ox-cheek.

Clemmie knocked on the door that Sarah had directed her to. The woman who opened the door was stout and smelled of potato parings. She was still dressed for the outdoors in a stiff black dress and cloak, both mud-spattered around the hem. Her faded but cheery bonnet with its cerise velvet trim, bouncing cherries and turquoise ribbon looked out of place above the heavily wrinkled face. "Aye, hen?"

"Sarah Loag sent me, Mrs Burnie. She says you're a middlewoman for Avery's in Prince's Square." Sarah had also told her that Mrs Burnie was not to be trusted and worked desperate women who had no other option into the ground for a pittance. That, however, Clemmie didn't think it wise to mention.

"Aye, hen, that's right. I've just come back from picking up a new load."

Clemmie knew that. She had followed the woman as she'd wheeled the rickety baby carriage up the lane, followed by an awkward boy who was obviously wanting. He had a lolling tongue and a face like a frightened moon and was the grubbiest person Clemmie had ever seen. The carriage had protested and squealed as it bounced over the cobbles and the contents inside had rattled and shifted. Mrs Burnie had stopped at several doors, each time reaching into the carriage and pulling out packages which she gave to the people behind the doors, or to the vacant boy to take up close stairs while she waited below.

"Sarah was wondering if we could have some to do. She said as you'd asked her if she wanted to do some before, but she wasn't able to do it because of Reuben and having to look after him and the children. I'm here now, so I can help her." The words came out in a rush. Her continued presence at the Loags depended upon finding work and bringing in some money. She was outstaying her welcome and Sarah had been muttering about her having to leave soon. Mrs Burnie was her last hope.

Mrs Burnie's eyes narrowed as she took this information in. "And who might you be, hen?"

Clemmie side-stepped the question. "A cousin of hers. Come to help out."

"And have you ever carded hooks and eyes before?" Clemmie shook her head. Mrs Burnie sighed but ushered her into the dark hallway. "Come away in, then. I haven't got all day. I wouldn't do this for everyone, but bein' as you're a cousin of Sarah's..."

The room was cold and unhomely, lit only by a flickering gas lantern which Mrs Burnie brought over to the table, motioning for Clemmie to sit down. "Here, you take one of these cards and sew the hook on first. Then you link the eye to it and sew that on." Her fingers were swift and sure, even though they looked like sausages exploding from their skins. "Six on a card, all like that. And they've got to be straight."

"How much do we get paid?"

"Rate for these is six pence a gross. Nine pence a gross for these smaller ones."

"May we take two gross of the smaller ones?"

Mrs Burnie looked at her and sniffed. "You may not. You may take one gross of the bigger ones, until I see how you do. And you have to supply your own needles and thread." She looked at Clemmie slyly. "I can give you a loan of threepence so that you can buy them. Good rates."

"No, that's alright. Sarah told me to tell you she has some."

Mrs Burnie looked disappointed. "I need the finished cards back by Wednesday noon. An' don't make me come looking for them. If I have to climb all those stairs, I'll dock you a penny." Clemmie looked at the hollow-eyed boy feasting noisily on bread and cheese in the corner. He'd no doubt be the one who had to climb the stairs, but she doubted that he'd be the beneficiary of the docked penny.

Clemmie was worried. Since she'd been at Sarah's she'd gone to meet Jeannie at the Home every Wednesday morning. It meant that she had to stay up until the early hours to finish the carding and Sarah hadn't been happy, but Clemmie insisted. She had to go every Wednesday morning. And every Wednesday morning, Jeannie was there at the window. When Clemmie arrived, Jeannie scrambled over the wall and they talked and laughed and cried, both of them speaking fast to get out all their news in the short time Jeannie had before she had to sneak back into the Home.

Clemmie told Jeannie that she was living with a good family, that she was kept busy with the carding, and that she was starting to feel heavy and out of breath with the weight of the baby. She didn't tell her that Sarah took almost every penny she made, that she also had to look after the children and that the carding was torture on her knuckles and eyes.

Jeannie told Clemmie that Mrs McCombe was furious when Clemmie disappeared, and that Miss Adair had taken her aside and asked after Clemmie. Jeannie had told neither of them anything. Mrs McCombe had given her a beating and Miss Adair pressed a shilling into her hand and told her to give Clemmie an address in Blythswood Square if she saw her. Jeannie forgot the number of the house, though she remembered to put the shilling in the wee hidey hole Clemmie had showed her.

Then, for the last two Wednesdays, Jeannie was pale and silent, her eyes huge and ringed with darkness. She cried the whole time they were together but refused to tell Clemmie what was wrong. And now, for the first Wednesday since Clemmie had left, Jeannie hadn't turned up. The window where Jeannie always watched for her was empty. Clemmie waited in the dampness of the timber merchant's close for five hours, her eyes fixed on the gap in the wall from where she could look up and see the window, ready to wave. But Jeannie didn't appear.

Clemmie stayed there until it was dark. Jeannie wouldn't come now and, besides, she was feeling weak and stiff and her back and feet were aching fiercely. Several times during the day she had squeezed herself into the stinking space underneath the stairs to avoid the timber merchant as he came and went. All she'd eaten was the small piece of gingerbread sponge she had bought for Jeannie from Lockharts with the little bit of money she had saved from what was left of her wages.

With a final glance at the window, Clemmie made her way out into Rottenrow. She was supposed to have taken the finished cards back to Mrs Burnie and picked up some new ones hours ago. If Sarah or one of the children hadn't been able to take them back before midday, the amount they would get for the cards would be even smaller and Sarah would be angry with her.

Clemmie's feet were heavy as she walked back to Tontine Lane. The darkness sucked her in. Although she had come to know the alleyways and passages, she hadn't yet been out after dark. Sarah kept them all in after dusk, barring the door and ignoring every knock and shout. The rat's nest of alleyways was dangerous enough during the day; if you didn't keep your wits about you, there was always someone ready to take advantage. At night, however, wits weren't enough. Thefts, knifings and even murder were common occurrences, and not even the police ventured in after dark. The only people about at night, Sarah said, were those with evil in their hearts and weapons in their hands.

Clemmie drew Sarah's tartan shawl close about her body, shivering in the dank atmosphere. She kept to the walls as she made her way as swiftly and quietly as she could through the closes; up and down staircases, in and out of doors, avoiding the worst of the taverns. The darkness seemed to deaden the usual sounds of the Tontine, leaving Clemmie with only fragmented whispers and muffled footsteps. A man had been beaten to the point of death for his pocketwatch here last week; a young woman had her throat slashed the week before. It was not a place to linger and Clemmie went as quickly as the dark, the ruts under her feet and her heavy body would allow her.

She caught her breath as a rat ran over her foot. Further along, a sickly yellow light spilled out of a brothel door as it opened to eject a drunken man. He fell headlong into a shallow puddle before standing up with difficulty and weaving his way towards Clemmie, shouting unintelligible words at the open door. Clemmie pulled herself back into a close entrance. She wrapped the ends of the shawl around her face to cover her pale skin.

The man staggered off without even glancing in her direction and the door of the brothel closed, pitching the alleyway into darkness once more. Clemmie took a step out of her hiding place but paused when she heard footsteps and a loud whistling. She made out the tune of *The Ratcatcher's Daughter* and smiled, but drew herself back into the shadows. Perhaps the man had spent an evening at the Britannia? There was precious little whistling in the Tontine at night, other than from the drunks rolling out of the taverns and brothels. Most innocents abroad were too wary of their surroundings and scurried about their business. This man, however, was confident and assured and, seemingly, unafraid of being jumped.

Underneath the whistling, though, she could hear another sound, one that she recognised. With every step towards her the jingling of a heavy watchchain became louder. Clemmie's hand flew to her mouth to trap the fear inside. Other watchchains must jingle like that, musn't they? Other boots must meet the ground with such assurance? At that moment, the whistling stopped and the man began to sing the words: "*But the ratcatcher's daughter she had a dream, that she wouldn't be alive on Monday. She went once more to buy some sprats, and she tumbled into the water...*"

A sudden pain flared in her belly and her breathing stopped. The jingling devil came closer, his voice now almost upon her. "*And down to the bottom, all covered up with mud, went the pretty little ratcatcher's daughter.*" She bent over, her hands clutching at the wall beside her as spasm after spasm gripped her. The devil's footsteps halted and the singing became a quiet humming. It took all Clemmie's remaining strength to stop shaking. Clemmie felt a wetness between her thighs as a searing pain shot through her.

The humming stopped and, over the thudding in her own head, Clemmie heard the rasping breath from her nightmares. Then the assured footsteps started once again, in time with the song. With every other step, the jingle accompanied the words. "...*So he cut his throat with a pane of glass, and stabbed his donkey after...*"

Clemmie collapsed to the ground with her waters around her, biting her lips to stop herself crying out. She couldn't give birth here. She needed to get back to Sarah's, but she couldn't leave the relative safety of the dark close. Not with the jingling devil nearby. As the footsteps and the humming became fainter, the pains in her whole body became stronger, eventually forcing her out of the mouth of the close, tumbling to the stinking, wet ground. She struggled onto all fours, feeling a temporary respite from the contractions. Then the waves returned ever fiercer. A stabbing pain in her groin forced her back onto the ground where she lay sobbing and exhausted. She was going to die, and the baby along with her, she was sure. And perhaps that was best.

Clemmie's mind disconnected and she felt a deep sorrow for the girl writhing in agony in the filthy gutter. As she faded into darkness, the door of the brothel opened once more, spilling out light and raucous laughter.

Mabel's face turned bright red and screwed up in what Clemmie had come to recognise as her pre-wail look. "Sh-sh-sh." She loosened her bodice and hoisted the baby and swaddling shawl up to her breast. She didn't want anything to give her away as she waited in the close next to the Home. It was Wednesday. Surely Jeannie would appear at the window today? Clemmie wanted to tell her Mabel Jean Watt's full name. Well, Mabel Jean Gilfillan, really, of course, but that would have to stay a secret. Jeannie would love it when she found out that Mabel Jean was named after her.

Clemmie had been up until four, finishing the carding so that she wouldn't fall behind, and had then come straight here. Sarah had promised to deliver the finished cards to Mrs Burnie, although she had only agreed to do so when Clemmie told her she could keep *all* the money she got for them. Clemmie had gone back to work on the carding only hours after Mabel had been born, determined to prove to Sarah that she could cope, but Sarah had become increasingly reluctant to keep Clemmie there in the three weeks since Mabel's birth. She kept hinting that it would be better for all of them if Clemmie would agree to give Mabel up. The hints were becoming more frequent and more demanding. Sarah, too, was up and about at all hours. While Clemmie finished the carding, she fussed about, seeing to Reuben and mending a threadbare garment which had already covered four of her children. As each one grew out of it, it was passed down to the next, Sarah's neat stitches disguising the rents and tears that were the legacy of each child.

Sarah looked slyly over at Clemmie as she threaded her needle with a new piece of cotton. "Have you...thought any more about what I said?"

Clemmie looked up from the hooks and eyes, pausing for a costly moment from the intricate work. Sarah looked away, her face colouring. "There's nothing to think about, Sarah."

"That baby will—"

"Her name is Mabel. Do you think that if you don't say her name, she's less real? That it makes it easier to give her up?"

Sarah sighed. "It's just...well, you haven't been able to work as much. I'm keeping you here out of kindness and, right now, you're repaying me by taking food out of my own bairns' mouths."

Clemmie knew this was partly true. She was eating less than she needed because she felt guilty; but she couldn't eat any less than she already was because she needed to be strong and nourished to feed Mabel. "I'm working more than I did just after Mabel was born. And I'll keep on working harder."

"Not if you keep on with this nonsense about finding your friend."

"I've told you; you can keep *all* the money this week. I'll find Jeannie; I know I will."

Sarah's look was sly. "Just think how much easier it would be to find her without a bairn at your breast." Clemmie didn't answer. Her anger made her fingers clumsy and she dropped hooks and eyes onto the floor. "She cries at night. Keeps us all awake." Clemmie looked pointedly at Reuben moaning and coughing in the corner. Sarah hurried on. "I know someone," she said. "A good woman."

Clemmie snorted. "A baby farmer. *Not* a good woman."

"She's no' a baby farmer; she disnae want money. She'll take the bairn as a favour and have it adopted."

Clemmie stared at her, horrified. "You've *already* discussed taking my baby away with one of those wicked, wicked women?"

"Clemmie, I…Mabel will have the chance of a better life. You'll have a fresh start."

Clemmie grabbed Mabel from where she lay, swaddled up inside an old wooden box, and clutched her to her breast, forgetting that she had attached the needle to her chemise. Mabel started to wail. "Just think, Sarah. Just think how you'd feel if someone took Maggie, or wee Sarah, or George."

Sarah glanced over at Reuben, sitting in front of the fire that constantly burned, no matter what the temperature, shivering under the weight of the three blankets they possessed, while Clemmie and Sarah sweated in their calico chemises and drawers. "Perhaps…it would be a good thing," she had said, quietly.

Clemmie sighed. She knew that conversation was not finished, but her main concern was that another week had passed without seeing Jeannie. Next week, she would come even earlier.

At half past four in the morning, the closes and alleyways of Tontine Lane were relatively quiet. Away from the suffocating atmosphere of the small apartment, with dawn breaking and a slight breeze starting to shoo away the fetid air, Clemmie felt relief. The knots in her belly were abating. She scurried as fast as she could, given the weight of the growing baby wrapped in the shawl bound tightly around her. A lamplighter in the High Street was alternately snuffing out the lamps and using his long pole to knock up the workers. He stopped to watch her curiously as she came up the street towards him. She bent her head and hurried past.

Eventually, she had to stop to take a breath, a pain in her belly reminding her that it was only recently that she had given birth. Mabel snorted and opened her eyes, a chubby arm forcing its way outside the shawl. Clemmie nuzzled her face into Mabel's head and tucked the arm back inside the warmth of the shawl. It was the same shawl her own mother had wrapped her in, a shawl that was badly knitted and full of holes but which was also the blue of her mother's eyes. She had rescued it from her hiding place under the floorboards, along with her other treasures before she left the Home. Mabel's eyes flickered shut once more. The clearing of a throat and the clinking of a chain further up the street stopped her. Was it him? Did he roam these streets looking for her, trying to sniff her out? She withdrew into a low, recessed doorway, trying to blend into the shadows.

Chink. There it was again. Footsteps came closer. A purposeful stride. Another clearing of the throat.

Clemmie drew back as far as she could, clasping Mabel to her so hard that Mabel let out a muffled whimper but didn't open her eyes. Clemmie relaxed her grip and gently stroked the downy head.

The footsteps stopped, a few paces up from Clemmie's refuge. He had found her. The jingling devil had found her. She should have left Mabel with Sarah. That wouldn't have been so bad. Not as bad as...

A loud, blustering sneeze made Mabel's eyes pop open, startled. "Damnation." A keychain jingled and the man sneezed again, suppressed this time. A portly man in a thick coat walked past the doorway, blowing his nose on a handkerchief. Attached to his coat button was a chain holding a large set of keys which he tossed into the air every few steps. Clemmie sobbed and let out the breath she had been holding in. She poked her head out of the doorway to see the large man slapping the lamplighter on the back before unlocking the cartwright's shop. Her heart slowly returning to normal, Clemmie carried on up the street and turned into Rottenrow.

Even though the day looked set to be a warm one for spring, there was a chill in the timber merchant's close, where the sunlight never found its way, and the walls ran with a slimy wetness that turned your fingers green when you touched it. Mabel had fallen asleep once more, her tiny pink lips still clamped around Clemmie's nipple. She prised the baby gently away and tucked her back into the shawl. Clemmie waited, her eyes never leaving the window, willing Jeannie to appear. Another half an hour went by. Then Clemmie heard familiar sounds. The heavy wooden gates of the courtyard opened, the rusted hinges rebelling, followed by the harsh sound of chains on cobblestones. Wednesday morning: they would be taking the foul patients to the Lock Hospital, of course. Perhaps this was her chance. Clemmie couldn't go into the Home and ask for Jeannie, but she could ask the canary women if any of them knew her and what had happened to stop her coming to the window these past few weeks.

She waited until the Home's gates had closed once more and four canaries made their ungainly way down Rottenrow, accompanied by three policemen and two wardresses from the Lock. The girls looked skinny and malnourished compared to their sturdy captors. Clemmie bound Mabel more closely to her and followed. The heads of the patients were bowed and Clemmie wasn't able to tell from this distance if she knew any of them. She crossed to the other side of the road and hurried on ahead. She stopped at the corner of Weaver Street and looked back up Rottenrow, waiting for the procession to come closer.

As the group neared the Industrial School, an unholy row broke out. In a flurry of arms and legs, a whirligig of boys spilled from the entrance to the school and into the street, throwing out punches and curses. As they spun, they overturned a barrow piled with rags. The hawker, too, was spilled to the ground, her skirts catching in the wheels of her barrow. Her curses joined those of the boys. The policemen accompanying the canary women stopped and laughed as the hawker and boys tussled. Eventually, one of them moved over, his huge hands grabbing an arm here and a leg there, flinging the boys out of the way. The other two policemen reluctantly joined in, as a crowd gathered around the fighting boys and screeching hawker. The wardresses, too, moved closer to watch, leaving the four canary women, shoulders hunched, staring at the floor: the only people – other than Clemmie – uninterested in the entertainment. This was Clemmie's chance.

She moved into the middle of the road, only to stop abruptly. One of the canaries, the smallest one, had lifted her head. A large, open sore festered on her top lip and her face was drawn and wan. Her hair was no longer corn-coloured and glossy. Instead, it looked dark and greasy and was shaved close to her head. Patches of skin could now be seen on her scalp. Above all else, though, it was the dull eyes that now stared at Clemmie, the eyelids swollen, whites reddened, that had made Clemmie pull up short. "Jeannie." Clemmie was not sure if she had uttered her friend's name or just thought it; her throat was tight and dry. "Jeannie!" she tried again. The girl stared back at her, unmoving.

As the policemen left the boys to their fight, one of them pulled the first girl roughly by the arm, causing all four to stumble and almost overbalance. The crowd which had gathered to watch the fighting boys now sniggered at this new entertainment. Jeannie's eyes never left Clemmie's. As Clemmie moved towards her, arms outstretched, Jeannie briefly shook her head and turned her eyes to the front. The procession shuffled off once again. Clemmie tottered behind, unsure of what to do. She stood in the middle of Rottenrow, watching as the group climbed the steps up to the Lock. As the door opened to admit them, Jeannie turned around. A small and obviously painful smile appeared briefly on her crusted lips and, with a small movement of her index finger, she gestured to Mabel, still asleep. Then the smile disappeared and she turned her head away once more, stumbling up the steps and inside the building. The door closed firmly behind her.

"It's no good, you'll have to go. We cannae afford to keep you here if you're no' working." Sarah's voice was wary. She and Clemmie had slipped into an uneasy truce since the row about the baby farmer.

Clemmie was carding hooks and eyes, with Mabel balanced awkwardly on her skirts. "I *am* working." She knew what Sarah meant, though. Since she had seen Jeannie disappear into the Lock Hospital her mind had been elsewhere. She had taken to trudging up and down Rottenrow every day for the past week, the shawl bound tightly around her, holding Mabel close, from the Lock to the Home, from the Home to the Lock. She didn't know to what purpose. She had to get news of Jeannie; she just didn't know how. As a result, her work rate had gone down and both Sarah and Mrs Burnie were complaining about it. Sarah was threatening to throw her onto the streets and Mrs Burnie was threatening to take away the work.

"Look, I'm sorry, Sarah. I need to find my friend." She had told Sarah only that a good friend was missing; she hadn't told her from where, or the circumstances behind her disappearance. Something also kept her from telling Sarah that she knew where Jeannie was; she just couldn't get to her. She didn't altogether trust Sarah, especially where Mabel was concerned, and that made things even more difficult.

"Well, you need to do it in your own time." Her own time? When did Clemmie ever have her own time? "Mrs Burnie was complaining yesterday. She says the only reason she hasnae got rid of you afore now is because you've been a good worker until now. But you're falling behind and I cannae keep you here if you're not bringing anything in."

"I work every hour I'm here. I give you everything I earn."

"It's no' enough." Sarah was intent on getting as much money as possible. Clemmie didn't entirely blame her; with Reuben's health as it was and a houseful of mouths to feed, Sarah was determined to look after her family. And Clemmie wasn't family, was she? She was a drain on the family and, if she was refusing to work, as Sarah saw it, then she was of no use to the Loags.

Sarah cast her eyes down at her darning. "It would be better if you left the bairn here while you went out to try and find your friend."

Clemmie looked at the pink cheeks that gave Sarah away. "I'll not do that, and you know it. I'll find somewhere else to live."

Sarah slammed her sewing down and moved to the cooking pot over the fire. "Please yourself. You're a stubborn lass, and no mistake. And you'll find it difficult to even get into a Model with a child. They won't take you, even in the worst of them. You'll end up in Barnhill and Mabel will be taken off you anyway." As she stirred the pot furiously, the fight went out of her. "I'm sorry, hen; it's just…" she gestured around her.

Clemmie nodded. "I know. And I *will* work as hard as I did before, I promise. Look, give me another week to try and find Jeannie. That's all. I'll go and see…" She was about to say that she would go and see Mrs McCombe, but something held her back. If she couldn't trust Sarah not to give Mabel to a baby farmer, she also couldn't trust her not to sell information. Clemmie sighed. She needed to talk to Mrs McCombe, but she couldn't take Mabel with her, just in case. And she couldn't leave Mabel with Sarah, just in case. There was nobody around her that she could trust.

*

Clemmie wasn't sure which house Miss Adair lived in – all Jeannie had told her was that it was in Blythswood Square – and she had been walking round and round in circles since she got here, Mabel fretting in her arms. She didn't dare to sit on the pavement or, worse still, in the gardens. If she stopped moving, someone would call a policeman and she would be moved on. She had already drawn curious glances from the fashionable passers-by. Even the maids and menservants going about their business here were well-dressed and tidy and looked down their noses at her. She looked out of place and she felt out of place, but she had to see Miss Adair. It was Wednesday and Clemmie was hoping that Miss Adair still visited the Home. She also hoped that she didn't pay other calls or go out for tea after her visit. Clemmie couldn't stay out much longer; Sarah was coming to the end of her tether.

A smart navy blue and cream brougham drew up at the other side of the Square and a footman jumped down from the box-seat next to the driver and moved out of Clemmie's sight to the door at the kerb. Clemmie crossed the Square. "Miss Adair?"

The woman stopped on the steps to the house, between the sand-coloured pillars and turned towards her. She looked puzzled for a moment, then her face broke into a surprised smile. "Clementina!"

Clemmie nodded and stepped towards her. As she did, the footman, who was hovering in the doorway, holding the door open to allow his mistress to enter, stepped forwards protectively.

Miss Adair held out a gloved hand. "No, John; everything is fine." Then, spotting Mabel, she gasped. "Oh, come inside, do, and introduce me to this little one."

Inside? In the house? "Oh, no, Miss, I couldn't."

"You couldn't? Whyever not? Of course you can. You look tired and pale. I'll arrange for some tea for you."

"I can't, Miss. I need to find out what happened to Jeannie."

"Jeannie? Your friend from the Home?" Clemmie nodded. "I did wonder about her as I haven't seen her for some weeks. Did she run away?"

Clemmie shook her head. "I know where she is. I just need to get to her. And I need your help." The language of the streets that Clemmie had cultivated since coming to Glasgow fell away and the careful, proper speech her mother had instilled in her felt unfamiliar but necessary.

"My help?" Miss Adair looked out at Blythswood Square. "Heavens. We are attracting rather too much interest. I can see Mrs Campbell's lips pursing from here. Come inside, do, away from prying eyes. I will arrange for some food and drink for you and then you can tell me all about it."

Clemmie was still unsure. She didn't want to go inside. What if she broke something? What if someone accused her of stealing something? What if she dragged in the filth of the Tontine's middens? "What about your...?" Clemmie realised that she had no idea who a fine lady like this might live with.

"My what, child?"

"Your people. What if they throw me out?"

Miss Adair swept down the stair towards her, laughing, and put a firm hand on her back, steering her up the stairs to the door. "I have no people, my dear. This is my house, and I can invite into it anyone I please." They entered the house and Miss Adair went on ahead. Clemmie tiptoed across the hallway, not wanting to sully the beautiful burgundy, grey and blue tiles laid out in an intricate pattern. She hopped about, trying to step only on the darker ones, earning a gurgle of glee from Mabel.

A young woman of around Clemmie's age hurried towards them from the dark recesses at the other end of the hallway. She stopped abruptly when she saw the unlikely trio. Miss Adair took off her gloves. "Ah, Ellen. My guest is thirsty. Do please see about getting some tea and cake. Maybe some of Mrs Dugan's delicious pear tart and we'll have it in the morning room. Oh, and Ellen? If you keep your mouth open like that, it might be very tempting for a fly." The girl's mouth snapped shut and she bobbed a curtsy and scurried back down the dim passageway. Clemmie heard the word 'lice' muttered in dark tones. Miss Adair ushered Clemmie through one of the doors that lined the hall. "We'll go in here. It's cosier than the parlour."

Cosy? Clemmie had never seen such a large, uncomfortable-looking room. Everything looked so perfect; she was scared to move, for fear that she might knock into one of the precious-looking ornaments or delicate tables and break it.

"Do sit down. Ellen will bring us something to eat and drink soon. What about the baby? Little...?"

"Mabel, Miss. Mabel Jean." Clemmie looked around. There had to be a hundred places to sit in this room. She headed towards the one which looked the least fancy and perched herself gingerly on the edge of it, hoisting Mabel onto her lap.

Miss Adair bustled over, laughing. "That's a footstool, my dear. Come, sit over here on the chaise longue. It's very comfortable." She scooped Mabel off Clemmie's knee and cooed at her as she led Clemmie by the arm to a sumptuous couch covered in a deep rose-coloured fabric. She patted the seat at the end with a high buttoned back and took a seat herself at the narrower end. "May I hold her while we talk? Does she need anything?"

"No, Miss...I mean...yes, Miss. You can hold her, and I fed her a wee while ago." Clemmie blushed. A lady like Miss Adair didn't need to know that. Watching Mabel in Miss Adair's arms, she was suddenly ashamed of the thin blue shawl that was wrapped around the baby. She had washed it in boiling water until her knuckles were red raw, but it still looked dirty and tattered, in comparison to the fine materials Miss Adair was wearing. Clemmie continued to stand, conscious of her own attire, the skirt dusty at best, and who knows what else at worst.

"Sit down, Clementina, do." Miss Adair smoothed the little cowlick of hair on Mabel's forehead and bent her slim neck until her nose was almost touching the top of the baby's head. "She's so tiny. How old is she?"

Clemmie sat down carefully, making sure as little of her as possible touched the seat. "Four weeks ago I had her, Miss." Was that all it was? The pain, the fear, the jingling devil, it all felt so long ago.

Miss Adair continued to coo over Mabel. Finally, she looked up at Clemmie. "Now, my dear. You said that you wanted my help?"

Clemmie opened her mouth to speak, but a tap at the door stopped her. Ellen entered, carrying a tray containing a tea set which she placed on a delicate table. Picking up table and tray, she placed them in front of the chaise longue and stood back. Miss Adair smiled at her. "Thank you, Ellen. You may serve the tea and then you can go and ask Mrs Dugan to prepare a nice basket of food for Clementina to take home with her."

Ellen stepped forward to the tray, pursing her tiny mouth. She poured tea into the two cups with their intricate pattern of cobalt blue and iron red intertwined flowers. She handed one cup to Miss Adair with a curtsy and the other to Clemmie, holding on to the saucer and glaring at Clemmie as if she were worried that the intruder might steal the gilt from around the edges. Clemmie grinned at the thought; although the grin quickly disappeared as Ellen let go of the saucer, setting the cup rattling and Clemmie's nerves jangling, worried that she would spill the tea or break the delicate china. Ellen looked at Miss Adair to check that she wasn't watching, stuck her tongue out at Clemmie, then spun on her heel and left the room, with a final curtsy for Miss Adair.

Miss Adair was rocking the now sleeping Mabel. "Well, I don't think you made any friends there."

"No, Miss. I don't think she likes my sort."

Miss Adair snorted in an unladylike fashion. "Take it from me, Clemmie, it simply doesn't do, to worry about what people think of you. In my experience, one should be bold, take chances in life and please oneself." Clemmie shuffled in her seat in discomfort and Miss Adair looked at Clemmie and frowned. "I'm sorry. That was inconsiderate and thoughtless of me. I have the wealth and the privilege to be able to make those choices, and I do realise that not everyone is so fortunate. So, my dear, what is it that I can do for you?"

Clemmie looked at the kindly eyes that gazed quizzically at her and shook her head. She didn't know where to start, nor how this woman could help.

Clemmie stopped halfway up Balmano Brae to catch her breath. Even without the weight of Mabel, this hill was a struggle. Clemmie felt a twinge of guilt and fear as she thought of Mabel. She didn't know whether she should have left her with Miss Adair, or told Miss Adair so much about her worries for Jeannie. What if Miss Adair went to the police; or refused to give Mabel back? Clemmie had had to go with what her gut told her to do and had allowed herself to be persuaded by Miss Adair's bold plan. Her fingers moved once again to the small but heavy bag tucked into the waist of her skirt. She had tied it firmly, but she needed to check that it was still there, that it hadn't been lost or stolen. She felt as though everyone she passed was looking at her with suspicion. Could they tell she had ten gold sovereigns about her person? Ten gold sovereigns. Surely Miss Adair wouldn't have given her all that money if she was going to go to the police? She had said it was less than she had paid that very morning for a coat, but it was more than Clemmie had seen, or would ever see in her whole life, she was sure.

Clemmie kept her hand over the wee bag as she turned into Rottenrow, conscious more than ever before of the jostling and elbowing that she experienced as she walked down towards the Home. She stepped into the timber merchant's doorway and drew herself as far back as she could in the mouth of the close, without losing sight of the gates of the Home. The Chapel clock struck the hour and Clemmie settled in to wait.

It was not long before Mrs McCombe appeared at the small staff gate. She stopped to tie the ribbons of her dark blue bonnet and set off down Rottenrow. Clemmie followed behind, keeping as far back as she dared without danger of losing her. Mrs McCombe's pace was swift and assured and she strode along without glancing to either left or right. At the foot of Rottenrow she turned into Castle Street and walked up the hill, crossing over the street at the Blind Asylum to inspect a stall of brooms and baskets outside. Clemmie hung back, waiting until Mrs McCombe set off smartly once again, towards the looming, black hulk of Tennant's Stalk. The tall chimney did little to take the noxious smoke and sulphurous odour away from the area's residents, even though that was its sole aim. The sky was darker here, the buildings indistinct and the air laden with caustic fumes which nipped at Clemmie's eyes. She was glad when Mrs McCombe turned away from the chemical works and into Garngad Road, but the heavy cloud remained above, and the sulphurous smell was joined by the bloody tang of the copper works which made Clemmie feel sick to her stomach.

The streets were much quieter here and, when Mrs McCombe turned into a narrow street, Clemmie speeded up to catch up with her. "Mrs McCombe!"

Mrs McCombe stopped with a jerk and spun round to face Clemmie. "Clementina Watt. Well, well, well."

Clemmie closed the gap between them but made sure to still keep well out of the way. Mrs McCombe was not carrying her tawse – she must leave that at the Home – but Clemmie did not trust her. She was sure that the Matron would love to take her back to the Home, back into the hands of the jingling devil. "I need your help."

Mrs McCombe laughed. It was an unfamiliar and uncomfortable sound. "And why would I help *you*, Watt? I could drag you back to the Home right now. Then we'll see exactly how much help you need."

Clemmie raised her chin. "If I'm not back within two hours, people will come looking for me. And they know where to come." She sounded more confident than she felt.

Mrs McCombe snorted. "People. What people could possibly come looking for *you*?"

"Important people." Clemmie's voice was more assured than she felt. She had no idea if Miss Adair would come looking for her, or what use the young woman could possibly be if Clemmie were to disappear, but it made Mrs McCombe hesitate. "And I have money." She took out the bag of sovereigns and shook it. The chink of coins chased away the look of concern and puzzlement on Mrs McCombe's face. She stepped towards Clemmie. Clemmie backed away, still holding the wee bag in the air. "Ten gold sovereigns. And you can have that now, with double that to come afterwards."

Before Mrs McCombe could answer, two little girls barrelled along the road towards them and flung their arms around Mrs McCombe's knees. Clemmie's mind went back to the conversation she had overheard months before. "Aren't you worried for your granddaughters, Mrs McCombe? What will you do if what happened to me happens to them?"

Mrs McCombe's face hardened and she put a protective hand on each of the small golden heads. "What is it you think I can do, Watt?

Clemmie drew in a breath. "I want you to get me into the Lock Hospital."

Mrs McCombe let out that uncomfortable laugh once more and Clemmie shuddered.

Clemmie plunged her spoon into the bowl of apple and plum charlotte. The exterior was crisp and buttery; the fruit inside was both tart and sweet and made her mouth water. Miss Adair watched her, frowning, a snuffling Mabel tucked into the crook of one arm. "Are you sure this is wise, Clemmie?"

"No," said Clemmie, indistinctly. This was her third trip to Miss Adair's in as many days and she had lost her fear of eating and drinking in front of this graceful woman and had stopped worrying about spilling things on the beautifully upholstered furniture. She had even lost her wariness of the perpetually scornful Ellen…almost. She swallowed the huge mouthful of pudding. "But there's nothing else I can do. I have to get in and see Jeannie."

"And you're sure it wouldn't be best to involve the constabulary? I have a distant cousin—"

"Aye, I'm quite sure. Some of the lassies at the Home told us stories. No offence, Miss, but even if your cousin was the Chief Constable…naw. Please, you mustn't. Promise me you willnae."

"Oh, my dear, don't worry. I wouldn't do anything without your say so. You know your own circumstances better than I. I promise I'll be guided by you. I'm not sure how much they would listen to me, truth be told, but it *is* an option you should consider."

"Well, Miss, I'm sorry to say, but the likes of me don't trust the police. No, I have to get into the Lock and find out what happened to Jeannie and what I can do to help her. I feel like it's my fault. I left her in there, knowing what the jingling devil was like."

"And are you sure it will have been him who gave her this...
dreadful illness?"

"Well, she didn't catch it off the bedsheets, Miss. Despite
what they say when it's a lassie as young as Jeannie that falls to
it."

"And what about you, Clemmie? Did you ever...?" Miss
Adair's face turned pink, and she gave all her attention to
adjusting Mabel's little bonnet.

"No, Miss. I was lucky. Besides, I was one of their regular
girls. And so I wasn't pure anymore. Girls like Jeannie...well...
they're special to any of these men that have the pox." Clemmie
felt uncomfortable talking like this to Miss Adair. She hadn't
even wanted to tell Jeannie.

"You mean this 'Abominable Superstition'?"

"Abom...?" Clemmie didn't understand the word.

"This ridiculous notion that having sexual relations with a
virgin will cure them of syphilis?"

Clemmie looked at her, aghast. The word Miss Adair used
might have been new to her, but this wasn't. "Aye, but...how do
you...?"

"I asked the family physician. Don't look like that, Clemmie.
I kept your name completely out of it, of course."

Clemmie put a hand in front of her face to hide her grin.
"It's not that, Miss. I'm just imagining his face when you asked."

"Yes, he *was* rather shocked, to say the least. He gave me
a lecture about not concerning myself with irrelevancies
outside my purview and that I should take up some healthy and
pleasant employment more fitted to my station. He suggested
embroidery, or tatting."

"And what did you say?"

Miss Adair stroked her fingers across the baby's puckered
brow. "I told him that the health and safety of young women
was well within my purview now it has come to my attention
and that I knew I could count on his assistance in the future. He

tried to dissuade me, of course."

Clemmie watched Miss Adair as she fussed over Mabel, rearranging the soft lemon shawl she had been wearing around her own shoulders on top of Mabel's own little blue one. "I have…another favour to ask of you. A great one." Miss Adair looked at her enquiringly. "I just don't…have anyone else I can ask. I know I cannae ever repay you for your kindness to me already, but as soon as I can get a job, I'll repay the money, even if I have to work all my life to do it." The words cannoned into each other as Clemmie rushed to get them out.

"Nonsense, my dear. There's nothing to repay. And you are to join my staff. Jeannie, too. Do please tell her that as soon as she leaves that dreadful place she is to come here, where there will be a home and a position for her for as long as she wants them."

"Thank you, but…" Clemmie took a deep breath.

"If you're hesitating to ask me whether I will look after Mabel while you're away, then there is no question to ask. Of course I will. Now, pass me that napkin; this little tyrant has been sick on the chaise."

Miss Adair had given Clemmie three days. She had not wanted to give her even that long, but Clemmie had insisted and countered Miss Adair's alternative suggestions at every turn.

"I shall simply become a Subscriber." Clemmie didn't know what this meant, and it must have showed in her face. "With voluntary institutions such as the Lock, they rely somewhat on rich benefactors. By paying an annual subscription I may propose a certain number of women for admission. That would also ensure that you are treated fairly and properly, or they will have me to answer to."

"There's no time for all that, Miss Adair. I need to get in there right now."

Miss Adair sighed heavily. "I really don't like the idea of you having to go back to the Home in order to be admitted to the Lock. Can you be sure that Mrs McCombe will stand by her word? What if she's told this jingling devil, as you call him, and he's waiting there for you?"

This was also something which worried Clemmie, but voicing those fears would do her no good. "She's a greedy woman; she won't want to risk her purse."

"Well, I could simply go in as a visitor and ask to see Jeannie. They are always advertising in *The Herald* for donations. And I am sure they have lady visitors, just as they do at the Home. That way, you don't need to be involved at all."

However, Clemmie was insistent. She felt guilty for leaving Jeannie behind and she needed to see her personally. "You're doing more than enough, Miss, looking after Mabel and loaning me the money and all."

"*Giving*, Clemmie, giving. At least let me do that."

And so here Clemmie was, climbing over the wall into the courtyard of the Home, Mrs McCombe striding towards her, the keys on her belt clanking ominously.

"Well, girl, where's my money?"

Clemmie tried to keep the fluttering in her belly out of her voice. "Once I'm inside the Lock, the money will be delivered to you." Miss Adair had insisted on sending John, the footman, with her and he was to deliver the money to Mrs McCombe. John had followed her to Rottenrow, grumbling the whole way. He was Ellen's young man and his tongue was just as sharp as hers. Clemmie had left him lounging disconsolately in a doorway opposite the gates while she disappeared up the timber merchant's close to climb over the wall. She didn't want to tell him that he was making himself comfortable in the doorway of a house of ill repute. Let him find that out for himself.

Mrs McCombe unhooked a large pair of scissors from her belt. The sudden movement of her mouth scarcely resembled a smile, but Clemmie realised that was what it must be – a bitter rictus of pleasure. "Get over here." Clemmie hesitated and Mrs McCombe gave her a look of scorn. "What, do you think I'm going to stab you? I need to cut your hair. Just like the other slatterns going with you today."

Clemmie hadn't thought about this. Losing her hair didn't worry her; but Mabel wouldn't be able to wrap her little fingers in it and tug it and bite it as she liked to do. What if her own child didn't recognise her afterwards? The cold steel flew around her head, the blades crunching shut close to her ears. Clemmie's hair fell in curls about her feet like apple parings. Several times, the blades touched her scalp and Clemmie felt the warm slowness of a drop of blood as it made its way down towards her chin. She kept her head held high, staring at Mrs McCombe's right eye as it loomed up close to her. The crows' feet at the outside corner deepened with effort at every bite of the blades. Mrs McCombe stepped back to admire her handiwork and Clemmie couldn't resist reaching up to touch her shorn scalp. In places, it was almost smooth; in others, she could feel rough tufts sticking up. She must look a sight.

Mrs McCombe thrust a dingy yellow dress at her. "Take that fancy dress off and put this on." She watched her undress, snickering nastily when Clemmie turned away modestly to pull the dress over her head. Mrs McCombe snatched the dress Miss Adair had given Clemmie and inspected it with interest. It was one of Ellen's and Clemmie knew that she wouldn't see it again. Yet another thing for Ellen to hold against her.

She followed Mrs McCombe around the corner, hitching her shoulders in an attempt to relieve the itch caused by the rough fabric, or the lice within it. Two other women in identical yellow dresses turned at their approach, their eyes registering a flicker of interest at the newcomer. Clemmie didn't recognise either of them. The younger one – just a year or two older than her, Clemmie guessed – with skin the colour of a rich ginger parkin, smiled briefly and then dropped her gaze to the floor again. Clemmie stared at her curiously; girls who looked like this one were uncommon here. The heads of the other two girls were shaved, like her, but Clemmie noted that their barber had been more industrious and neater than hers.

As Clemmie composed herself, the gates opened. Two policemen strolled in, followed by two nurses from the Lock – one dark, one fair. "Three, Mrs McCombe? I thought we were only to receive two today?"

Mrs McCombe grunted and shrugged, taking the large black record book from the proffered hand, kicking the chains and manacles out from under her stool as she wrote in the book in her cramped writing.

"Finlayson, Lillie."

"Yes, Matron." The voice matched the skin – warm and dark with the hint of an accent Clemmie didn't recognise.

"Cherry, Marion."

"Yes, Matron." The other woman was older, in her early twenties. Her voice was hoarse but held an impudence that caused Mrs McCombe to look up from the register and narrow her eyes, before turning back to the book in front of her. There was a brief silence as she wrote something down.

"Watt, Clementina."

"Yes...Matron."

Mrs McCombe's pen scratched on the pages of the book once more, before she slammed it shut. "Get them out of here."

One of the policemen herded the girls together – roughly pulling on an arm or pushing at a shoulder until the three of them were awkwardly pressed together, the touch of another's breath bringing a familiarity and warmth none of them felt. Their shorn heads were bowed as they avoided each other's eyes. Despite the closeness and the warmth of the day, Clemmie felt suddenly cold and alone in her strange yellow dress. The policemen bent down to clasp the cuffs around their ankles. As hers were fastened on, the policeman's hand snaked up Clemmie's leg and pinched the back of her knee. Clemmie yelped and kicked her leg as far as the chain would allow. Her knee caught the policeman on the chin and he let out an oath, pulling the chain hard so that the cuff bit into her ankle, leaving a red welt. He lifted his hand to strike out at Clemmie, but the dark-haired nurse stopped him.

"Constable! I'll thank you not to touch the *patient*."

The stress on the word had its intended effect. "Aye, pox ridden whore, so she is." He lowered his hand and roughly pulled Clemmie into line, before shoving all three young women in front of him, forcing them to walk forwards.

Mrs McCombe caught them up at the gate and brought her lips to Clemmie's ear. "Enjoy the steel prick, Watt." Clemmie didn't ask what she meant.

As they left the Home behind them and made their way down Rottenrow, Clemmie saw the look of horror on John's face as he registered her shaved head, yellow dress and manacles. She smiled briefly, seeing that he had moved away from the door of the brothel. She remembered how she and Jeannie, following the canary women – it felt so long ago, now – had watched reactions to the chained women as they had passed by: scorn, sympathy, disgust, curiosity, and bent her head. Clemmie could feel her face reddening, her shorn head, too, felt like a beacon. She wanted to cry out: *I don't have the pox!*

She kept her eyes on the feet of the two women in front of her, concentrating on the careful steps and the shuffle, clank, shuffle, clank, shuffle, clank. She could feel the life of the street going on around them as they passed, could hear the raucous laughter and insolence in the voices of some of those who called out to them.

The outside world receded with every step, until it was just Clemmie and the two extra pairs of feet. She would see Jeannie. Everything would be alright. She would have Mabel snuggling into her breast again soon. She would—

They came to a sudden halt and Clemmie looked up. The words Treatment – Knowledge – Reformation were spelled out on the sign above her head. The two nurses raised their hems as they climbed the steps and into the open doorway where they stood, one on either side of the door, beckoning. The policeman pushed Clemmie in the back and she stumbled forwards into Marion Cherry, who was only an inch or so in front of her. The three of them tumbled up the steps and into the gloom beyond. A knee – Clemmie had no idea whose – pinned her head to the floor and she inhaled the pine scent of turpentine and the honey warmth of beeswax from the highly polished floorboards.

The dark-haired nurse helped the three women to rise. "Constables, these are young women, not sacks of coal. Treat them with some respect." Her voice was quiet, but firm. "And you can take off the shackles. They are no longer needed."

Clemmie's ankles felt so light without the heavy iron around them that she felt she should hold on to the wall to keep from floating away. The nurses led them past a closed door and into a small room on the left. Here, a tiny elderly woman was perched up high, behind a tall desk. Like the floor, the desk was glowing with polish, reflecting the flicker of the gas lamps around the walls. She stretched out a spotted and wrinkled hand for the black book, which one of the nurses passed up to her. The woman opened the book and inspected it gravely, before looking up at Clemmie and the two canaries with her. "I am Mrs Condra. Matron, to you." Her voice was soft and deep with age, with a slight Irish lilt. She sighed. "Marion Cherry – I was not expecting to see you back yet again. The Superintendent will not be pleased; nor will the Chaplain. It took us a long time to find a suitable place for you, and then it was only thanks to one of our subscribers, given your…history. What went wrong this time?"

Clemmie could feel Marion Cherry stiffening beside her. "The Master, Matron. *That's* what went wrong."

"Ah, the pity." Mrs Condra shook her head, tutting, until Clemmie was sure she had forgotten about them. "And you, Lillie Finlayson? What's your story?"

"I'm a biscuit packer, Matron. At Gray, Dunn."

"In Kinning Park?"

"Yes, Matron."

"Not a prostitute, then? As it says here?"

"No, Ma'am. A biscuit packer." Their shoulders touching, Clemmie could feel Lillie's back stiffening. Her melodic voice sounded aggrieved.

"And where are you from, Lillie Finlayson?"

"I was born in Govan, Matron."

"And your parents?"

"Aye, them too."

The Matron raised her eyebrows. "Grandparents?"

"The West Indies, Matron. Demerara."

"Slaves in one of the sugar houses?" Lillie Finlayson nodded. A brief smile flickered on Mrs Condra's lips. "And here you are, drowning in the stuff, working in a biscuit factory making Florador Fingers and Windsor Wafers for Her Majesty." She turned to Clemmie. "Clementina Watt."

It wasn't a question, but Clemmie responded anyway. "Yes, Matron."

"Mrs McCombe doesn't seem to like you very much, Clementina Watt." Clemmie said nothing. "Would you like to know what she has written about you here?"

"No' really, Matron, no."

Mrs Condra's cheeks concertinaed as she smiled and shut the book. "A wise decision, indeed. Now, Marion Cherry, shall I tell the rules of this house, or will you? You know them just as well as me, by now."

Marion Cherry recited, as if by rote. "We are to remain here until we are discharged. We are not to go out on any pretence, and, if we do, we will not be allowed to return. We are to behave ourselves soberly and decently——"

"And that means?"

"No swearing, quarrelling and the like."

"Indeed. No fighting. We had cause to send three girls to the Police Office only last week. God Himself only knows what will become of them. Carry on, Marion Cherry."

"We are to be out of our beds by seven o'clock in the morning and in our beds by eight o'clock at night. We are to wash and ready ourselves before breakfast and, for the rest of the day we are to clean the wards and assist in the Wash House when required to do so." Marion paused and looked at Mrs Condra.

"Divine Service, child."

"Oh, aye. We are to attend Divine Service and listen to the Chaplain in a quiet and orderly fashion…" her voice trailed off.

"Liquor, Marion Cherry, the bane of your life. God knows you should remember this rule, even if you can't follow it."

"Aye…aye. We're not to have any liquor nor bring in or receive any provisions not supplied by the Hospital."

"Tea, bread, butter and sugar excepted. You may receive those items if you have people who would like to leave them for you. And you are not to receive any books other than those that the Chaplain has approved. Thank you, Marion Cherry. Let's see if you can stick to them this time, shall we?"

Mrs Condra closed the book, hauled herself off her high seat and came around the front of the desk. Her blue serge dress was starched and pristine. Although a good few inches under five feet tall, her presence was imposing and Clemmie and the other two canary women stepped back and bobbed their heads. "Now, Nurse Henderson and Nurse Fulton will take you to be bathed." She looked at each of them in turn, her eyes lingering on Marion Cherry. "Plenty of soap and water, Henderson, I think. And take their clothing away to be boiled. All three of you will then be examined." She looked soberly at each of them in turn. "It will not be pleasant, but try to withstand it without movement; it will go better for you, if you do."

As the nurses started to lead them out of the room, she called after them. "Nurse Henderson?" The dark-haired nurse turned towards her. "It's that young doctor today. Make sure he has chloroform ready."

Shiny duck's bill...cold...cold... *Shhhhhhhhh, shhhhhhhhh.* Stabbing...duck bites. *Shhhhhhhhh. There, there.* Have to get the baby out...have to... *Stop pushing, child. Don't push.* Cold and hard. Why is the baby cold and hard? Take it out...take it out. *Stop pushing against the speculum so. Hold her down, Nurse.* The face. The face blots out the light. The dark hurts. *For pity's sake, Doctor, give her the chloroform.* Pressing my shoulders down. Is it him? Climbing on top of me? *What does the girl mean...The Devil?* Stop it! Stop. Tearing me. It hurts! *Shhhhhhhhhh, shhh...shhh.* It hurts! *Help her.* Gravy-stained handkerchief covering my face. Sweet... sickly. *That's it; breathe deeply. Breathe in.* Stinks of rotting paper and rum. Sickly and sweet. *Breathe in, child.* Cold...cold. Tastes like pennies. Pennies in my mouth. Heavy. *That's it, that's it.* Heavy...where have I gone?

When Clemmie awoke, Nurse Henderson was standing over her, holding a steaming bowl out to her. "Have some of this, child. Rice and milk."

Clemmie struggled to sit up. She was still in the examination room. "Have I...? Have I been here long?" The coppery taste was still there, but she felt rested, as though she had slept for days.

Nurse Henderson smiled. "Only ten minutes. Now, take this, so that I can give this other bowl to Lillie."

Clemmie saw Lillie awakening on the table next to her. "Where's Marion?"

Nurse Henderson picked up a second bowl. "Oh, Marion

didn't need the chloroform. She was on and off the table in a matter of seconds. Don't you worry about her; she's well used to the speculum."

"The steel prick." Nurse Henderson's mouth dropped open and she stared at Clemmie. "Somebody said that to me. I didn't know what they meant."

"Yes…well…that's as may be. But it has to be done."

"And now?"

"The doctor found no discharge and recommended a short course of mercury treatment, just to be sure. Then you can go back to the Home. It would seem that you have been lucky."

Lucky.

Clemmie stood, wincing a little at the soreness she felt inside. Nurse Henderson touched her shoulder briefly. Clemmie sensed a warmth that was not just skin deep. "I have a friend here – Jeannie Jack. Do you know where I can find her?"

"Jeannie?" Nurse Henderson's voice was concerned.

"Yes. Isn't she here?"

"Oh yes, she's still here…but…"

But what? Clemmie kept her voice calm. "Can I see her?"

"She's very ill. She's kept in a room on her own."

"The pox?" Surely Jeannie couldn't be that bad. It had only been a few weeks, after all. Clemmie had seen the ravages caused by syphilis, but it took longer than that.

"She is syphilitic, yes. But…it's not that. Her mind is… unbalanced. We have to keep her locked up and isolated until she leaves."

"Leaves? Where's she going?"

Nurse Henderson hesitated. "Once the signs of syphilis have gone, she'll be going to the asylum."

"The *lunatic* asylum?"

"I'm afraid so, child. She's very unwell."

Clemmie was silent. She should have taken Jeannie with her when she left; they would have managed somehow. It was her fault. "Can I see her?" she said again.

It was Nurse Henderson's turn to be silent. "I don't—"

"I *have* to see her. Please."

Nurse Henderson patted the hand that had reached out to grab her forearm and appeared to come to a decision. "Well, perhaps it will do her good to see a friendly face. She's to have a mercury fumigation tomorrow morning. Usually, she's there on her own as it is too distressing…She is so young…" She cleared her throat. "I'll take you down at the same time. But just this once."

Clemmie had not slept well. Although the beds were more comfortable than those in the Home, and the dormitory less crowded, the coughing, screeching and moaning of the other women had kept her awake most of the night. And the pervasive smell sickened her: a cloying mixture of festering sores, fetid breath and an antiseptic that burned her eyes and nose. Despite the smell, though, she was weak with hunger. Last night's dinner had been a bowl of watery-looking pea soup, ladled out by an older woman with copper-coloured scabs on her face and hands. The woman's hair was thin and patchy, and her mouth and nose were puckered at the edges. One of her eyes was an angry red, the pupil misshapen and unseeing. She would ladle a portion of soup into a bowl from an enormous iron cauldron, then take the discoloured rag tucked into the waist of her apron and press it to her mouth, from which saliva streamed almost constantly. Clemmie decided to forgo the soup and make do with a mug of the sarsaparilla which was offered to each of them. Several other women in the dining room held similar rags to their mouths or used their sleeves, slurping loudly and constantly to suck the saliva back in. Marion Cherry had whispered to Clemmie and Lillie that it was an effect of the mercury, adding spitefully that they would find out soon enough. Clemmie looked around for

Jeannie, but she was not in the dining room. She tucked into a bowl of thick porridge – thankfully, the woman with the sores was nowhere to be seen and they all helped themselves from the large saucepan.

After breakfast, Nurse Henderson came into the dining room and beckoned to her. "I'll take you in and bring Jeannie to you," she said, as she made her way downstairs. "Once I bring her, you can have ten minutes with her."

"But…" Ten minutes! Was that all?

"Ten minutes." Nurse Henderson's voice was firm. "And I shouldn't even be allowing you that." She opened a door at the bottom of the stairs and led Clemmie into a windowless basement room which smelled of damp. Three long, narrow wooden benches took up most of the room. Under each of the benches, spaced at regular intervals, was a contraption Clemmie had never seen the like of before, five to each bench. Each contraption consisted of a large spirit lamp, over which was a circular tin bath. The centre of the bath was raised, giving the whole thing the look of the inside of a jelly mould.

Nurse Henderson motioned to Clemmie to wait, then unlocked a cabinet on the wall and pulled out a bottle and a pair of goggles which she put on. She poured water from a pan into the jelly mould at the furthest away bench and, on the raised central plate, she measured out grey liquid from the bottle. She repeated the procedure at the next bath before carefully replacing the stopper in the bottle. She then lit the two spirit lamps below the tin baths.

"You'll find some cloaks in the cupboard in the corner. Get out of your clothes, put a cloak over yourself and sit on the bench over one of the baths. The cloak needs to cover the mercury bath. I'll bring you a fresh nightgown to wear afterwards."

Clemmie did as she was told, shivering a little. She tied the cord of the cloak around her neck. It was made of an oil cloth lined with flannel and she was grateful for the warmth. She climbed onto the bench, carefully positioning the cloak around the bath with the lamp underneath. At first, the warmth of the steam on her skin underneath the cloak was pleasant and soothing, but she soon began to feel itchy. The vapours also made their way into her eyes and nose and the steam stuck what was left of her hair to her forehead. Her scalp felt cold and damp. As she began to fidget on the bench, the door opened and Nurse Henderson came in, guiding Jeannie in front of her, gently loosening the strings of Jeannie's nightgown as she did so.

Clemmie gasped in horror. A dark and angry ulcer the size of a dinnerplate was spread across her friend's neck and narrow chest. She looked so fragile. "Jeannie!"

But Jeannie did not react. She stood, her eyes vacant and unfocused, mouth open, saliva spilling out. Nurse Henderson tied a cloak around her neck and led her over to the bench next to Clemmie. "She may not speak much. She's on opium for the pain from the ulcers in her throat." She arranged the folds of the oilskin cloak around the tin bath and withdrew to the edge of the room.

"Jeannie!" No reaction. Clemmie wanted to reach out and grab Jeannie's hand, but their arms were inside the cloaks. She shuffled slightly along to get a little closer to her friend. "Jeannie, it's me, Clemmie."

Jeannie's eyes remained dull, but her ragged breathing seemed to catch and whistle. Clemmie tried again. "Mabel wants to meet you, Jeannie. My little Mabel Jean. And I have a home for you to come to. Somewhere safe and kind. Miss Adair has promised you a home, too…" Her voice faltered as Jeannie lifted her head and her eyes seemed to focus briefly. Her mouth moved, the cracked lips opening in a grimace to reveal bright red gums and spaces where teeth should have been. "Oh, Jeannie. I'm so sorry. I shouldn't have left you there. I should have known that the jingling devil would—"

Jeannie's body twitched and she started to say something. Her voice was low and raspy and it was as though her mouth and tongue couldn't form the words. Clemmie leaned her head closer. "What is it?"

"Thedevilthedevilthedevilthedevil..." Jeannie's voice became louder, and her body shook and convulsed underneath the oilskin.

"Thedevilthedevilthedevilthedevil." The bench shook beneath them as Jeannie's convulsions became more violent.

"Shhhhh, Jeannie, shhhhhhh. It's me, Clemmie. He's not here. The devil's not here!"

But Jeannie's voice only became more frantic and panicked. "Thedevilthedevilthedevil..."

Nurse Henderson rose, alarmed, and took a step towards them as Jeannie's jerking caused the tin bath beneath her to rock and rattle.

"Thedevilthedevilthedevilthedevilthedevilthedevil..." Jeannie's voice was almost a shriek, now.

The bench tipped and fell to the floor with a crash. Clemmie jumped out of the way, but Jeannie seemed oblivious to anything, falling limply to the floor with the bench on top of her. Her spasms knocked over the tin bath and spirit lamp, the water extinguishing the lamp with a hiss. As Jeannie thrashed uncontrollably, the bath clattered and the end of the bench thumped against the floor. Through it all, Jeannie's tormented cry continued. "Thedevilthedevilthedevilthedevilthedevil..."

Clemmie stood, trembling and helpless in her oilcloth cloak, watching the bony limbs and damaged skin of her friend as she jerked and twisted on the ground. The water from the bath pooled around Jeannie and soaked into the packed earth. Tiny beads of quicksilver shivered and shimmered in the lamplight as they found each other, forming perfect shining circles in dips and hollows.

Nurse Henderson wrapped her arms around Jeannie, comforting. "Shhhhhhhh, Jeannie, there, there, my child." She looked at Clemmie. "I shouldn't have allowed this. She's too far gone. I'll take her to bed and give her a sedative. Take the cloak off and let the air dry you before putting on the new nightgown I brought you. Don't rub the mercury off." She stroked Jeannie's head and whispered in her ear, words that Clemmie couldn't make out but which were said in a soothing voice. Jeannie was whimpering, but the shuddering and shaking had mostly stopped. Nurse Henderson turned her attention to Clemmie, one hand stroking Jeannie's cheek. "Wait here. I'll come back down for you soon."

She unwrapped the cloak from around Jeannie, soothing her all the time. Clemmie stood, unmoving, her own cloak heavy around her. Jeannie was silent and calm now and her head lifted for a moment. The dullness seemed to leave her eyes and she gave a broken attempt at a smile. "Clemmie…"

Clemmie stepped towards her, but Nurse Henderson stopped her. "No. I need to take her up while she's calm." She put her arm around Jeannie and led her quickly to the door. She opened it to reveal a waiting party outside, summoned, no doubt, by the clattering and screaming from the basement – two nurses accompanied a group of women, including Marion Cherry and Lillie Finlayson, as well as the drooling woman from the canteen. They all looked on as Nurse Henderson ushered Jeannie through the door. Jeannie put out a hand and grasped the frame. Turning back to Clemmie, she spoke. Her voice was quiet but clear. "I know who he is. The jingling devil."

Clemmie had been unable to eat any of the hard bread on offer at lunchtime. Her gums were red and sore and running her tongue along the back of her teeth made her mouth feel as though she was chewing down on hot cinders. Marion Cherry hovered over her as she tried to eat and swooped down on Clemmie's portion of bread and broth at the first sign of a grimace.

"Doesn't your mouth hurt?"

"Aye, but if you suck the broth through the bread until it softens, it's not so bad." Marion proceeded to show them by slurping and swooshing, finally opening her mouth to reveal semi-masticated pieces on her tongue.

Lillie drew back, horrified. "You have only three teeth, anyway, you have to suck *all* your food."

Marion shrugged and took another piece of Clemmie's bread. "It's a long time until supper, and only rice and milk then."

Clemmie didn't much care. It wasn't just her gums that stopped her from eating. She needed to find out what Jeannie knew, and she was running out of time. Miss Adair had given her only three days and tomorrow was the third day. A big part of Clemmie wished it was today. She was tired and sick and sweating and drooling and she would love to lie down and go to sleep. She wanted to leave this place and go back to her comfortable bed at Miss Adair's house and hug Mabel and hug her and hug her. She wanted to breathe in the violet soap that Miss Adair had given her for Mabel's hair and which reminded her of her mother, fresh from her weekly bath. And she wanted to eat a warm fruit cobbler off delicate china. Miss Adair would go to the police and she would make them find the jingling devil and save Jeannie and—

At the thought of Jeannie, Clemmie felt immediately guilty. Of course she couldn't just give up. It was up to her to save her friend.

Nurse Henderson had said that Jeannie was kept locked up and isolated. Tonight, she would try to find her.

*

This was not the Home. She didn't know which floorboards creaked, which doors groaned, which windows rattled when they were disturbed by changes in the air around them. She didn't even know if the next door would open onto the darkness of a sleeping dormitory, the firelight of a nurse's room, or the cold cleanliness of the room with the steel pricks. She slipped out of her own dormitory and started her search at the top of the building. On the top floor were storage rooms and one large room of sleeping women. Clemmie checked each bed, just in case, but none of the sleepers, whether fitful or quiet, was Jeannie. One young woman opened her eyes as Clemmie passed and stared at her before turning her head away; doped with opium, perhaps, or simply past caring.

Clemmie made her way down through the building, pressing her ear to every door, moving on from it where she heard voices, carefully opening it where there was silence. She grew bolder as she went. She felt like a wraith, an insubstantial wisp announcing death. She slipped through the cramped kitchen, avoiding copper pots stacked in a higgeldy-piggeldy heap by the scullery door; in through the laundry, with its piles of neat sheets and linens; before slipping outside into a small courtyard, grey with soot and only a wooden bench to relieve its drabness.

In the basement she avoided the fumigation room. She already knew what was in there – the cloth pressed to her mouth to catch the drool was testimony to that. The next door was locked. Was this where Jeannie was kept? Should she call out and see if Jeannie was inside? She decided to investigate the remaining two rooms first. She tried the handle of the room next to the locked door and it opened soundlessly. The blackness inside was heavy and oppressive, with no windows to allow even a sliver of light through.

Clemmie stepped into the darkness, hoping that her eyes would adjust, but the blackness seemed to close in around her even more. She breathed in a sickly-sweet scent, mixed in with illness and something rotten. She turned her head, listening for the slightest sound, but there was nothing. She needed light. The lamps in the fumigation room would be perfect. She backed out, into the corridor. Thankfully, the fumigation room was open, and she lit one of the smaller spirit lamps and carried it back.

As she held the lamp in front of her and moved it in an arc, the blackness receded. It was just an ordinary room, small and windowless, cold and unwelcoming, but ordinary. A chair in one corner, a thin rug on the damp stone floor and a bed. Lying on the bed was a thin form. Clemmie moved over to the bed and, shielding the lamp with one hand, she moved the light upwards to the pillow.

"Oh, thank God! I've found you." Jeannie's eyes were on her, unblinking. "Oh, Jeannie, they've tied you to the bed. Let me get these loose."

But the ropes binding Jeannie to the bed were not needed any more. Clemmie gently reached out to touch her friend's face. Her skin was cold and damp and unmoving beneath Clemmie's fingers; nothing like the plump, warm cheeks Clemmie wanted to remember.

"Let's get these ropes undone." Clemmie's fingers felt numb and useless, as she struggled with the bindings. She had to do it; Jeannie shouldn't be tied up like this. "I'll get you out of here, Jeannie." But the knots were stubborn and Clemmie knew it didn't matter anymore. Her numb hands moved from the knots to Jeannie's fingers and she clasped them between her own. She started to cry, silently at first and then, as the grief and guilt and rage bubbled up inside her, her sobs turned to screams.

*

"Shhhhh, child, shhhhhh." Nurse Henderson tucked the blanket under Clemmie's chin.

Clemmie struggled to sit up anyway, her head heavy and her eyes refusing to stay open. "What...?"

"We found you in the basement, screaming." Nurse Henderson bit her lip. "I'm...sorry about your friend. She wasn't well, you know. It was probably for the best, the poor bairn."

Jeannie. Clemmie felt her loss like a physical pain balling up in her stomach and chest. "I need to see her."

"You can't, the undertaker's carriage came to take her away."

"Away? But...?"

Nurse Henderson fussed with her sleeves. "We had to give you a sleeping draught to calm you down."

"It's still dark, I can't have been asleep that long."

"It's ten o'clock. At night. You've been asleep nearly twenty-four hours." Clemmie gasped, thoughts of Jeannie temporarily chased away by thoughts of Mabel and Miss Adair, who would have been expecting her hours ago. Nurse Henderson patted her arm. "It's natural after a shock like that. You needed the sleep. I've been sitting here with you most of the day."

"No, you don't understand." Clemmie threw off the blanket and gingerly stood up, the cold stone floor jolting her awake. "I have to go. I was only supposed to be here... They'll be worried."

Nurse Henderson gave a tight smile. "Your...friend... Miss Adair?" Clemmie nodded. "Yes. The lady has made her presence felt." She looked at Clemmie, her eyes full of curiosity. "Her footman arrived with a letter at about three this afternoon. The letter said that you were to be removed to her house, immediately, and that you were to have no further treatment. We sent him away. And then the lady came herself." She pressed Clemmie back onto the bed. "She wouldn't listen to me, of course." Her words were as sharp as a poke of acid drops. "Mrs Condra set her straight. Told her that we would give you no more treatment but that you were in a hysterical state after finding your friend dead and that she couldn't possibly take you away."

"What did she say?"

"She seemed quite upset about it. She said she was going to speak to the Board of Governors, Dr Patterson, the Chief Constable, and goodness only knew who else." Nurse Henderson sniffed. "Matron told her that she could speak to the King of Siam for all she cared, but that you were going nowhere for the time being." She touched Clemmie's shoulder. "Not after your reaction to your friend's death. We know Miss Adair meant well, but we couldn't let you go like that. We have a duty and I think she understood that in the end."

Clemmie started pulling on her clothes. "I have to go."

"Now? Don't be ridiculous, child. You can't go wandering around Glasgow at this hour. Besides, you're still faint from the draught."

"I'm going." Her legs felt as though they weren't part of her body, but she was determined to leave. Nurse Henderson kept up the persuasion all the way to the door of the Lock, only reluctantly fetching Matron when Clemmie shook the handle as if she would never stop.

Mrs Condra twirled the set of keys from finger to finger as she surveyed Clementina. "And why are you wanting to leave us, Clementina Watt? Tell me that."

"I just...have to go, Matron. I came here to see Jeannie and now she's dead. I have nothing to stay for."

"Mmmmm-hmmm." Mrs Condra looked up at her. "And Nurse Henderson here tells me you have a bairn. Is that right?" Clemmie nodded. "And you don't have the syphilis." It wasn't a question, but Clemmie lowered her eyes and shook her head. Mrs Condra hummed tunelessly under her breath for a moment. "There are not many who willingly enter this place. And, correct me if I'm wrong, Nurse Henderson, but I don't think we've had any *healthy* residents before. Not any who decided to stay after the examination, anyway." Again, it didn't appear that any response was expected, and Nurse Henderson didn't give her one. "Well, you must have been very close to your young friend, Jeannie Jack. She was lucky."

"No' very lucky, Matron." A hot, red anger rose from Clemmie's belly. "Mistreated and misused by those men. For their pleasure and because of this evil superstition that an innocent like her could be their cure from the pox. Broken, out of her wits and left to die. Not lucky, Matron. Not lucky at all."

Mrs Condra tutted, the wrinkles around her kindly eyes deepening. "Ah, is that how it was? The poor wee thing; I thought as much, given her age. But, despite all that, she *was* lucky. To have such a friend; she *was* lucky."

Clemmie's anger disappeared, falling back into a burning, throbbing ache somewhere deep inside her, and leaving her with only sadness. "I failed her. I left her in the Home and I didn't come back for her soon enough."

"You *did* come back, though, Clementina Watt. You did come back." She took off her sturdy Melton cape and reached up to lay it over Clemmie's shoulders. "It's cold outside and you'll be needing this. It's dark, too, and dangerous in these parts. You know that, though. Are you sure you won't wait until morning?"

"No. I have to go, now."

"Where are you going?"

"Blythswood Square."

Mrs Condra smiled, briefly. "Blythswood Square, is it? They surely won't be expecting visitors at this time of night. Wait until morning."

"They'll be expecting me. She knows I'll come."

"This Miss Adair of yours?"

Her Miss Adair. Clemmie's eyes prickled with pain, sadness and relief. "Aye."

"Then Nurse Henderson will accompany you. And that cheeky skinamalink of a footman can bring her back." She smiled at Nurse Henderson who nodded and moved to get her cape and hat.

Clemmie stopped her. "No. I'll be fine. It's not far and I know these streets. I'll go on my own."

Mrs Condra looked dubious but unlocked the door for her, drawing back the bolts and sliding the largest of the keys on the ring into the lock. "Then take good care, Clementina Watt. Watch out for yourself." She put a hand on Clemmie's shoulder as if in a final attempt to keep her there and then patted her gently. "I tell all the girls who leave here to lead a good life and be kind to others. I don't think I need to tell *you* that. So, instead, be kind to yourself."

Clemmie nodded. "I'll send your cloak back with the cheeky skinamalink of a footman tomorrow."

The door closed, the key turned and the bolts slid back into place. Clemmie drew the warm cloak around herself and turned up Rottenrow. Mrs Condra was right: she needed to watch out. She could go along George Street. It would be wider and lighter, and there would be lots of people around. However, Rottenrow was quicker, more familiar. All the way up the top to Cathedral Street and then along Bath Street. There would be light there, too, and grand people coming back from dinner and the theatre.

Keeping close to the walls she made her way up Rottenrow, crossing the road from time to time to avoid the worst of the taverns and brothels. Pockets of light illuminated her way like a string of glow-worms and she made her way from one to the other, resting in the safety of each one before scurrying to the next.

Rottenrow was a different place at night, devoid of merchants and small boys and red-faced women in closes talking to their neighbours. Head bowed, she went as fast as she could, trying to keep her footing in the gloom. She criss-crossed the street to avoid not only the taverns but also the shadowy loners with their faces hidden by mufflers. She skirted raucous men and women with their arms around one another. Two men lounging in the doorway of a brothel whistled to her and called something out, but she kept her pace brisk.

Clemmie paused just past Hopetoun Street. She could see the lights of the Church Mission Hall up ahead and outside it a small group of men were standing around a carriage, one of them holding on to the bridle of a horse which was whinnying and bucking. She ducked into Catherine Lane. It might be unwise to pass the men; besides, the lane was short and would take her out on to Cathedral Street.

The darkness closed about her and she slowed, the ground uneven beneath her feet. There were no lamps up ahead and a slight bend in the lane cut off any possible sighting of the street at the other end. Picking up her skirts she carefully felt her way, keeping to the middle of the lane to avoid the silent closes she passed. She halted, one foot poised in mid-air. Was that clinking sound coming from in front of her or behind her? She held her breath. Nothing. She put her foot down on the ground and listened again.

Nothing. She let out her breath in a nervous laugh.

Clink.

There it was again. She hadn't imagined it. Behind her, definitely behind her.

She took two short steps forward and then another.

Clink.

She ran.

Rounding the bend, she could see the lights on Cathedral Street ahead of her. A figure was shuffling slowly past the end of the lane and she opened her mouth to call out.

A hand clamped over her mouth. "Miss Watt, as I live and breathe," said the jingling devil. "It's been a long time. Far too long."

Hearing his voice in her ear like that made her remember all the times she had heard it before. She started to struggle, flailing at him, trying to cry out. The jingling devil grabbed her to him even more tightly. "Calm down, you little bitch. Your interfering friends in high places can't help you now, can they?" He laughed, humourlessly. "You have your Lady Bountiful to thank for tipping me off as to your whereabouts. And Lady Luck for just opening the door and delivering you to me as I waited outside thinking up my excuse to go in and fetch you."

His breath was like a snake's tongue on her neck. She tried to move her head away from him, peering up the lane, willing some passer-by to turn into the lane. Why should they, though? There was nothing here for them.

"But you only have yourself to thank for this." He gripped her tighter. "You couldn't just fade away or die like the other little whores, could you?" The hand over her mouth loosened as he ran it almost gently over her cheek and across her brow. "Like your little friend did. Was that her I saw earlier being carted away by the carrion hunter? She wouldn't tell me where you were, you know. I told her you'd deserted her."

No. Jeannie would never have believed that. And, in the end, she knew it. Clemmie squirmed, trying to free herself from his grip and the hand which had been stroking her hair clamped itself over her mouth once more. "Do you know how much trouble you've caused me? Hmmmmm?"

The jingling devil took her chin in his hand. "You're going to take a look at me."

Clemmie shook her head, making moaning noises against his hand, trying to dislodge it from her chin. She didn't want to see him. He had never let her see him. If she saw him, that would be the end, she just knew it.

His hand forced her chin around to face him. Anyone seeing them now would mistake them for lovers, locked in passionate embrace. "Open your eyes, girl." She mewled with fear. "Look at me, bitch."

He squeezed her chin, hard and she opened her eyes. And then she knew. Knew who he was, the very horror of him, the darkness, the power. And she knew.

THE TURNKEY

Friday 31st January 1919

From the Post Office on one side of George Square, to the North British Hotel on the other, all I could see was a seething mass of people. I jumped onto the steps of the Great Western Railway Company and from that vantage point I could see the tops of cloth-capped heads all turned towards the Municipal Buildings. A red flag flew in one corner of the square and men had climbed onto the plinths of all the statues, clapping each other on the shoulders and grinning good-naturedly. I pulled a half-eaten lemon bun out of my pocket and bit into it. I'd been sitting in Miss Rombach's Tea Rooms reflecting on my unpleasant interview with Superintendent Orr when a crowd of men had barrelled past the window shouting and gesticulating. Without thinking, I'd shoved the bun into my coat pocket, thrown some coppers down on the table for the harried waitress and dashed outside to follow the men.

I turned my head as a cry went up from the crowd. Police flooded into the Square from Cochrane Street at the far end, batons aloft, and a great rush of people came my way. I tried to duck behind a pillar but was swept off the steps and into the crowd. The lemon bun was soon lost and, as I was buffeted this way and that, it wasn't long before my hat flew off too. I watched it bowling its merry way over the heads of the crowd. Then it disappeared out of sight, no doubt to be immediately trampled to a pancake.

Feeling up into my hair, I pulled out a hatpin that hadn't gone the way of my hat. I jabbed it into the arm of the man in front of me. As he pulled the arm out of the way, I insinuated myself

161

into the tiny gap freed up. I continued this hatpin and shimmy manoeuvre. In this way, I managed to force my way through the jostling crowds almost to the tram stop at the Graham Statue. I stopped to catch my breath. Suddenly, there was an almighty crash followed by even more shouting and screaming.

A hand grabbed my arm and I found myself hoisted off the ground and onto the plinth of the statue. I was about to protest at the effrontery, when I realised that I now had a superb place from which to survey the assembled mass, so I smiled my thanks to the man who had plucked me out of the crowd. At the bottom of North Frederick Street, a lorry had been overturned and the awning had come off. Boxes of bottles now formed a barrier across the street. Some of the crowd were throwing the bottles at the police, who were still charging around hitting out with their batons. Stones and daffodil bulbs from the parterres surrounding George Square were also thrown by the rioters. I knew they were daffodil bulbs because Floss and I had watched them being planted a few months before. And because one of them hit me on the nose before I managed to duck out of its way.

A green tramcar, heading east, forced its way into the Square, gong clanging, trying to clear the crowds in front of it. I could hear the shrieking of the warehouse girls on board. Men in front of the car jumped onto the splashboard to get out of the way, climbing up and over, and soon there were heaps of them hanging off the car like baubles on a Christmas tree. A man jumped from the car, brandishing the reversing handle, followed by the tramcar driver, a woman who seemed determined to get this vital piece of equipment back.

More shouts drew my attention back to the City Chambers. A man ran down the steps of the building, his arms held aloft, seemingly trying to get the crowd to calm down. It was like King Canute trying to hold back the waves. He bent down, disappearing from view, before reappearing holding onto a dishevelled-looking woman. I gingerly made my way around the plinth to get to a spot where I was close enough to see that the woman had a boot print on the side of her face. He thrust her behind him onto the relative safety of the steps and remonstrated with the policemen surrounding him. They went at him with their batons and the crowd reacted by surging forward angrily and engulfing the group. Another police baton charge had people flying out of George Square into the streets leading off it.

I began to hear people talk of heading to Glasgow Green – peacefully, seemed to be the idea – to be addressed by the leaders of the strike. I jumped down from the plinth and threaded my way in the opposite direction, towards Blythswood Square and home. The streets away from George Square were much quieter. I turned off St Vincent Street and headed up the hill, shoulders hunched against the chill, very sorry that I'd lost my hat. As I passed one of the wee lanes, something caught my eye. A man was standing tucked into a doorway and I gasped. He was only wearing his combination drawers. I put a hand to my mouth and hurried on, but a hoarse "Miss" drew me cautiously back to the mouth of the lane.

I averted my eyes. "What is it?"

"Can you help me? I…I…some ruffians set about me and stole my uniform."

"Your uniform?"

"Yes, Miss, I'm a police sergeant. Look," he said, picking something up from the ground. "They left me my helmet."

"That doesn't prove anything. Show me your warrant card."

"I can't. It was in my pocket. Look, I'm not asking you to come anywhere near me, but I would be most obliged if you would nip into the temperance place – The Vigilance Association at number 45 – and let them know that Constable Ferguson is in a wee bit of a bind. They know me in there. Please, Miss."

I relaxed a little and approached further. He was a skinny, pathetic looking specimen and I was trained in ju-jitsu, thanks to Floss and her Suffragette pals. I didn't think I'd have any trouble with him. The poor man was shivering like a wet kitten. "Of course. I'll be as quick as I can."

"Thank you, Miss. Please ask them to bring a coat, would you. And some shoes."

I looked down at his feet. A grubby big toe was poking out of his left sock and I felt rather sorry for him. I took off my coat. "Here, put this around you until I get back. It will keep you warm and preserve your dignity."

He reached out a hand for the coat. "Oh, thanks awfy, Miss."

"Well, we police have to stick together, don't we?"

"Sorry, Miss?"

"Us police." I beamed at him. "I just got a job as a policewoman."

"You, Miss, a policewoman?" He rocked back on his stockinged feet and cackled.

"Well, Constable Ferguson, it seems that you have your laughter to keep you warm, so you won't be needing this." I snatched my coat back out of his hands and stalked off up the road.

I was still seething when I reached the house. Ellen let me in, concern on her face. "Are you alright, Miss? Only the way you banged on that door was fit to wake the dead." She looked at my head. "Oh, my heavens, where's your hat? Here, let me fix those pins a wee bit."

She reached up to tidy my hair which, no doubt, had gone indecorously haywire, but I batted her hands away gently. "Don't worry, Ellen, I'll do it later. Where's Floss?"

Ellen folded her arms. "Your mother's in the morning room, Miss. She'll be glad to see you, been fretting all morning about this…lark of yours." She sniffed, just to underline her displeasure at the thought that the daughter – adopted or not – of the fine Miss Florence Frances Adair should wish to join the police force. That she should wish to do any job at all, in fact.

I tried to suppress a grin, as she turned on the heel of her pristinely polished shoe and marched to the morning room doors. She opened them with a flourish, as if announcing the Queen of Sheba. "Here's Miss Mabel, Miss Adair."

Floss looked up from the papers she was studying. "Thank you, Ellen. I have no idea how I would have recognised this bedraggled specimen without you telling me who she was." She rose from her desk and moved to the couch, patting the seat beside her. "Come and sit down and tell me all your adventures, my dear."

"Only if it will stop you fretting, Flossie."

"Fretting?" She glanced over at Ellen and her brow cleared. "Ah, of course."

Ellen shrugged and turned to leave. "I'll bring tea," she announced as she pulled the doors closed behind her. We didn't deserve it, but she would bring it anyway. Poor, long-suffering Ellen, who'd been with my adoptive mother even longer than I had.

Before throwing myself into an armchair with a sigh, I kissed Floss and her best friend Josephine, who sat by the fire reading the newspaper and smoking a cigarette. Flo and Jo — spinsters, firm friends and rabble-rousers since the early days of the Suffrage movement.

I gave them a blow-by-blow account of my whole day, starting with my interview with Superintendent Orr. "He barely even glanced at my references from the munitions factories. As he so eloquently put it: 'Swanning around in an ugly uniform and catching wee lassies sneaking hairpins into a factory isnae the same as arresting dangerous criminals, hen.' According to him, 'lady policemen' aren't wanted in the force." Floss snorted. "Oh, you haven't heard the best part. I reminded him that Glasgow already had one policewoman and that the Chief Constable seems to think highly of her abilities. He just called Miss Miller a glorified secretary and said he'd forgotten that Mr Stevenson gets invited to your... soirees. That was the very word he used."

Jo laughed. "And no doubt these soirees that Flo has are the reason he's forced to employ you?"

I plumped up my cushion. "Exactly. He made it perfectly clear that it was only thanks to my connections that I was being reluctantly – I lost count of the number of times he said the word – admitted into the police service at all."

Jo stood and kissed the top of my head before getting us all a whisky. "But you have been admitted, and that's the main thing."

"I'm beginning to wonder why I want to. Twenty-one shillings is all I'm getting. That's less than I got on factory patrol." Floss laughed and waved a hand at the splendour of the room around her. "I know. I know it's not the point for me, but it's the principle. I don't even get a boot allowance. And you know why?" I glared at them both and they shook their heads, amused. "Well, apparently I'll not *need* boots. According to *him*, I'll not be stirring from my desk, so I can have bare feet for all he cares. No boot allowance, no uniform, no warrant card, no patrols and no fraternising with the men. That's what he said." I gulped down my whisky and Jo took my glass to refill it for me.

Floss put the papers she had been working on back into their envelope. "And is that why you're so late? Fraternising with the men?"

I told her about the strikers in George Square, although I may have slightly over-egged my own part in the riots.

"Well, dear girl, it seems as though Ellen was right: I *should* have been fretting about you." She sighed. "It all sounds *very* exciting, and I wish I'd been there to witness it."

I snorted. "You? Witness it? Nothing less than rushing into the fray and picking up a bottle to throw would have done you." Floss had always been a law unto herself. When she'd adopted me, she'd been the same age I was now, stubbornly insisting, despite the qualms of the two uncles who thought they were in charge of her. It had been a different time back then. Women had more freedom now, thanks to the Suffrage movement and the war, but it still wasn't easy. Floss had never let that stop her, however.

"Anyway, I have no doubt that this Superintendent Orr will soon come to see your worth."

I wasn't quite so sure. "I'm going to be stuck in the office, taking statements. I didn't join the police to be a secretary. I want to go out on patrol, speak to people, solve crimes…"

Floss put her hand on my knee. "It was a long time ago, my dear. You do know that you may never find out what happened to her, don't you?"

I sighed. "I know. But I have to try, at least."

She leaned down to the side of the couch and lifted the familiar coromandel box, inlaid with delicate mother of pearl, onto her knee. Jo sat quietly, watching us with a faint smile. It was a ritual we'd repeated ever since I could remember. I knew by heart what was inside it, of course, as well as the order we would pore over everything, and what Floss would say about each item. Until I was about twelve, the box had come out once a month or so, but then the gaps had become longer and longer, not because I cared any less as time went on, but because as I got older and understood more, and Floss told me more and more of the bad parts of my mother's story, I carried the contents of the glossy box in my head. It was almost a year since we had opened it.

I leaned across and unhooked the clasp – another ritual – lifting the lid to release the delicate, powdery scent of violets and reveal the purple padded satin inside. The contents were few but precious: a soft blue wool shawl inexpertly made with uneven edges and more holes than wool; two locks of hair wrapped in a frayed piece of muslin – one of them shiny gold, the other the darker brown of a freshly peeled conker, just like my own; a little doll made from a clothes peg and dressed in a rough, worn material; and the bar of violet soap that was the source of the box's scent. At the bottom, the two most precious things of all – two letters, both signed '*Mother*' but not by the same hand.

The first of these was a small, rough square, torn off a bigger piece of paper. It had been folded and refolded so many times that the creases were worn through in places and the edges were dirty. It had neat, tiny holes in it, and we surmised that the note had once been sewn into a garment. The letter was short: *You are Clementina Watt from now on. Never use your real name and remember that we all love you, Mary Grace, Henrietta and I. All my love, my dearest Clemmie. Mother.*

In the corner, in a different handwriting was a name – Sarah Loag – and an address in Tontine Lane, the number rubbed away. When I was small, Floss had hired an investigator to make enquiries, but all he'd got for his trouble was a black eye. No-one knew a Sarah Loag – or was willing to admit to it – and the place was a warren of closes and alleyways, most of them without numbers. I didn't tell Floss, but I'd also gone there early one morning in my factory patrol uniform during the War. There were few people about, but, even with the dawning of a summer day, the alleyways were dark and foul-smelling and the sound of a throat clearing in a nearby doorway had sent me scurrying out into the relative freshness of Argyle Street.

The second letter was a different matter. Written on Floss' thick, creamy paper, with her crest at the top, my mother formed her letters like the child she had been: *Little Mabel Jean, if I don't come back, be good for Miss Adair and make sure she tells you all about Jeannie and me. If something happens to me, Miss Adair should christen you Mabel Jean Lillias. I wasn't allowed to say my maw's name after I left her in that place, but if I've gone, it won't matter. Lillias, that was her. All my love, my dearest Mabel, just as my own maw wrote to me.*

Floss had told me everything she knew about my mother, and

about her friend Jeannie, but it wasn't a lot. It wasn't enough. I didn't even know my mother's real surname, or the name of the asylum where she had lived with my grandmother, Lillias, until she was in her early teens. I wanted to know so much more about my mother and these two women I had been named for. Floss had tried to find Lillias when I was a baby, but all she knew about her was what my mother had told her: that she was young, just a girl, really and had been betrayed by her husband who had committed her to an asylum. Floss had visited every asylum in and around Glasgow. However, with only the names Lillias, Mary Grace and Henrietta, there had been frustratingly little she could do.

I watched Floss now as she ran her fingers over the letters. "She left it tucked under her pillow. I didn't find it until..."

"I know," I smiled at Floss. She always told me this, and I always responded in the same way.

"If I'd known she thought she was in danger..."

"I know," I said and hugged her. "I know."

I dressed very carefully on the morning of my first day: a tailored jacket and skirt in navy and a pale blue blouse with neat pintucks; sensible black buttoned boots and a black felt hat with a sedate blue ribbon. I made sure to pin it on especially firmly; I didn't want to lose another hat. Someone – probably Ellen – had crept into my room before I was awake and lit the fire, for which I was grateful; the morning was cold and dreich. She had also left me the newspaper and I skimmed through it as I gulped down a slice of toast. The news was still full of the riots on Friday – Manny Shinwell, the final ringleader, had been arrested at his home in Govan and several rioters were due to appear in court later that day.

I left the house at eight, determined to be at Central Station well before nine, so as not to set off on a bad foot. I told the desk sergeant who I was; he seemed singularly unimpressed but nodded his head towards a large room where a sizeable crowd was gathered. Policemen, both in uniform and plain clothes, were taking their orders from Superintendent Orr and another, older Superintendent. Orr glowered at me as I slipped in at the back of the room and most of the room's occupants turned to look at me. I was relieved not to see Constable Ferguson amongst them. I was regretting my actions of the previous day; for a start, he had looked so pathetic standing there. Also, if he told everyone what I had done…well, it was already clear that I wasn't welcome here, and that would just put the cherry on top. The stares made me nervous, but I stuck out my chin and put my hands in my pockets, trying to look nonchalant.

I was relieved when heads swung back to Orr as he cleared his throat. "One more thing. I have a letter from the Chief Constable." He held it out in front of him as though he'd just plucked it from a stinking gutter. "Miss Mabel Adair has been appointed as female officer…" he paused and sniffed before continuing pointedly, "…for the purpose of obtaining statements of evidence in cases of criminal assault on women and girls and generally to assist in any way in which her service can be made available." The latter part of this sentence was skipped over as if an irrelevance, but I stored it away for future reference.

"Miss Adair will be attached to the Detective Department, Central Division. Superintendents and Detective Officers requiring her assistance may communicate with her by telephone or in person." He folded the letter and dropped it onto the table in front of him. "Now, get about your duties."

With a scraping of chairs and a few more curious and appraising glances in my direction, the men left the room. Orr picked up the letter once more and thoughtfully started to pick his teeth with the folded corner. "I'll show you your office, Miss Adair, but first, tea."

"Oh, thank you, Sir," I said, gratefully.

"The kitchen's at the far end of the hall. Black, strong, two sugars. My office is across the hall."

My own 'office' still had a sign saying 'Store Cupboard' on the door, but someone – I wasn't sure who, although I guessed that it was unlikely to have been Superintendent Orr – had made an effort to make it bearable, with a desk, chair, coat stand and a rather sorry-looking potted plant. A couple of mops and brooms were tucked into one corner behind a pile of cardboard boxes. Orr looked around the room. "As you can see, this has quite put us out. We can't have you sharing an office with any of the men, and we've had to go to some effort to accommodate you."

Some effort, but not much, apparently. "So, what am I to do today? Are there any cases requiring my attention?"

A brief smile curled his lip. "Oh, I'm sure you'll be positively flooded with *cases* soon enough. For now, though, you can read this." He flung down a large tome on the desk, as well as some forms. "Regulations, conditions of enrolment, your duty roster. You'll work six days out of seven. At the moment, I've given you Sundays off; you'll want to be at church, I'm sure."

"Thank you, Sir." I looked down at the forms and noted the handwritten amendments scribbled on them; references to uniform and boot allowance had been struck through, 'he' and 'his' had been changed to 'she' and 'her'.

"You'll need to have a medical examination, of course. This is usually done beforehand. As are these." He threw down two sheets of paper. On one of them were four arithmetic problems: addition, subtraction, multiplication and division. On the other, the sentence: *The British girl's cream and roses complexion, it is said, is becoming a myth'*. I looked at him, puzzled.

"To test your skills at composition and spelling and to make sure you can write legibly. I've made it easier for you by giving you a topic in which I'm sure you can excel."

I looked down at the arithmetic sheet and picked up the pencil he'd also thrown onto my desk, so that he couldn't see the flush of annoyance that I felt blooming on my face.

He placed a few more forms on my desk. His voice was smug. "I'll leave you to get on with that for the next hour or so. The arithmetic is rather complicated." He turned on his heel and marched to the door.

"Sir," I said, in my pleasantest voice.

He turned. "Yes?"

I waved a piece of paper at him. "I've finished the arithmetic questions if you want to take them away and mark them."

On Tuesday, the highlight of my day was a visit from the cleaning woman, Mrs Wilson, who came to retrieve her mops and brooms. I apologised for having usurped her cupboard. "It's alright, dearie. I've got a bigger room now: one of the cells in the basement." With that, she clanked and muttered her way out of the room.

On Wednesday, I made up my mind to go and find someone who could show me where the old case files were. I wasn't sure if this would be allowed, but I could use the excuse that I was familiarising myself with some of the cases the station handled that I might be required to get involved in. Really, of course, I would be looking for information about my mother. I was debating my strategy – I hadn't yet identified a friendly face – when there was a tentative knock at the door. Perhaps this would be some actual work to do. Instead, a sheepish-looking Constable Ferguson poked his head around the door. "Can I have a word, Miss?"

"Of course, do come in Constable." I waved him to the seat at the other side of the desk and he perched uncomfortably on the edge of it. In his uniform he didn't look quite as scrawny and, despite his sheepishness, he had an air of quiet authority about him. "I'm… errrrr… glad to see that you've got your uniform back. As a matter of fact, I wanted to see you. I'd like to apologise for my conduct; I shouldn't have been so rude. It was too cold a day to have left you in that…predicament."

"Nae bother, Miss. It's me as should apologise. I was a wee bit rude to you, too. I shouldnae have laughed. It's just, well, I've a daughter about your age and I cannae imagine her being in the police; it just disnae seem right." He was looking down at the helmet he was turning round and round in his hands.

"Well, the world's changed these last few years, Constable Ferguson. We all have to get used to new things, I suppose."

He sighed and his eyes darkened. "Aye, that we do, Miss. I lost my son. Passchendaele. Anyway, Miss. It was my daughter who tellt me off and said I should apologise, and she was right. An' thanks for letting the Temperance Society know. You would have been well within your rights to forget you ever saw me."

"I would have found that a very difficult thing to do, Constable."

He blushed. "Aye, I was a right sight for sore eyes, eh, Miss?" He hesitated. "I've not…told anyone about it, Miss Adair." He shrugged. "I'd never live it down with this lot."

"Don't worry, your secret's safe with me."

The relief was apparent on his face. "Thank you, Miss. I really appreciate that." He stood up. "And if there's ever anything I can do for you, just you let me know."

I stood up too. "Actually, Constable Ferguson, I believe there *is* something you can do."

I spent the rest of the week being mostly ignored and, when I wasn't, wishing I had been. I was glad when Saturday afternoon came and I was free to enjoy the rest of the weekend. Floss had planned a dinner party for the Saturday evening and had purposefully placed me next to the Chief Constable.

"Ah, Mabel, my dear. And how has your first fortnight been? Are my men keeping you busy?"

I took a sip of champagne, wondering how to answer. I had been expecting this question since the soup and sherry had been served. It was delicate, however. I didn't want to undermine either him or his men, nor did I want to get a reputation as a tattle-tale.

"Everyone has been very kind to me, James." Only a little white lie. Most of them had simply ignored me, and only Superintendent Orr had been positively *un*kind. "I'm sure it will take a little while for them to get used to me and feel comfortable trusting me to take witness statements for them, when they're so used to taking their own."

He lowered his glass and looked at me. "They *are* bringing you cases, though?"

"I haven't had any yet, no."

"I see." Stevenson looked at me, thoughtfully. "Well, we must make sure that the detectives make use of your abilities. Your mother did warn me that this might be the case. I…well, I shall get the issue resolved, my dear. Now then, let us give this magnificent joint of beef the attention it deserves, shall we?"

It was with renewed hope and vigour that I went back to my broom cupboard on the Monday.

My first visitor was Constable Ferguson. "You'd best keep your head down, hen. Superintendent Orr's on the warpath."

"Why, what have I done?" He grinned widely and cleared his throat, taking from behind his back a piece of paper, which he proceeded to read. "To remove any misapprehension as to the meaning of the order of 3rd February, 1919, it should be understood that Miss Adair should be informed of all cases of criminal or indecent assault upon women or girls and should be asked to take their statements."

I groaned.

"Anyway, hen, just thought I'd better warn you." Constable Ferguson gave me a cheery salute and left the office.

I didn't have long to wait before there was a sharp rap on the door. I steeled myself for a glowering Superintendent Orr, but it was a plain-clothes detective I'd seen around the station a few times. I'd noticed him because of his pinned sleeve. As he entered my office now, I saw that his neck on the same side was shiny with scars, pink and puckered.

He bowed his head to me slightly. "Miss Adair, I'm Detective Inspector James Lorrimer. I was wondering if you would be free to take a statement for me?"

I tried to hide my excitement. "Of course. I'd be very happy to."

"Thank you. I was hoping I'd get in before you get too busy." He was older than I'd first thought, and his face was very difficult to read, unsmiling and somehow closed off. I wasn't sure if he was being sarcastic. However, before I could open my mouth to speak, there was another knock at the door which opened to reveal a man of around the same age as Lorrimer, in his fifties, but much more relaxed and approachable. "Ah, sorry Lorrimer, I see you got here first." He smiled at us both, but Lorrimer's face remained set and he said nothing.

The newcomer turned to me. "Miss Adair, my name is Detective Chief Inspector Pritchard; Alexander Pritchard." It seemed to me as though he stressed the 'Chief'. "I'd like you to take a statement from an elderly spinster who was attacked in her own home last week. So badly has the incident affected her that she's only felt able to report it now, poor lady."

"Certainly, Detective Chief Inspector." I pulled over the leather-bound notepad Floss had given me on my first day and made a note on its pristine first page. "I'll be with you as soon as I've spoken to Detective Inspector Lorrimer's witness."

"She'll wait," said Lorrimer abruptly. He nodded to us both

as he left the room.

Pritchard smiled his charming smile once more. "Excellent. I'll bring Miss Keyes in and get someone to make you both a cup of tea."

I was kept busy for the rest of the day. Having taken a statement from a nervous and tearful Miss Keyes, I interviewed Nellie Mellors, Detective Inspector Lorrimer's young music hall artiste who was accused of stealing a fellow performer's purse after the evening performance; a seamstress who had been attacked by another seamstress who suspected her of stealing her clients; and a bruised and battered woman who was scared to go home to her drunken husband. The policeman who brought her in had sneeringly referred to her as 'a shrew who couldn't cook'. I also saw a middle-aged woman who had been arrested for disorderly conduct. This case was not, strictly speaking, within my job description and it was my opinion that the Detective Constable who had arrested her had just wanted to get rid of her, given her language and attitude. However, we parted at the end of the interview on relatively friendly terms as she was taken down to the cells to cool off.

My final interview of the day was a young woman who had been attempting to steal a pair of boots from a shop in Queen Street. She had broken-in during the early hours of the morning and was caught surrounded by a pile of boots which she was trying on. The constable who had arrested her was covered with scratches and bruises where she'd fought to escape his clutches. The only thing he'd managed to get out of her was that she was sorry she'd been arrested before she found a pair that fitted. The constable laughed when I asked him to bring her into my office and told me that I was to interview her in the cells where she couldn't do any more damage.

It was my first trip down to the cells and I went with some trepidation. The turnkey, a cheerful-looking woman with a glowing red face, opened the gate to let me in and pointed down the corridor. "Third door on the left, hen. Watch it, yon lassie can fair spit." The corridor was lined with flickering lights and the walls were white tiles down which rivulets of water ran and pooled on the stone floor at intervals. Heavy wooden doors with black painted iron fittings lined both sides. I stopped outside the one the turnkey had pointed to and she took a huge ring of keys from her belt and unlocked the door, standing back to let me into the cell. "Just bang when you want out." She pushed me inside the cell and slammed the door behind me.

I felt a flutter of fear in my chest, but one glance at the young woman sitting on the uncomfortable-looking bed banished my concerns. She looked as though she would blow away if I breathed heavily on her. Her knees were drawn up to her chest and her skinny arms were wrapped around them. "An' what are you, some sort o' do-gooder come tae make me repent?"

"No. I've come to take your statement."

She laughed. "Aye? That wee nyaff o' a constable too feart is he? What are ye? His sister?"

"No. I'm a policewoman."

She unfurled from her position and rocked with laughter as she continued to stare at me. Her laughter was eventually ended by a fit of coughing that culminated in a ball of phlegm. I looked away, grateful that it hadn't landed on my shoe, given the turnkey's warning.

"Let's start with your name."

Janet turned out to be a young woman of sixteen whose only real crime was to be homeless and shoeless. She'd tied whatever dirty rags she could find onto her feet to protect them and keep them warm. It wasn't her first offence: she'd been arrested twice within the past month, both times for stealing a meat pie from a shop on the Trongate. The same shop each time, it turned out, since she'd taken against the proprietor. She was resigned to the fact that these previous crimes meant that when she was taken the short walk upstairs from the cells to the courtroom, she would be sentenced to a month in Duke Street Prison. At least she would be fed, there, and, I hoped, come out with a pair of boots to her name.

Less than a month into the job and I was beginning to wonder whether I had done the right thing, joining the police. For the most part, I felt that my statement taking was a pointless exercise. The women I spoke to fell into two camps: those who had been arrested – the majority for theft, assault or soliciting – and those who were the victims or witnesses of crime.

In the case of the former, I generally took their statements in the damp, dark cells in the basement. In the case of the latter, I interviewed them in my windowless office, the walls of which seemed to close in more oppressively the more women I heard from: drawn-faced women with blank stares who told of terrible beatings in quiet, toneless voices; elderly widows who were trying to earn a pittance to keep themselves alive and were being taken advantage of by callous employers or grasping landlords; young girls with scared eyes who hinted in whispers at terrible things. All I could do was listen and send them home to violent brutes; send them home to wrap hairpins or card buttons or bead slippers for eighteen hours a day; send them home to poverty, sickness, fears and nightmares.

And every day I faced reluctance, resistance and rancour from the men I worked with. I was still being mostly ignored, the statements I took were snatched from me with a sneer and I had to bite my tongue on several occasions when personal comments were made about me within my hearing. They were waiting for me to swoon at the first sight of blood and were annoyed that they had to modify their language around me. When I heard that one, I really struggled to stay silent; I could easily have held my own with any one of them on that front. The thing that most annoyed them was that I had my own office. Didn't they realise that I wasn't allowed to sit in the same room as them?

"When I went into the Factory Patrol, I was praised by men like them for carrying out a role that set a man free to become a soldier and serve his country. Now I'm being told that I'm taking the bread out of the mouth of that same soldier by stealing his job."

I was telling all this to Floss and Jo over a large bowl of Mrs Dugan's melt-in-the-mouth apricot pithivier. It had been my mother's favourite, too, apparently, and Mrs Dugan always knew when it was most needed.

I dipped my spoon into the smooth and creamy egg custard that accompanied the dessert and took a big mouthful. "And it's not the lower ranks who are the worst, by any means. In fact, I've met more kindness from them than I have from their superiors. One of the Inspectors referred to me as a Copperette yesterday, and then told me not to get hysterical when I finally became fed up biting my tongue and told him I had every right to be there."

Jo's laugh was more of a wheeze and I glanced over at Floss. Jo's health had never fully recovered from being force-fed in Perth Prison and she was subject to bouts of pneumonia that had left her thin and drawn and looking far older than her fifty years. However, Floss didn't seem to be too concerned. "Well, my dear girl," she said now, resting her plump hand on Jo's bony one. "You'll just need to get used to it, I'm afraid. They don't like us in their worlds. It scares them."

"I'm not even allowed to go into the Courtroom. I took a statement from an extremely nervous young woman – a child, really – who was arrested for keeping a house of ill repute. *She* doesn't keep it, of course; there's a man behind it, but he stays out of the way and the three women who live there take it in turns to confess to brothel-keeping when there's a raid. The police know that's the case, but they don't care. They're not interested in getting the real criminals and they treat the women terribly.

I wanted to accompany her to Court, but Superintendent Orr said it wouldn't be seemly for a woman to hear such things. And when I tried to argue my case, he told me it was *me* that wasn't seemly."

I stuck my spoon into the pithivier so hard that a piece of apricot flew out and landed on Josephine's neat suit. She picked it up and popped it into her mouth. "Mabel, dear, welcome to the vinegary spinsters club. There are only two positions available to you: *un*feminine and *too* feminine."

"And what about the mice? What do I do about those?"

"The mice?" Floss swirled the ice in her glass and took a sip of whisky.

"Yes. Today was the third dead mouse left on my desk. Constable Ferguson says that I shouldn't worry, that it's a rite of passage for all new recruits."

"Dead *mice*?"

"Well, he said it's not always dead mice, just some sort of prank or trick that they do to initiate new policemen."

"And what did you do with them?" Jo's wide smile indicated that she wasn't taking this very seriously.

"The first two I threw in the waste-paper basket."

"And today's?"

I fumed at the memory of the latest gift, placed in the middle of my neat desk. "It was wearing a doll's bonnet and apron, so I picked it up by its tail, took it into the general office and dropped it on the floor."

Jo had her head bent and her shoulders were shaking. Floss' grin was wide behind her hand. She reached over and squeezed my knee. "Don't you think you over-reacted, my dear?"

I glowered at her. "The bonnet and apron were embroidered with my initials. Very badly. Very badly indeed."

Now Floss and Jo didn't even bother to try and hide their amusement. "Besides, it's not just me. I try and keep my head down and get on with things, rather than causing a fuss, as I've been accused of. On several occasions I've had cause to speak to the policemen who brought either the women or their cases to me. It doesn't matter if they're the victim or the supposed criminal, they're treated most dreadfully and subject to the most terrible insults, just for being women."

Jo sighed and looked at Floss. Jo's mouth was set into a thin line and Floss' hands were gently stroking the fabric of her dress at her knees, something she always did when she was troubled or thoughtful. "We saw that in prison, didn't we, Floss?"

Floss nodded. "Generally, we were treated much better than most of the ordinary women who were in there. Presumably because none of them had influential relatives who could kick up a fuss. Most of them were poor and just trying to feed their families. Generally, as I say. Apart from the force feeding." We all fell silent. Floss and Jo had talked before about their experiences as suffragettes and I never knew quite what to say. Floss reached over and touched Jo's hand once more.

"Hurry up will ye, Miss Adair." A nervous Constable Ferguson hopped from one foot to the other.

I ignored him and flicked through the file I had taken from the dusty shelves in the records room. It had a name on it I recognised from Floss' stories of my mother: Euphemia McCombe. It was an unusual name and the closest I had come to anything useful so far.

"Miss!" Ferguson's voice was now urgent. "Someone's coming. I'm aff." He slipped out of the door and disappeared. So much for helping me with a cover story. I had watched the file room sergeant, McGillivray, leave the station a quarter of an hour ago and the sprightliness in his step told me he was headed to the pub for an early dinner, so it was unlikely to be him coming back.

I cast about for something I could use to hide the file in my hand and my eyes lit on a neat pile of new files at the end of the counter. I picked up a handful and slipped Euphemia McCombe's file in the middle of them. Not a moment too soon.

"Ah, Miss Adair. Are you...alright?"

"Yes, thank you, Detective Inspector Lorrimer." I tapped the files I was holding. "I came down to see if Sergeant McGillivray had some spare files I could use. My paperwork is starting to look a little messy and I wouldn't want to get in trouble from Superintendent Orr." I realised I was starting to babble and closed my mouth firmly.

Lorrimer nodded, all seriousness. I had never seen him smile, I realised. I tried to edge round him and make my escape. "Did nobody tell you that all stationery requisitions go through the Desk Sergeant?" He stood his ground.

"No," I lied. "They didn't. Ah well, I shall be better informed next time, won't I?" I put my hand on the heavy door and forced it open another couple of inches to try and get through. "Well, please don't let me keep you." The door screeched along the ground, until I could neither push it further open nor pull it shut.

Lorrimer reached out with his good arm and, seemingly effortlessly, pushed the door open another few inches, finally giving me enough room to get through. However, his outstretched hand remained on the door and blocked my way. "Actually, it was you I was looking for."

After I had interviewed Lorrimer's young music hall artiste, Nellie Mellors, the previous week, I had told Lorrimer that she had admitted to stealing her friend's purse, but that I thought she was holding something back. She seemed jumpy and scared and kept repeating that she'd stolen the purse because she had to get away. She'd clammed up entirely when I asked her from what and had steadfastly refused to open her mouth again.

Lorrimer had let her off with a warning, on the proviso that she pay her friend back the money she had taken. Now, however, it seemed that she was in more trouble.

"She and a friend – not the same one she stole the purse from – were attacked two nights ago in one of the closes off the New Wynd, not far from here."

"Is Nellie alright?"

Lorrimer nodded. "She's fine, managed to squirm out of the man's grip and run off. A few bruises, a black eye, some cuts and scrapes."

"And her friend?"

"Betty McKay. Unfortunately, she wasn't so lucky. Died in the Royal a couple of hours ago. I want to question Nellie, but she's not at home – her landlady says she moved out, all of a palaver, as Mrs Anstruther put it, the same night she was attacked."

"And the landlady has no idea where Nellie moved to?"

Lorrimer shook his head. "No, but she called round at her old place earlier, to pick up one or two things she'd left behind and to pay Mrs Anstruther her outstanding rent. Told her she was back at work."

I shifted the files in my arms. Lorrimer held out his hand to take them from me and I almost accepted. Just in time I remembered my plunder and pulled them away. "So how can I help?"

He hesitated. "Well, this is quite irregular, but I was thinking about what you were saying before. I don't think we'd get anything out of her by bringing her here. I got the impression she's not fond of the authorities. She's been arrested at least twice for prostitution, although she swears blind she wasn't soliciting." I opened my mouth to speak, but he continued hurriedly. "I thought I'd go and speak to her at her place of work. And...well, I'd like you to come with me. For some reason, she seemed to at least find you tolerable when you spoke to her last time."

"Thank you." My tone was dry, but he didn't seem to notice. "Where's she working?"

He hesitated again. "The Coliseum. Eglinton Street. There's a variety show on this week; Gertie Gitana, the Idol of the People. I thought we might see if we can catch Nellie between performances. There's one just before seven and the second's at nine." He looked down at his feet. "Superintendent Orr doesn't know about this, and I'd rather keep it that way, if you don't mind." I must have looked shocked because he hurried on. "We've all had strict instructions that we're to consult with you only if necessary and only on the premises."

"Really?"

"Yes. If you want to know his exact words, they were: 'That wee madam's to stay in her cupboard.' He said some other things, too, but I'll not trouble you with those." His face was still hard and closed off, although his mouth twitched as if he was trying to restrain a smile.

"Oh, I'll bet he did. Well, I'll not stay in my cupboard like a broom."

"So, you'll assist me in taking Nellie's statement this evening?" I nodded firmly. "Thank you. If you'll tell me where you live, I'll come and pick you up just before eight. We can speak to Nellie before the second performance."

"Oh, no, Detective Inspector Lorrimer." I pulled the files close to my chest.

He looked puzzled. "No?"

I looked at my watch. I was famished and Floss always said I made my worst decisions on an empty stomach. "It's nearly five and time for me to escape from my cupboard. We should just have time for a spot of dinner before the first performance. You at least owe me that, if you want me to risk the likely wrath of Superintendent Orr." He opened his mouth as if to protest. "Besides, I've never been to a variety show."

*

I told Lorrimer I would collect my coat and meet him at the corner of Buchanan Street outside Fraser & Sons in about an hour. Far enough away that it was likely that nobody would see us together, but also busy enough that it wouldn't seem strange if they did. When I got back to my office, I couldn't resist a look at the file I'd stolen from the records room. It was several years old, pre-War, and this Euphemia McCombe was a widow who'd been arrested for entrapping young girls and luring them into a life of prostitution. There was very little information, and nothing seemed to have happened in the case, at least according to the file. My mother had told Floss that the Mrs McCombe who ruled the roost at the Home, had – at the very least – been neglectful of the girls in her care. At worst, my mother had hinted, Mrs McCombe had allowed danger into the Home at night. She'd been reluctant to say more, and Floss had always blamed herself that she didn't make her tell the whole story. Floss tried to get the Home, and Mrs McCombe, investigated after my mother was murdered, but the only result was that she'd been politely requested never to visit again.

It was definitely worth paying Euphemia McCombe a visit. There was an address for her in the file. I checked the city map that had been one of Floss' presents to me on joining the police force.

"Moncur Street...not far away."

I closed the file and left it in the middle of my desk and headed out of the station. At the Trongate clock, I hesitated. Turn left and it was a ten-minute walk to Frasers. The clock told me I had plenty of time and if I went to Frasers now, I would be waiting in the cold for ages, so I turned right and continued along Gallowgate until I reached the washhouse at Bain Street. At the next corner, I stood back for a moment to watch the workers streaming out through the archway at the front of the clay pipe factory. The building, with its small, neat red and white bricks continued around the corner into Moncur Street and I followed the wall round.

The close I was looking for was past a women's model lodging house. Mrs McCombe would be in her sixties now if she was still alive and she might not be at the address any longer. None of the doors seemed to have any names or numbers. I put my ear to the first one on the ground floor. Nothing. I hesitated and then knocked softly. Nobody answered and, after trying the other doors with the same result, I went upstairs. There were no lamps in the stairwell and the only light came in from a dusty window. On the next landing the tired-looking woman who opened the door to my knock promptly shut it again as soon as she saw me. I could hear children crying in the background and, since she clearly wasn't the woman I was looking for, I carried on upwards. The light coming in from outside seemed even dimmer here on the top floor. I knocked on the door to the left of the stairs. I was about to turn away and try one of the others when I heard shuffling behind the door. It opened a few inches and a woman peered out. She looked to be in her sixties or seventies and her sparse grey hair was pulled back and pinned on top of her head. She was wearing a black wool coat that had seen better days. Her eyes narrowed and a look that I couldn't work out flashed across her face. She glared at me, pulling the door even closer so that only her head was visible in the flickering light from the hallway behind her. "What do you want? I don't need any do-gooder trying to sell me Jesus." She wheezed out a short, humourless laugh. "An' if it's money you're wantin', I've no' got any, neither I have."

She moved to close the door, but I put out my hand. "Mrs McCombe? Euphemia McCombe?" She pushed the door against my hand again, but I stopped her. "You were the Matron at the Home for wayward girls in Rottenrow?"

She scowled at me. "An' what if I was?"

"I'm looking for information about my mother. She was there."

She blinked and then laughed her nasty laugh once again. "And what makes you think I can remember one slattern over another after all these years?"

I could feel my face and chest reddening with anger. "My mother was murdered. Her friend lost her life after being mistreated whilst in your care. As did other girls, I understand."

Now it was her turn to be angry. She flung the door open and reached out and grabbed my arm. Despite her advanced years, she was strong, and her fingers dug into my flesh, even through my coat sleeve. "I did nothing to any of those girls." Her face was close to mine and I could see the thin, purple veins criss-crossing her nose and spreading out across her cheeks.

I tried to pull my arm away. "I'm a police officer. You'd better let go of me now."

She did let go of me but only to laugh. "A polis officer? And you think that will help you? Far from it, you stupid wee bitch." She leaned forward and her sour breath made my eyes water. "Your mother's dead and nobody's interested. You don't go knocking on the gates of hell unless you want to raise the devil. No, you get back to that fancy house you came from and take tea with your fancy lady friends, instead of interfering where you don't belong, or that devil will see you can't close the gates again." I staggered backwards as she gave me a push and went back inside, slamming the door behind her.

What a mess I'd made of that. I ran back down the stairs, unsettled by the encounter and didn't pause for breath until I reached the bright lights of Trongate once more. It took a moment standing in the middle of the pavement to recall what I was doing there. Should I still go to meet Lorrimer, after my discomfiting encounter? Should I give this whole thing up and, as Mrs McCombe had said, go back to my fancy house? No, I had to carry on.

It was fully dark now and passers-by jostled and pressed and laughed, as they headed out for their evening's entertainment. The tantalising scent of hot pies, fried fish and cocoa coming from stalls and shop fronts made me realise how hungry I was. As I passed The Britannia, I realised that the next lane was New Wynd, where Detective Inspector Lorrimer had said Nellie and Betty were attacked. I looked back at the clock on the Tolbooth Steeple; I still had quarter of an hour before I was due to meet Lorrimer. I hesitated for only a moment before ducking inside the narrow entrance to the lane.

The buildings loomed above me and, away from the streetlights and shop windows on Argyle Street, it felt suddenly dark and enclosed. There was a faint light spilling out ahead and I made my way towards it. The window of a dingy restaurant with no name showed off a large piece of pale and unappetising roast, surrounded by dusty blue dishes of forbidding-looking pigs' trotters, potted head and black puddings that looked as though they would lay like lead pipes in even the strongest of stomachs. The dish was artistically decorated with pickles from which all colour had long since departed. I shuddered and moved on, past several dark and unappealing closes. From one of the closes, I could hear an accordion playing a polka exuberantly and surprisingly well. I poked my head into the close mouth.

A narrow, turnpike stair led upwards into the darkness and I could just make out the three globes of a pawnbroker's on the next landing. The accordion was louder now and accompanied by the rhythmic thumping of feet landing on bare boards which echoed down the stairs. A harsh cough from above made me jump. My nerves were already somewhat frayed from my encounter with Euphemia McCombe and this music and merriment was not one of Floss' balls. This was somewhere else I had absolutely no business being.

*

My evening was a revelation in more ways than one. From the start I regretted my spur of the moment suggestion of dinner. It was a silent, stilted affair, not improved by a plateful of braised veal which looked and tasted like the police issue boots I wasn't allowed. The vegetables had been boiled to an unappetising mush and the potatoes seemingly hadn't been boiled at all. The meal was only saved by a rather decent rhubarb flummery. Lorrimer spent the entire time looking morose and as though he regretted asking me to help. I tried to initiate conversation and raised all manner of topics, but he showed no interest in any of them. I didn't think it was wise to tell him about my detour into the street where Nellie and Betty were attacked, so I lapsed into the same morose silence as him and ordered another helping of rhubarb flummery.

The Coliseum was a modern, red sandstone building from the outside. Inside, however, was a different matter. It was very grand and Baroque, with mosaic doors, white marble columns and ornamental pilasters, as well as a superb white marble staircase and bold, rich Turkey red carpets. We purchased seats towards the back of the stalls and settled in.

Once conversation was off the menu, the evening improved. We were thrilled and entertained by a comedy acrobatic act, Cornalla and Eddie, who tumbled and juggled and kept up a smooth and funny banter with the orchestra and audience. Serio-comedienne Miss Dora Lyric danced and sang. I laughed uproariously at her coquettish performance of *Coax Me* and Lorrimer glanced at me and raised an eyebrow. Haley's juveniles, a dance troupe of around twenty talented children, performed a human pyramid and comedian Harry Merrylees had the entire audience in fits of laughter with his droll skits. I sneaked a couple of glances at Lorrimer. It was the first time I had seen him muster up a smile. His face became less drawn and slightly lopsided, as the puckered skin on the side of his neck closest to me seemed to stretch to its limits each time the smile appeared. I turned away, feeling as though I shouldn't be watching and took in the rest of the audience instead. The atmosphere between Lorrimer and me in the interval was not quite as stilted or uncomfortable as we discussed the acts of the first half.

The second half began with a chorus line of young women.

"That's Nellie Mellors, second from the end."

"Goodness, I hardly recognise her with her hair curled and her face painted like that." Nellie's costume seemed to consist entirely of jewels and feathers, and she was very different from the rather dowdy-looking mouse whose statement I had recently taken.

After the dancers left the stage, I leaned over towards Lorrimer.

"Should we go and interview Nellie straight away?"

"No, we'll wait until the end." He glanced at me. "Unless you want to go, that is?"

"Oh no! I'm enjoying myself immensely." A brief smile touched his lips and I settled into my seat to watch the rest of the show. My enjoyment only increased as the evening wore on. An exceptionally fine quartet sang unaccompanied a repertoire of popular songs from the last hundred years or so. Some were very grave, some humorous. My particular favourite was *The Organ Grinder's Serenade*. I made a note to see if I could get copies of some of the songs to play on the gramophone I had bought Floss at Christmas.

The star of the show, however, was most definitely Miss Gertie Gitana. When her name was announced, the audience broke into loud applause and cheering. Lorrimer leaned across, "She was the Forces' sweetheart, you know."

"I didn't know. Have you seen her before?"

Lorrimer nodded. "She came to the hospital where I was recuperating to entertain the troops."

I was taken aback and didn't know how to respond, as this was the first piece of personal information he had shared, but I was saved as Miss Gitana was no sooner out on the stage than she started to sing. Her charm and personality came through in her act as she worked her way through what were, apparently, old favourites of the audience. The song I liked most was called *Iola*, which involved some energetic yodelling, and I made a note of that one for Floss, too. The absolute favourite of the audience, however, was *Nellie Dean*, which Miss Gitana was persuaded to perform twice. The second time she sang it, the audience joined in with such gusto – if not exactly skill – that Miss Gitana was practically drowned out. However, nobody seemed to mind too much.

After Miss Gitana's several encores, we made our way backstage. Lorrimer's warrant card was a magic ticket that got us past every obstacle, and I was annoyed all over again that I wasn't allowed one. The scene that greeted us backstage was one that appeared to be utter chaos and my eyes watered at the mingled scents of greasepaint, sawdust, cigar smoke and the perfumes of Houbigant, Coty, Guerlain, Rubenstein and their cheaper imitators. I stood with my back pressed against the cold stone of the passage, letting my ears and nose acclimatise.

It was a long passage, leading from the stage at one end to the dressing rooms and offices at the other. We made our way through the throng of men, women and children flowing purposefully around us, like a busy colony of ants. Stagehands scurried about carrying painted scenery that looked a lot less grand close-up than it had on stage. Harry Merrylees was leaning against a door talking glumly to a large man in a suit, while half-dressed dancers with white, cold-creamed faces and shivering in their thin wraps, stretched and twirled and bent themselves into strange shapes.

I wanted to reach out and touch the silks and satins, the chiffon and crepe de chine, the furs and feathers of each costume as the wearers passed me, but I put my hands firmly in my pockets and followed Lorrimer along the corridor. Eventually, we were directed to the Stage Manager's office and, after Lorrimer told him why we were there, the Manager summoned a boy to go and fetch Nellie Mellors.

Soon enough, there was a tentative knock on the door and the Stage Manager stood up. "I'll leave you to it." He gave me a curious glance as he left, holding the door open for an anxious Nellie to come in. "Now, Nellie, I hope you've not been doing anything wrong. We keep a respectable establishment here, you know."

"No, sir. I've done nowt wrong." She looked at us, pleadingly. She was dressed for the outside, in a brown coat that had seen better days and a pair of black buttoned boots. Her face was pink and scrubbed and free of make-up, but her hair was still the neat helmet of curls she had sported on stage. A couple of faint scratches on her face and a vague yellowing around her left eye were the only signs of the attack she had experienced.

"She's correct," said Lorrimer. "Miss Mellors is helping us as a witness to a very serious assault, that's all."

The Stage Manager nodded, looking from Nellie to me once more, and left the room.

Nellie hovered by the door, looking as though she was on the verge of escaping. I pulled over the chair next to me. "Come and sit down, Nellie."

She settled herself in the chair. "How's Betty? I'm gonnae go and see her tomorrow, I have the matinee off."

I looked at Lorrimer and he nodded. I put my hand on her arm. "I'm so very sorry to tell you that Betty passed away earlier today."

Nellie's bottom lip wobbled, and her hand fluttered up to touch one of the scratches on her face, but then she nodded and looked down at her hands, worrying at the skin around her bitten nails.

"Can you tell us what happened to you and Betty that night?"

She gestured with a nod of her head towards Lorrimer, without looking up. "Ah've already told him."

"I know, but I'd like to hear it from you."

She sighed and sat on her hands. "We wis walking up New Wynd on the way home an' this man came out of nowhere. He hit me to the ground and then set after Betty, who was running down the lane."

"Did you see his face?"

She hesitated. "Naw. It wis too dark. An' he was turned away from me. He just kept hitting her. Awfy it was." She put her face in her hands, as if to shut out the picture.

"Did he say anything?"

"He said, 'That'll teach you, you can't get away from me, none of you.' An' then he tellt her he knew where she stayed."

"Do you know what he meant by not getting away from him?"

She lifted her head and glanced at Lorrimer. "Naw."

I thought she was lying but carried on with the questions Lorrimer and I had agreed on. "What did you do then?"

"I wanted to help her, but I wis scared. After I got maself up aff the ground, I ran out onto Argyle Street, an' shouted for help. People just thought I wis drunk an' ignored me, but the man from the hot pie stall outside the railway station at the Cross saw I was bleeding and came with me. It wis too late. The man had gone an' Betty wis just lyin' there." She started to sob. "I shouldnae have left her. I should have stayed."

"No, you did absolutely the right thing. You went to get help for your friend. Did you get the impression Betty knew who he was? Do you have any idea why he attacked her?" Again, she gave a sideways glance towards Lorrimer and I gestured that he should leave the room. He shook his head, but I continued to gaze at him as Nellie remained silent. Eventually he gave a sigh and left the room. I turned back to Nellie. "It's very important that you tell the truth, Nellie, you know that, don't you?"

She wiped her nose on her coat sleeve. "Aye, Miss, but ah'm scared."

"What are you scared of? Do you think he'll come after you?"

She was silent. Just when I was about to ask another question she said, "Betty...she were only young, just fifteen, an' a wee innocent. Not used to fendin' for hersel', an' she wasn't managing on her wages." She looked at me and I nodded encouragingly. "She'd met this man an' he said he could help her. Put her in the way of some extra money."

"I see. And when was this?"

"About a month ago." She pulled herself up straight in her chair. "We couldnae get any work efter the pantomime finished, not for ages. Then I got taken on at the Coliseum and tried to help Betty out, but it's hard..."

Had I sounded as though I was judging her and Betty? "I'm sorry."

She shrugged. "Anyway, I tried to tell her no' to do it. An' I tellt her I'd been to see one o' they fortune tellers an' the woman said a friend was in danger, an' I knew she meant Betty, so I tellt her." Her words were piling on top of each other, and I laid a hand on her shoulder. "I said she could come an' stay wi' me. An' she did, but she started doin' it anyway. I tellt her it was dangerous, but she said it wisnae so bad if you had a wee drink before." She suddenly stood up. "I shouldnae be saying anything."

"Nellie, the police can help you."

"The polis?" Her laugh was short and bitter. "The polis cannae help me."

"We can. *I* can."

She looked me up and down, the scorn clear on her face. "You? You have nae idea."

"Then tell me."

She shook her head and buttoned her worn coat. "Can I go? I've said everything ah'm gonnae."

"*Please*, Nellie."

She walked to the door. "Don't worry about me, ah'll be fine." She pushed her way past Lorrimer who was hovering outside the door and carried on down the corridor without a backwards glance.

The file I had placed in the middle of my desk was no longer there. I double-checked my drawers and the pile of paperwork in a tray at the edge of the desk. Had the cleaner moved it? I doubted it. She gave my room a wide berth and Constable Ferguson had told me that she'd quite categorically refused to clean it. Ferguson had laughed as he enumerated the reasons for her refusal and did a passable impression of Mrs Wilson's gravelly voice. "Wan, ah've tae go doon two flights o' stairs tae get ma cleanin' stuff noo'; two, ah've enough tae dae cleanin' up efter aw yous men; an' three, there's only two women belong in this polis station – me an' the turnkey. She can clean it hersel', it'll dae her guid."

I was annoyed with myself for leaving the file out. Superintendent Orr generally gave my office as wide a berth as Mrs Wilson, but it would be typical for him to come in and discover the file. Another black mark against my name, no doubt. I swore under my breath and decided that there was nothing else for it but to broach Sergeant McGillivray in his lair. Before I could think better of the plan, I strode down to the file room.

"Ah, Sergeant McGillivray. I was working on a file yesterday and I believe someone may have inadvertently brought it back, thinking I'd finished with it."

He looked at me thoughtfully, his bottom jaw moving slowly

from side to side, like a cow chewing its cud. "Nobody's been in here, Miss. Not for... ooooh..." he raised his eyes, his jaw moving all the time. Apparently, he found the answer on the soot-grimed ceiling. "Not for the last two days."

"Ah, well, maybe they came in while you were...out." I smiled brightly at him as I moved to pass him towards the shelves of files. "I'll just pop back there and see if it's been returned."

He held out a hand to stop me. "Not so fast, young lady. Let's have a look in the logbook, shall we?" He hoisted the heavy black book onto the counter in front of him with a grunt and opened it, turning the pages as slowly as if they had been dipped in treacle. Every new turn of the page was accompanied by his little pink tongue poking out to lick a dusty finger. The moist and glistening digit was then used to flick the bottom corner of the page up so that he could turn it. I noticed with some distaste that this bottom corner was thicker and grubbier than the rest of the book.

I tapped my foot as the pages turned torturously slowly. What he saw on the page in front of him didn't seem to make him happy. "No, Miss. No files signed out to you, as far as I can see."

"Really?" I reached a hand over to turn the logbook towards me, but he batted my hand away and pulled it protectively towards him.

"No. Naebody has taken a file out in the last two days. And certainly, nothing for *you*."

I pushed past him, taking him off guard. "No matter, I know exactly where the file I want is, so I'll just get it myself." I continued a stream of comments to myself, my voice getting increasingly louder, to block out his blusterings.

Finally, he grabbed hold of my arm. "Miss, you *cannot* go into the files yourself. If you want a file, you must go through the proper channels." He pulled me forcibly back through to the other side of his counter, closing the hatch firmly behind me.

"I'm afraid I'll have to tell Superintendent Orr about this breach of regulations."

"No matter, Sergeant. I'll just explain that the breach must have occurred on one of your regular...absences from your post." I had well and truly scuppered any chances of making an ally of him, but I didn't think that was ever likely to happen anyway. Besides, I'd seen all I needed to. The file was no longer there. Whoever had taken it from my desk had not returned it to its rightful place. I was annoyed at myself for not having had a proper look at it when I had the chance.

I returned to my office and checked everywhere once again. Should I just bite the bullet and go and put my side of the story to Superintendent Orr before McGillivray did? Before I could decide, there was a knock at the door. My 'Come in' was sharper than I had meant it to be, but Detective Chief Inspector Pritchard didn't seem to notice.

"Ah, Miss Adair, I've been looking for you all morning." I looked at my watch. It was only half past nine and Pritchard laughed easily. "Sorry, been in since seven – I have a case on at the moment that I'm trying to make headway on. Actually, it's that I want to speak to you about. Are you engaged?"

In answer, I waved him to the chair in front of my desk, pulled over my notepad and pen and looked at him expectantly.

He took his time getting settled, crossing his feet at the ankles and brushing an invisible speck of dust off the leg of his navy worsted suit. I'd noticed before that he was always immaculately dressed. "A palmist. One Madame Christine. Intent to deceive."

"A fortune teller? They seem to be cropping up all over the place."

He frowned. "How do you mean?"

"Oh, just one of Detective Inspector Lorrimer's cases. A young music hall artiste who witnessed an attack on her friend. She'd recently been to one."

"Ah, I see. Well, it seems to be the fashion for young – and not so young – ladies these days to tempt fate in this way."

"Is this woman in the cells?"

"In the cells?"

"Yes." I stood up. "For the interview?"

"Ah." He laughed. "No, Miss Adair. She's not in the cells. I haven't arrested her yet. For that, I need *your* help." He bowed slightly. "I want you to pose as a customer, and have your fortune told."

Another opportunity to go outside my remit. "Posing as a not so young lady, I take it?"

He had the grace to look slightly sheepish. "Um…well, not…I mean…"

"Don't worry, Detective Chief Inspector. I'm not quite so thin-skinned as that. What does Superintendent Orr say about this?"

I expected him, as Lorrimer had, to say that the superintendent didn't know, but he just shook his head and shrugged. "It was he who suggested it, Miss Adair."

After Pritchard left, I sat at my desk to make my preparations for the following day. I was excited at the thought of being part of an investigation and wanted to get my cover story just right. Madame Christine specialised in telling the fortunes of factory girls, lovelorn spinsters and widows. Pritchard, after looking me up and down appraisingly, reluctantly decided that I was probably too old to pass as a factory girl, far too cheerful-looking to be a widow, and that it was probably best if I pass myself off as an unmarried typist desperate for love. Part of me wanted to tell him that, at the age of twenty-five, yes, I might technically be a spinster, but I had chosen that path.

After Pritchard left, I was busy spinning quite the backstory for myself when a quick-fire rapping at the door made me jump. Constable Ferguson poked his head around the door, "Got a wee minute, Miss?"

I waved him in, and he entered, bearing two steaming mugs of tea and something wrapped in waxed paper. As he put the tea on the desk, I looked up at him. "Mrs Ferguson's clootie dumpling?" Ferguson and I had taken to having a cup of tea together on his tea break, and it often came accompanied by some of his wife's superb baking – treacle scones, perkins, Empire biscuits and Dundee cake. My absolute favourite, though, was her clootie dumpling.

He grinned at me and nodded. "Aye, Miss. It's to say sorry for running out on you in the filing room. I got Lizzie to make it special."

I unwrapped the paper and breathed in the familiar sweet warmth of ginger, cinnamon and golden syrup. I took the biggest slice and broke off a large, sticky chunk.

"Mmmmmm, you're forgiven for leaving me to my fate. You didn't take a file off my desk by any chance, did you?"

He looked puzzled. "No, Miss, course no'." He took a slurp of his own tea. "Listen, there's someone I think you ought to speak to. It's the lavvy…sorry, lavatory attendant…at the public conveniences in Wilson Street. You know the ones I mean?" I shook my head. "The ones at the corner of Glassford Street."

I shook my head once more. "I've never been in a public lavatory."

He raised his eyebrows and stared at me. "Anyway, the woman who works in there, old Winnie, I think she may be able to help you. She's been there for about thirty years an' all the lassies go in there. I was on my beat this morning and she was outside smoking her wee pipe an' I realised she might be able to help."

I'd told Constable Ferguson something of what I was investigating; telling him that I wanted to find out about a young woman who had been murdered in the city centre about twenty-five years ago. He'd clearly been curious as to why I would want to find out such a thing. I hadn't told him that the woman was my mother, of course. He found it as strange as I did that there were no records of her death at the station – which was the one nearest to where she had died, as well as being where most of the police records for the city centre were kept. The murder had been in the papers – briefly, Floss had told me, reported as the unfortunate death of an unnamed fallen woman at the hands of an unknown assailant – and I'd found records of crimes before and after my mother's murder in McGillivray's files. I think what I'd told Ferguson about the case intrigued him, even if he didn't entirely understand *my* interest.

I decided to call in and speak to the lavatory attendant on my way home. I'd seen these public lavatories, of course – they were all over Glasgow city centre – but I hadn't really taken much notice. This one was on a little island in the middle of the street. Steps flanked by iron railings led down at both ends of the island. I headed down to the door marked 'Ladies Public Lavatory', where a small board told me that admission was one penny.

I pushed open the door and entered the tiled lobby. Immediately, I was met with the tar-like scent of carbolic soap. From what I could see, the space was shaped like a T. At the end, the passageway opened out into a large open area that was all gleaming marble, white porcelain floors and shining brass. I had never seen anywhere so clean. There were three stout mahogany doors on each side, each one with an intricate mechanism of brass and glass which I assumed was where you put your penny. One of these doors was open and the porcelain and tiles inside were just as gleaming as those outside. The rear wall was patterned with coloured, glazed brick. I took another couple of steps forward. Two further cubicles at the end of each row of stalls contained a large marble washbasin with hot and cold taps. Hung over each basin was a gleaming plate-glass mirror with a shelf, on which lay a brush, a comb, and a fluffy-looking towel. Two comfortable chairs and a small table with a vase of flowers in front of the rear wall completed the furnishings of the room.

The place was toasty and warm and the reason for this became clear as I stepped further into the space. Tucked around the corners past the washbasins at the top of the T was a room at each side. The door to the one on the right was closed, the one on the left was wide open. Inside, it was surprisingly spacious, with a large iron range and neatly stacked shelves. On one side of the range a huge saucepan was steaming, its lid rattling slightly.

An oil-cloth covered table was set to one side and a tiny woman sat in a huge, battered armchair, reading. Her face was pressed up almost against the pages of Edith Wharton's *Summer*. On the shelf above her head was a neat row of books – I spotted several of my own favourites: John Buchan, Elizabeth Gaskell, and Alice Hegan Rice's *Mrs Wiggs of the Cabbage Patch*; as well as many that I hadn't read. I returned my attention to the woman. Her steel-grey hair was thick and abundant, piled on top of her head in a loose swirl, wisps of it curling around her pink cheeks. The retired Gibson Girl look was further enhanced by the pristine, high-necked white blouse, which looked to have been carefully hand-embroidered, and the burgundy A-Line skirt, sprigged with bluebells and primroses. A substantial and highly-polished pair of boots peeped out from under the skirt.

As I moved closer, she looked up. "Aw, sorry, hen, I didnae see you there. Did ye want change?" She fished into the pocket of her apron and pulled out a handful of pennies.

"No. No thank you. It was you I came to see, actually, Mrs..." I realised that Constable Ferguson hadn't told me her surname.

"Just Winnie'll dae, hen. It's what everybody calls me." She looked me up and down. "You'll be the lassie Archie was telling me about, then?"

I further realised that I didn't know Constable Ferguson's

first name. "Constable Ferguson?" She nodded. "Yes. He told me I should come to see you."

She jumped up from the chair and gestured that I should sit down, before scurrying past me and dragging over one of the chairs from the main room. My first impression that she was tiny had been wrong. Short and wiry she may have been, but her forearms under the rolled-up sleeves were plump and strong. When I didn't move towards the chair she had vacated, she nudged me towards it with her hip. "Aye, Archie tellt me that a fancy young lady would be coming to see me. Want some pudding?" She lifted the lid from the pot on the stove, reaching in with a metal ladle and pulling out a large, muslin-wrapped parcel. Lifting the lid released a rich and savoury scent. "Beef pudding. Wi' kidneys and oysters."

My mouth was watering, and I would have loved some, but I explained that we were expecting visitors that evening for dinner. Winnie nodded easily and popped the pudding back into the pot and put the lid back on. I took a final deep breath before the meaty perfume was trapped inside the pan once more.

Winnie settled herself down in her chair, crossed her legs at the ankles and surveyed me. Her cool, appraising gaze made me slightly uncomfortable. The skin around her sharp, grey eyes was criss-crossed with wrinkles, but her cheeks were smooth and pink. "So, hen, what can I do fir ye?"

"Constable Ferguson tells me you've been here a long time."

She laughed. "Aye, I have that, hen. I came in wi' the porcelain. That'll be more than thirty years ago, now."

"And you've been here ever since?"

"Aye. Nine in the morning until eleven at night. An' never a day aff sick." She nodded her head at me, proudly. "I took a couple of days off when my Murdo died, that's aw. And once I turned seventy-five, the Corporation tellt me I should retire. Tellt me they'd gie me a retiring allowance. Four shillings an' tenpence a week, if ye can believe that." She snorted. "An' whit am I gonnae do? Sit around on ma erse all day? Naw. I tellt them I'd get ma daughter in one day a week, to gie me a break, but that's aw." She nodded again and looked at me as though she was daring me to argue.

"You must enjoy it," I said.

"Aye, I do that, hen. Always somebody poppin' in – although we don't get many the likes of yourself, of course. An' I've got ma books when there's naebody here."

She jumped up as the door opened. "Marion, Ada – that yous two finished for the day?" I peered out of Winnie's room, to watch her greeting two young women in plain but fashionable coats with big buttons and wide belts. One of them looked as if she were about to disappear into her enormous roll collar.

"Aye, Winnie, that's us. I've been dying to go since three, but that Mr McKenzie wouldn't let us off the shop floor. Been quiet as the grave all day, too." She put her penny into the mechanism of one of the stall doors and disappeared inside. Her friend removed her jaunty red wool-felt hat and smoothed her hair.

When the other young woman came out of the stall with a sigh of relief, Winnie beamed at them. "Beef puddin'?"

They shook their heads. "Naw, thanks, Winnie, my young man's taking me to the Queen Anne for my supper. An' Marion's to go home and cook for her da, since her mammy's ill."

Winnie saw them to the door, chattering all the time and wishing good health to Marion's mammy, and then came back to me. "Where were we, hen? What was it you wanted to know about?"

I took a deep breath, wondering how much I could tell this woman, but before I could start, the door opened again. Winnie tapped me on the knee. "I'll no' be a minute." I peered out once more, to see her greeting a girl who was most unsuitably dressed for the chill early evening outside. "Come away in, Bridget, you look perished. That you just startin'?"

The girl looked at me and hesitated. "Aye."

"Don't you be worryin' about Miss Adair, she's a pal. Here," Winnie lifted the chain attaching one of the keys around her waist and unlocked one of the stalls. "There y'are. I'll get ye a wee bit puddin'."

"Ta, Winnie." The young woman closed the door of the stall behind her.

Winnie came bustling over and took the pot lid off once more, letting the gloriously scented steam escape. She unwrapped the pudding and served up a large portion onto a tin plate. She leaned across and whispered in my ear. "Don't let on you're with the polis, she'll only scarper an' she needs a good feed." I nodded, and she pointed her ladle at me. "And don't you be lettin' on to the Corpy that ah'm lettin' some of the lassies in for free. Lord knows, they've little enough. Ah'm no' gonnae take their money off them when the cludgies are goin' beggin'."

Bridget came out of the toilet stall and Winnie handed her the plate and a spoon. "Get that down you. It'll stick to your ribs."

The young woman spooned the steaming pudding into her mouth as if worried that it would be stolen. I watched her as she ate. Her eyes darted everywhere, nervous and haunted, and I could see that she was very young, just a girl. "Ta, Winnie." She handed back the plate and made to leave, but Winnie put a hand on her arm.

"Here, hen." She jumped onto a little stool, sprightly for all her advanced years and lifted something down from one of the shelves. She shook out a red woollen shawl with orange flowers crocheted onto the bottom of it and wrapped it around Bridget's painfully thin shoulders. "That's better. Now, remember and come back if you need a warm-up, or a wash or anything."

"Ta, Winnie." Bridget opened the door, letting in a blast of cold air, and left the lavatory.

Winnie stood for a moment, shaking her head, sadly, before settling herself back into her chair. "Now then, hen, whit is it?"

I might be proved wrong, but the kindness and respect she had shown to Bridget had persuaded me that I could trust her. "My mother was murdered not long after I was born," I started. "Her name was Clementina Watt."

I told Winnie about the Home, about Jeannie, about my mother's stay in the Tontine Close with Sarah Loag, about my birth, about the Lock Hospital and Jeannie's sad end, and about my mother's violent one. By the time I got to the end of my story, Winnie and I were sitting on the floor and I was wrapped in her arms as she rocked me, stilling my sobs with a rhythmic, "Sh-sh-sh."

At some point, she had closed the door to her little room, and we sat in the dim light, our voices stilled as women came and went; the sounds of chattering, coins clattering, doors banging and water running muffled by the thick mahogany door.

We stood now and I settled myself back in my chair. Winnie pressed a huge blue and white checked handkerchief into my hand and busied herself with a pot of water on the stove. Moments later, a mug of strong, hot tea was thrust into my hand. I could smell the sweetness of the sugar. Then she sat back down in her own chair.

"I'm afraid I don't remember a lassie called Clementina, hen," she said. "She wasnae one of my regulars. I remember them aw, every one." I sighed, and she held up a hand. "I do remember hearing about the murder of a lassie in a lane just off Cathedral Street." She shrugged. "I didnae get tellt a name, and it wisnae so unusual, a young lassie from the streets, dyin' by violence. The reason I remember it, was that they said the girl had been in the Lock, and it came just the day efter the death there of a lassie I *did* know."

I looked at her and she gazed back at me, nodding soberly. "Aye, hen. Jeannie Jack was her name. I hadn't seen her about for a wee while, right enough." She sighed. "So young, she were."

Winnie told me how Jeannie had appeared one day, dirty-faced and red-eyed. She had appeared distressed, and Winnie had helped her to wash, then fed her and talked to her.

"Her teeth didnae stop chatterin' the whole time. A lot of the other lassies who come in here are gallus and bold – it's often just a front, mind you. Jeannie was so shrunk in on hersel'. An' so *young*. Bridget reminds me of her." Winnie tutted and shook her head. "Bridget's not cut out for that life, and neither wis Jeannie. I could tell that."

"Did she say anything about what had brought her here?"

Winnie shrugged. "To tell you the truth, hen, she didnae say much of any note at aw. That first time, she was haverin' an' mutterin' to herself a good bit. She kept mentionin' the devil, like one o' they evangelists you see rantin' on the Green. I couldnae get much sense out of her. Eventually, she just left."

"But she came back? You said that was the first time she was here."

Winnie tamped down her clay pipe and lit it once more, taking long, slow puffs until it was to her satisfaction. "Aye, she came back almost every day after that, sometimes two or three times. I fed her, gave her a couple of things to wear, let her sit for a wee while if she wanted."

"Did she talk to you? Tell you why she was there?"

"Naw, hen. An' it wisnae for want of askin'. I got the feelin' she was in one o' they homes for wayward girls. A few of the other regulars seemed to know her, but they steered clear."

"Do you know why?"

Winnie looked at me before she answered, as though she was contemplating whether to say anything. "They were scared, likely enough."

"Scared? Of what?"

Winnie opened the door to her room and walked around the toilets, checking each of the stalls. She moved with the agility and strength of a woman forty years her junior. When she came back, she pulled her chair up closer to mine. "There was a man; a man most of the lassies were feart of. A very important man who could get you anything." Her calm, grey eyes gave me that appraising look once more. "Young, innocent lassies were his speciality. An' he had a whole load of other important men who were his...customers." She spat the word out with distaste.

"Do you know who he was?"

"Naw. Just that he was an important man. Not like the usual brothel keepers and pimps around here. If any of the lassies knew his name, they didnae tell me. Girls who talked were known to disappear. An' most of the lassies tended to avoid any of the girls they thought belonged to him, like they were poison. Wee Jeannie was right in her ramblings, he was the very devil, by all accounts."

"And Jeannie? What about her?"

Winnie sighed and sat back. "She wis here every day for one or two months. Then...she wisnae. One of the regular lassies told me she was in the Lock an' then a few days later, I heard she'd died. Somethin' terrible happened to that wee lassie, hen. I could see it in her eyes. You need to watch yourself."

"I do?"

"Aye, hen. He disnae like anyone interferin' in his business, so the lassies tell me." I was silent for a moment as the implication of Winnie's statement sank in. "Oh, he disnae roam the streets like he once did, too important for that, by all accounts, but he's still there. The trade in young innocents is still there. An' lassies are still bein' murdered."

"Well, ladies, do I look sufficiently spinster typist?" I gave Floss and Jo a twirl as they sat in the cosy little sitting room off Floss' bedroom, having a leisurely breakfast.

"Where on *earth* did you get *that?*" Floss pulled at the uneven hem of the rather misshapen brown wool coat I was wearing.

"I borrowed it off Ellen."

"Remind me to give her a pay rise. That's just about the ugliest garment I've ever seen."

"Well, don't tell Ellen that, she loves it. I had to withstand a half hour lecture on how to look after it before she'd let me take it out of the house."

Floss turned to her friend. "What do you think, Jo? Too dowdy?"

Jo took a bite of her toast and eyed me up and down. "Not dowdy enough, I would say, but that's more about your attitude than the clothes. This woman will be expecting a meek, downtrodden young woman who'll hang on her every syllable. You look more like you're going into battle, Mabel."

"She's right." Floss adjusted the brim of my hat. "Put some more powder on and hunch your shoulders a bit. Oh, and try to look less well fed."

"And more as though you're desperate for a husband."

I picked up the battered handbag I had found in a little shop selling second-hand goods when I was walking home from my visit to Winnie. "Thank you both. You're *so* helpful." I stalked out of the room, followed by the sound of their laughter.

Ellen caught up with me just outside the door. "The gentleman is waiting in his car, Miss. He said he didn't want to come in and that he'd see you outside." She looked me up and down, her face fretful. "You're a wee bit broad for that coat, Miss. Mind when you sit down not to rip the seams, won't you."

I glared at her and stopped in front of the hall mirror. I opened my handbag and took out a leaf of Papier Poudré to blot my face and the Moroccan leather Coty powder box that I had already used three times that morning. Damn my pink cheeks. As I applied the powder puff, I breathed in the fresh, mossy scent. A fine dusting of powder clung to my upper lip and I blotted it once more before leaving the house. Perhaps now I was sufficiently pale.

As I came out onto the steps, Detective Chief Inspector Pritchard jumped out of the car to come round and open my door, but I beat him to it, turning the handle, climbing in and closing the door behind me in one smooth move. Pritchard got back in behind the wheel and looked over at me. Even in his bulky Ulster coat he looked trim and elegant.

"Are you well, Miss Adair?"

"Perfectly, thank you."

"You look rather pale." I fumed all the way to Byres Road, although Pritchard didn't seem to notice, keeping up a cheery recounting of the woman we were going to see for most of the drive.

"She's not really from the South of France, of course, nor is her real name Madame Christine. It's actually Ada Austin and she's from Manchester, but I'm sure that wouldn't be as intriguing to her clientele. I understand that her French accent is impeccable – as long as you've never met an actual French person before."

"And how did she come to your attention?"

"Police in Partick have received several complaints about her over the months – deception, menacing behaviour, assault, that sort of thing – and they've even arrested her on several occasions but have never been able to bring a case against her."

"Assault?"

He turned towards me and grinned. "Yes indeed. She whacked a policeman over the head with a crystal ball. And no, before you ask, he didn't see it coming."

I laughed. "So how did she get out of that one?"

"She said it was an accident; it slipped out of her hands when the policeman grabbed her in what she described as a terribly ungentlemanly way. She can be very convincing, I understand. She doesn't charge for her services, which is how she stays within the law. Instead, she receives 'gifts', monetary, of course, from those whose fortunes she tells. And most of her victims are too embarrassed afterwards to complain when they realise they've been duped."

"But not this time?"

"No. Not this time. Partick received a visit from a distraught woman who finally decided to go to them after being blackmailed out of several hundred pounds over the last few months.

"Blackmail?"

Pritchard sighed. "Yes, particularly nasty the way Austin got her claws into this woman. She'd visited this so-called Madame Christine several times; had her palm read, then her cards, then paid more to have her fortune told with the crystal ball and have her horoscope written. The whole range of con tricks. It all culminated in her participating at a séance where Madame Christine supposedly conjured up the spirit of the woman's grandfather. And all the time during these sessions Austin gradually gleaned information about the woman through questions and sympathetic suggestion. Some of the information revealed was particularly embarrassing."

"Oh?"

Pritchard laughed. "No, I shan't tell you what it was. It would make one of us blush and I very much doubt it would be me."

I turned my head away and stared out of the window, annoyed. Just as the story was getting interesting. "And why did Partick call *you* in?" I knew the answer to this but wanted to see what Pritchard would say. Ferguson had told me that Pritchard had rather a reputation within the Glasgow police force for his knack of exposing fake fortune tellers, mediums and spiritualists, and was often called in for such cases, particularly where matters had become serious.

Pritchard shrugged. "Oh, I don't know. It's become customary now. I don't mind; I find these cases particularly nasty and very distressing for the victims."

"And are they always women?"

"No, indeed – a fair few men amongst them. Several months ago, I assisted in the case of a businessman who was conned out of a small fortune. It's the women whose cases get to me, though. It seems especially cruel to deceive a shop girl, or a spinster, or a grieving widow who lost her sons in the war."

As he lapsed into a brooding silence we arrived at the address of Madame Christine, in a narrow street not far from the Botanic Gardens. I'm not sure what I expected, but I was taken somewhat aback by the grandeur of the terrace of buildings, each with neat steps up to the entrance, and decorative ironwork along the front. Before I could stop him, Pritchard jumped out of the car and hurried round to my side to help me out. I climbed the steps, and a neatly uniformed young woman opened the door to me and showed me into a sumptuously decorated waiting room, one floor up.

The room was in complete contrast to the refined but unobtrusive exterior of the building. Brightly-coloured rugs were scattered over the shining parquet floor and the walls were crimson tinted, topped with a frieze of Egyptian lotus blossoms in rich blues, oranges and greens, picked out with gold leaf. Two middle aged women dressed in black sat at either end of a long divan scattered with multi-coloured silk cushions. Their mourning dress and their stillness made the women look almost like absences amongst the colour and brightness that characterised the rest of the room. A third woman, younger, and wearing a coat rather like my own – like Ellen's, I should say – sat on the edge of a comfortable-looking armchair upholstered in peacock blue taffeta. I sat down on the last remaining chair. The four of us sat in silence. The only movement in the room came from the younger girl who was picking at a thread on her coat. A window in the wall to my left was partially draped with something thin and filmy, but a narrow shaft of light crossed the parquet floor and illuminated one of the women in black. Dust motes floated slowly in front of her and settled on her coat.

The thick, red velvet curtain at the end of the room was pulled aside and a young woman came through, buttoning her coat. Her face was smiling and flushed. "Oh, thank you, Madame Christine, you've made me so happy!"

Madame Christine smiled and bowed. "My pleasure, my child." Her voice was deep and musical, with an accent that definitely wasn't French. Her clothes were as colourful as the waiting room: a silk georgette crepe dress which flowed in clean, straight lines from her shoulders to just above her ankles. It was dark blue, intricately embroidered with stitching and beads in lighter shades of blue and green that shimmered as she glided over to the door of the flat. The young woman left with one more breathless, "Thank you," and Madame Christine turned back to us. We all sat a little straighter in our chairs.

"Madame McGregor?" one of the black clad women stood up and followed Madame Christine through the curtain. The rest of us relaxed once more and settled into our seats to await our turn. Mine came half an hour later. I followed Madame Christine into her consulting room, as she called it. This room was furnished more plainly than the waiting room. The thick curtains were closed and the room was lit by lamps. In the centre an oval table was draped with a filmy purple scarf. On it was a crystal globe, resting on an ornate brass stand. Several similar items were displayed in a glass case in front of one wall, along with casts of hands in either porcelain or some sort of resin, decorated with lines, words and symbols.

"What reading will you have, ma chère?"

"I...I've never had my fortune told before, Madame Christine. What will the charge be?"

She looked affronted and her hand fluttered to the string of bright beads around her neck. "I never make a charge, my dear. Gifts only. But I take nothing under half a crown. For that, you may have an ordinary reading of the palm. For seven shillings and sixpence, I will use the crystal ball." She looked me up and down. "There are, of course, other, more expensive options."

Connie Atkins would be unlikely to be able to afford very much, so I told Madame Christine I would like her to tell my future from my palm and painstakingly counted out two shillings and sixpence. She tucked it into a small purse at her waist, placed a pink silk cushion on the oval table and gestured for me to place my hand on the cushion, palm up. She took my hand in her own delicate fingers and held it as if it were a prize orchid. She traced the contours of my hand, examining the lines on my palm. Her brow was furrowed and her lips sagely puckered. Then she took a magnifying glass and went through the entire ritual once more, her green eyes hovering over my future.

"The human hand, ma chère, is the truest guide to human character." I felt like telling her that I would sooner trust the creases of an old glove to tell my character, but simply put on what I hoped was a rapt smile. She took that as her cue to continue, waving her own hand expansively. "Character is destiny. And therefore, the lines which tell your character also tell your destiny."

I wasn't sure what the correct response should be and settled for a nod and a smile. "You have good heart, head and life lines. You can be somewhat stubborn and your ankles are weak." My ankles were most definitely not weak, but she might have been right about the stubbornness. "You have made a change this year and secured a very good position, which will be beneficial to you." She peered down at the story apparently written in my hand. "I see that you have been disappointed in love. However, there are two young men who are interested in you – one is dark and one is fair." She paused and looked up at me and I nodded again, trying to make it as non-committal as possible. This seemed to satisfy her.

"And…will I marry?" I tried to blush by holding my breath.

She stroked my palm and frowned. "You will receive two offers of marriage and will refuse the first. A man of good quality will marry you before your…" she looked up at my face and the frown deepened, "…thirtieth birthday, and you will enter society."

I sighed. "That *is* a relief, Madame Christine. My mother will be delighted."

Madame Christine beamed and brushed a stray curl off her forehead. "And now, ma chère, you have exhausted my gifts for the present. However, if you would like to make another appointment, we can continue."

She reached into one of her pockets and took out a small leather-bound book and a pen. As she opened it, I saw names, addresses and various sums of money. I committed as much as I could to memory, havering a little so that the notebook would remain open as long as possible. "Let me see…possibly next Tuesday? Or, wait…I won't be able to get away from work… what about Thursday?"

I left the building and turned back to look at the house. As I did so I glimpsed a man limping swiftly off along the street. His collar was up, and his hat was pulled down low, but something about his walk and the coat arm pinned to his side reminded me of Inspector Lorrimer. I shrugged. Perhaps it *was* Lorrimer. Or perhaps it was someone else. Sadly, it wasn't unusual to see a one-armed man these days. I walked back up to Byres Road to where Detective Chief Inspector Pritchard had said he would wait for me. I filled him in on what I had discovered, and he wrote down all the names and addresses I could remember in his notebook. "Well done. I'm impressed with your quick thinking and with your memory."

"Well, Madame Christine *did* say that I had secured a good position in which I would be successful."

He barked out a laugh. "We'll see what Superintendent Orr has to say about that, I'm sure."

"That reminds me; why did he allow me to come out on this investigation when he has made it clear that I'm never to leave the station?"

Pritchard shrugged. "He seems to be under the impression that you've been meddling in things which don't concern you and wanted a way to keep you busy with something. I make a suitable guardian, it seems." He grinned as I huffed at that. So it *was* Orr who had found the file on my desk. Pritchard came to a stop at the bottom of Byres Road, allowing pedestrians to cross in front of us. "*Have* you, Miss Adair? Been meddling, I mean?"

A smile twitched at his lips and I straightened my shoulders and glared at him. "I most certainly have *not*. If you must know, I inadvertently picked up an old file along with some empty files I wanted to use to organise my cases. When I realised my mistake, I put it on my desk to return it the next day."

He bit his bottom lip to stop the smile spreading. "And did you exercise a young lady's natural curiosity and look at the file when you realised your error?"

I folded my arms. How dare he. "No, I didn't. I left it on my desk unopened. Indeed, I can't even remember the woman's name." And, with that, I turned pointedly and looked out of the passenger window.

I decided to visit Euphemia McCombe again on my way to work the next day. As I made my way through the still-dark streets, I went over our conversation once more. A workman walking close behind me swore under his breath as I halted abruptly. He glared at me as he pushed his way past. I raised my hand to apologise, but my mind was on something Euphemia McCombe had said; '*Get back to your fancy house*'. Had that been a guess? '*Take tea with your fancy lady friends*'. No, I didn't think it was a guess. She knew who I was before I went to visit her. I ran the rest of the way to Mrs McCombe's close, taking the stairs two at a time. I paused at the dusty window on the second-floor landing to get my breath back. The weak early-morning sun hadn't yet penetrated into the back courts and I peered out at the grey mud below before continuing on up the stairs.

I heard the distinctive sound of a pair of tackety boots coming down from the top landing. Whoever it was, they were taking the steps at a fair pace, so I pressed myself into the wall so that I wouldn't get in the way on the narrow steps. As the man descended, pulling his cap low on his head, he jumped slightly as he saw me on the landing below. "I'm sorry…" I started, but he thrust his way past me, winding me slightly as his elbow caught me in the stomach, and I heard the nails on his boots crunching on the rough pavement outside the building.

I continued upwards, more slowly now. Mrs McCombe's door was slightly open. I knocked, but there was no response. "Hello?" I called. I poked my head inside, but all I could hear was the dripping of water. I pushed the door open wide and went in, calling out once more.

The hallway was dark and narrow and there was only one door at the end, which was ajar, letting in some light. Hooks in the wall of the hallway held a couple of items of clothing – the old, black coat Mrs McCombe had been wearing when I saw her and a brightly-coloured shawl that looked as though it had been painstakingly made from scraps of wool left over from some woollen hose here, a scarf or an old jumper there. Every now and then, pieces of brown sacking were sewn into holes in the wool.

The door at the end of the hall opened half-way before hitting up against something on the other side. I shoved a bit harder and the door opened fully. The source of the dripping sound was revealed as a large, white enamel jug lying on its side on the kitchen table. The table itself was the reason the door was difficult to open. I could tell that it was not in its usual place, thanks to four dust-free squares which put the normal position of the table further towards the middle of the room. A cane bottomed chair lay on its side.

A couple of wooden crates made up the rest of the furniture in the room, other than a fireplace and range at the other end. A pan of something bubbled on the range, spitting and hissing, and I could smell burning. I walked around the table, intending to take the pot off the fire, but I couldn't get near it. Euphemia McCombe was crumpled on the moth-eaten rug in front of the fire, her sparse grey hair spread out around her head.

Constable Ferguson glanced around him as he entered the tea shop. He looked very different in his everyday clothes, older and not as polished. I had arranged to meet him in Partick, as I thought it was unlikely we would be spotted by anyone who knew us. He made a beeline for the table. "What did you do?" His voice was a mixture of awe and concern. "Superintendent Orr is beelin'."

I pushed over the second cup and the plate of cakes I'd ordered. He waved away the cakes but poured himself a cup of tea. "Did he tell you I'd found a dead body?" My interview with Superintendent Orr had not been a pleasant one. I'd told him that I'd been visiting the poor and needy at the behest of Floss and my presence in that place was simply unfortunate. He clearly didn't believe me and was calling for me to be sacked, but Floss had backed up my cover story, even embellishing it with small details and Orr had been forced to back down. I was suspended until the end of the week. To recover from the shock, ostensibly.

"Is this something to do with that old case you're so interested in?"

"You haven't mentioned that to anybody, have you?" I took a slice of marble cake from the stand and idly picked it to pieces on my plate, releasing the scents of nutmeg, cinnamon and cloves.

Ferguson looked a little sheepish. "Not really, naw."

"What do you mean, 'not really'?"

He shrugged, "Detective Inspector Lorrimer asked me what you were doing down in the file room that day. He saw me disappearing along the corridor."

I sat back and glared at him. "And what did you tell him?"

"Just that you were lookin' at old murder cases. You know, to give you a feel for how things worked. That's what you tellt me, anyway. I wisnae meaning any harm."

I rested my chin on my hand. "I know. It's fine." I hadn't been fair with him, and he'd put himself out to help me. "Now, was there something else you wanted to tell me, or did you just want to find out the latest gossip?"

He laughed. "Naw, Miss. I've got a message from Winnie. She wants you to go and see her." He hesitated. "I wisnae going to tell you; you're already in enough bother. An' I know there's something you're not telling me. You're going to an awfy lot of trouble over a girl who's been dead for twenty-five years."

"I can make my own decisions, Archie." I popped a couple of the pieces of marble cake into my mouth and stood up. "I promise I'll tell you later. In the meantime, don't tell *anyone, anything.*"

I hopped on the tram into the city centre and walked the last few blocks to Wilson Street, keeping a wary eye out for anyone from the police station. I ran down the steps to the public convenience and pushed open the door. Once again, I was met with the carbolic soap smell which changed as I walked down the corridor to something savoury and delicious. My stomach grumbled. It was now nearly dinner time and, other than the piece of marble cake in the tea shop, I hadn't had anything since breakfast.

Winnie was mopping the already pristine floor, humming away to herself. Her smile grew wide when she saw me. "Hello, hen. Can I get you some steamed mince pudding?"

"I'd love some, Winnie, thank you."

She ushered me into her room and plumped the cushion on the chair for me, before patting it as an invitation that I should sit down. She fetched a plate and a spoon from a neat pile on one of the shelves and served up a steaming portion of the pudding. My mouth was watering as she handed it to me. "Sorry for the tin plate, hen."

I laughed. "Not at all, Winnie. Goodness, this smells amazing." I plunged the spoon in and blew on the contents to cool it down before taking a bite. The rich, meaty gravy had soaked into the spongy suet and the soft onion was juicy and almost sweet. It was glorious and it was a few minutes before I spoke again.

Winnie watched me with a smile on her round, red face, her arms crossed, still leaning on the mop. "Better, hen?"

I sighed happily. "Much, thank you. Archie said you wanted to see me?"

The smile disappeared and she dragged a chair over towards mine, taking the plate and spoon from my hands and placing them on the table. "Aye. I did. Some of the lassies have been a bit skittish in the last couple of days. I managed to get one or two of them to talk. They've been unsettled by the death of that woman Archie says you found."

"Euphemia McCombe?"

"Aye. And the young lassie that died recently in one of the closes off Trongate."

I leaned forward. "Betty McKay?"

"Aye, that's her."

The door opened and a well-dressed young woman scuttled in, pushed her coin into the slot and slammed the door behind her. We stayed silent until, just as quickly as she had come, she left again, without so much as looking at us.

"Do they think the deaths are related?"

"Aye. They do." Winnie's face was grim. "That man I tellt you about, the one who controls the trade in flesh in the city centre; he's a powerful man with other powerful men behind him. I tellt you afore about how he specialises in young girls. Very young girls." She waved a hand towards the toilet cubicles. "The lassies who come in here, the working girls, they're his bread an' butter. Then there's others, like Bridget."

"And like Jeannie."

"Aye, like Jeannie, too; the young girls. Well, that's a different matter. An' Euphemia McCombe knew all about that. Retired a good few years ago, apparently, an' she was no longer in a position to help this man once she retired, but her name and reputation still go on, like a witch in a fairy story. An' she had a hold over him; they say he protected her when she was arrested once." She looked at me, her grey eyes dark and troubled.

"Do you mean that…"

"Aye, hen, that Home your mother was in, the place this McCombe woman ran, that was like a wee sweetie shop for this devil and his…customers."

"But why would he kill my mother?"

Winnie tucked a stray lock of hair behind my ear. "Maybe he thought she would tell this grand lady of yours. An' he may not have done it himsel' you know, hen. He's very careful and has others do his dirty work for him, maist o' the time." She hesitated. "They tell me he likes it, though, hen. The killin'. 'Specially where the young lassies are concerned." She shuddered and then straightened her shoulders. "Some people must know who he is, of course, but the girls tell me they don't know and that they don't want tae know. An' he likes tae keep it that way. This Euphemia McCombe knew who he was, though."

"And Betty McKay?"

She nodded, slowly. "Aye, one or two o' the lassies say she knew, too, an' that's why she's dead."

Nellie. I had to speak to Nellie. I knew she was hiding something. I stood up and reached for my coat, which I had taken off when I came into Winnie's cosy den. But Winnie grabbed my hands. "An' you need to be very, very careful, hen." The outside door opened, and she drew me closer. "The lassies also tellt me of someone who's got him rattled."

It took a moment for her meaning to sink in. "And you think it's me?"

"Who else is it gonnae be?" She gripped my hands still tighter. "Don't trust anyone. Ye hear me?"

I nodded and gave her a brief hug. It felt extremely unpleasant, thinking that this man might be aware of me and I tried to put the thought aside. "Here, let me give you some money for the pudding." I reached into my purse.

"Ye'll not, hen." I could tell I had offended her and gave her another hug as two middle-aged women approached to ask for change for the cubicles.

"My dear, your friend is right. You *do* need to be careful." Floss took my hand, concern on her face. "Do you want me to speak to James?"

"Winnie said don't trust *anyone*."

Jo gave a half laugh. "I'm sure she didn't mean the Chief Constable, Mabel."

I glared at her. "No-one. Right now, the only people I trust are you two and Winnie."

Floss sighed. "Well, what can *we* do?"

I shrugged. "I need to see Nellie, but my actions have already got Euphemia McCombe killed—"

"You don't know that." Flossie's voice was uncharacteristically sharp as she paced the room.

"No, I don't. But I can't take the risk. I need to speak to Nellie, to find out what she knows, or, at the very least, to try and keep her safe, somehow. If someone *is* watching me, then I don't want to jeopardise her safety still further." I needed a way to contact Nellie.

"Perhaps I can help?" Floss picked up the deep blue velvet brocade shawl from the back of the ottoman and wrapped it around her head. With swift and graceful movements, she twirled around and passed the fringes of the shawl across her face. Jo clapped her hands, delighted.

Floss and Jo insisted I stay at home over the next two days. I was not due back at the Station until the following week and they wanted to keep me out of harm's way until then. It took only those two days for them to rent, furnish and decorate a small flat on the second floor of a very smart building just around the corner from Copland and Lye on Sauchiehall Street. They'd used my descriptions of Madame Christine's flat in their decorating spree, apparently. They'd also had an advertisement printed and delivered to the Coliseum offering 'the young ladies of the chorus a free half-hour sitting with the world-renowned palmist, psychometrist and clairvoyante, Madame Varvara, in Glasgow for just one week. Hours 10am to 2pm'.

"And what, may I ask, is a psychometrist?"

"I really have no idea. But after studying such advertisements in the newspapers, we thought it sounded rather fine."

"And you, I suppose, are Madame Varvara?"

Floss waved a dramatic hand. "I am she, yes."

I laughed. "You're going to be inundated with chorus girls all wanting their fortunes told."

"Ah, no. You see my maid," Floss gestured towards Jo, who gave a curtsy, "my maid is going to the Coliseum to take bookings. She'll take just enough for it to seem real, making sure your Nellie is amongst them."

"And what if Nellie doesn't sign up?"

It was Jo's turn to be dramatic. "Then I shall receive a… what did you call it, Flo?"

"Materialisation."

"A materialisation which will mean that I have to seek her out by name."

Floss clapped her hands. "Exactly. Nobody would be able to resist that!"

And they had been absolutely right. Nellie had been one of the first to sign up. For appearances sake, Jo signed up four other young women, too.

All this was why I'd left the house that morning at eleven, spent the next hour and a half wandering round the shops, buying a pair of gloves here, a purse there, all of which I tucked into the voluminous but rather battered brown leather bag I was carrying, hoping to bore any possible person following me. In the bag was also a change of clothes and, shortly before Nellie was due to arrive to see Madame Varvara, I sauntered into Copland and Lye. I headed up to the dressmaking department, where I went into one of the changing rooms.

Fifteen minutes later, an altogether different young woman came out. I wore a coat that was too big for me, an unbecoming hat pulled down low over my forehead, rather shabby boots, and a pair of round glasses with a heavy, dark frame. I folded all my original clothes as tightly as they would go into my bag and left by a different entrance around the corner.

The flat Floss had chosen was perfect. There was also a milliner and a photographer in the building, so the close was well-used. I climbed the stairs to the second floor. A sign outside announced one of the flats as 'Madame Varvara – Consulting Rooms' and I smiled to myself. How had they managed to do all this in such a short time? I bit my lip as Jo, neat as a pin in her maid's uniform, opened the door to me. Her short hair, which usually stood out in all directions, was plastered to her head and pinned underneath a frilled cap, and her pristine apron was tied with a perfectly symmetrical bow. "Madame Varvara is presently consulting, but please do sit down and take some tea."

Nellie was sitting on the edge of her seat, nervously worrying the clasp of her tooled brown leather handbag, thumbing it open and snapping it shut. Jo led me to a seat which was turned away from Nellie and I nodded in thanks. I didn't want Nellie to recognise me until Floss' client had left. Jo fetched me a cup of tea in a delicate china cup that I recognised as part of our best tea service. Ellen would not be happy about this, I was sure. We sat in silence; the only sound being the regular dull click made by Nellie's handbag as she pressed the clasp shut.

After a few minutes, an excited young woman emerged from a door on the other side of the room. She walked backwards, her gloved hands to her chin, as if trying to stop her head from rotating. "Oh, *thank* you, Madame Varvara, thank you so much. I'm *ever* so grateful. I shall go straight round to the Art School and sign up. Then my da *cannae* do anything about it."

A vision swathed in amethyst taffeta and silk followed the young woman into the room, bracelets rattling as she reached out to touch the girl on the arm. "Excellent decision, my dear. And should you meet the very talented Ann Macbeth, tell her Floss and Jo send their love."

The young woman gasped. "A message from the other side?"

Madame Varvara bowed, mostly to hide her smile, I thought. "Something like that, my dear, yes." I too, lowered my head to hide my smile. Ann was a friend of Floss and Jo, and, like them, a former Suffragette.

The young woman left the flat in a flurry of excited squeals and Floss sat on the chaise next to Nellie. Nellie looked up at her expectantly yet fearfully. Floss grabbed hold of Nellie's hands. "Now, don't be afraid. Mabel here has something she wants to talk to you about. I'm sorry for the subterfuge, but it was the only way we felt we could safely get you here."

I moved over and sat on the floor in front of Nellie. She looked at me, her face confused, as if trying to place where she knew me from. Her eyes opened wide. "Oh! You're the lady that came to the theatre with the polis! Is this about Betty?"

"Well, yes, but it's also about you. I think you're in danger." Her eyes opened even wider, and she shifted on the chaise as if to get up and flee. "You're safe here, I promise you. We just want to keep it that way."

"Why do ye think I'm in danger?"

"You more or less said it yourself that night at the Coliseum. And I think you know something that you're not telling us." She looked down at her hands, still tightly clutching her handbag. "Do you know something? Did you see something? The face of the man who killed Betty?"

She hesitated. "No. I didnae."

"But you know *something*. Please, you have to tell me."

"I cannae. You'll tell them. An' then he'll find me."

"I'll tell who?"

"The polis. An' he'll come after me."

"If you report what you know, then the police will keep you safe. They'll find him." She looked down at me, horrified. I reached up and gripped Nellie's hands so tight that she winced and tried to pull them away. "Tell me. Tell me what you saw."

Nellie started to cry. Floss put an arm around her, and I relaxed my grip a little, a sick feeling in the pit of my stomach. Her voice when she spoke was so soft that I had to lean forward to catch her words. "There wis another man there that night. He wis the one that told Betty that she couldnae get away from him."

"And you saw him?"

She shook her head. "Naw. But I know what he is. Betty tellt me there's this man who's in charge of it all. No one sees him; none o' the lasses, anyway. He keeps his face covered an' hires others to do his dirty work. But Betty heard his voice one day in one o' they pubs at the Tron and knew it wis him."

I stroked her hands gently. "And what did she do?"

Nellie was silent. Then she shrugged and looked at me, her eyes full of bitterness that made me draw back slightly. "Nothin'. She couldnae dae nothin', could she? He wis there with all his polis pals."

"Police? He's a policeman?"

She looked straight at me. "Aye, Miss. He's one o' they polismen who's going to protect me, so you tellt me."

When I turned up at the station for my shift on the Monday, my stomach was still churning. Was this man one of my colleagues, or was he from a different division? Floss had tried to persuade me not to go into work, but I knew I had to. After what had happened, any absence would look like an admission that I couldn't cope with the job. Besides, I had decided that the only thing I could do would be to flush the evil out. I hadn't told Floss that, though. I'd simply told her that if I didn't turn up for work it might look suspicious, particularly as Nellie had been spirited away from under this man's nose.

Nellie had finally agreed that she needed to disappear for a little while. We'd disguised her in Floss' coat and the rather magnificent wig that Floss had been wearing as Madame Varvara, and Jo had taken her through the back court, over a wall and into the basement of Copland and Lye, where a tunnel under Wellington Lane led up into the Haberdashery Department. From there, they could go out onto Bath Street. I left through the front entrance to the close at the same time, and anyone following would have been led a merry dance to shop after shop before a well-earned tea-room stop. Nellie was now ensconced in one of our spare bedrooms, much to the displeasure of Ellen, who looked unfavourably on 'chorus girls'.

A knock on the door of my office announced Constable Ferguson. "Did you go and see Winnie, Miss?"

My noncommittal "Mmmm," surprised him somewhat and he shuffled his feet awkwardly. "Was there something you wanted to see me about, Constable Ferguson?"

"Errrr…no, not really, Miss. Just wanted to see…" His voice trailed away, and I regretted my sharpness. I was almost sure that I could trust him; he was probably slightly too young and, I suspected, too junior in rank to be this man, but I didn't want to risk it. Nor did I want to cause him trouble if he inadvertently let something slip.

"Sorry, Archie. Just a bit out of sorts this morning."

"No problem, Miss. I just came to tell you that Superintendent Orr is wantin' to see everyone."

"Now?"

"Aye, Miss. 'Fraid so."

I let out a sigh. "Oh well, we'd better go then, Archie. We don't want to poke the bear, do we?"

He grinned at me, and I was relieved that he seemed to have forgiven me my sharpness. We walked together to where the whole station was congregated, and I looked around at the sea of faces. One of them might be a murderer; might have murdered my own mother, in fact. Many of them I still didn't know. I let my gaze linger on each of them in turn. Too young, too junior, too prone to being drunk on duty, too lazy. I ruled out the Desk Sergeant and Sergeant McGillivray – the Desk Sergeant was too comfortable and too fat; it took him several minutes to raise himself from his chair and McGillivray, although a nasty, weaselly piece of work who was quite capable of bullying women, didn't seem the type to have carried out something on this scale for so many years.

Superintendent Orr was a possibility, of course. His face as he blustered on at the front of the room about numbers and reports and wasting time became increasingly choleric. He had a temper, that was certain. I looked over to my right, at Detective Inspector Lorrimer, checking his watch, his forehead furrowed. The puckered scar on his neck was white, which I'd come to recognise was a sign that he was under stress. Detective Chief Inspector Pritchard was leaning against the wall, his stance easy and casual, his mouth curled into a bored half smile. He must have felt me watching because he turned his head and nodded slightly, mouthing clearly 'Good to see you back'. I gave no sign that I had seen him and continued scanning the crowd. A couple of the other plainclothes policemen I hadn't had much to do with also caught my eye. One, a burly man in a tight-fitting suit, stood with his arms crossed and a scowl directed firmly at Superintendent Orr. I thought his name was Davies but wasn't sure. The other was Detective Chief Inspector Mackie, a small, wiry man who was perpetually sniffing. Archie had told me he had a reputation for cruelty, particularly when arresting women. Could he be the one? I was suddenly more aware than ever of my status as the only woman present. My discomfort grew when I heard Orr say my name.

"Miss Adair, did you hear me?" I let out a small squeak and Orr laughed nastily. "I see that Miss Adair is too busy thinking of fripperies and furbelows to be troubled by the smooth running of this station." Hoots of laughter from around the room followed. The men's faces were all turned towards me – some of them smirking, some glowering, a couple of them kind – and I could feel my face burning. I held my head up and made tight fists of my hands behind my back. "I was asking, Miss Adair, if your recent fright had made you think twice about a career in the police. Or, at least, convinced you to keep at your desk, doing what you are paid to do, rather than poking your nose in where it's not needed or wanted?"

His sneer and the sniggers from some in the room were exactly what I needed. I took a deep breath and tried to keep my voice calm and level. "On the contrary, Superintendent

Orr. Recent events have made me even more determined in my choice of career. And I shall be poking my nose exactly where I feel it necessary to do so."

Lorrimer caught up with me in the corridor after I stormed out of Superintendent Orr's meeting. "Nellie Mellors is missing."

"She's…"

"I went to speak to her again yesterday evening, as I was worried about her and she's not at her lodgings, nor did she turn up at the Coliseum yesterday." He pushed me gently against the wall as the other policemen streamed out, looking at us curiously as they passed.

Archie hesitated as if he was going to stop, and I briefly shook my head at him. "Perhaps she's moved on, left Glasgow and got another job."

Lorrimer shook his head. "I looked in her room. Her clothes and belongings are all still there. And her landlady said she was excited about going to see a fortune teller of some description but would be back just after lunch."

"A fortune teller?" I tried to keep my voice level.

"Yes. Apparently, this is the third time in just a couple of months. Haven't you been helping Pritchard with some case he's working on involving a fortune teller?"

"Yes…yes, but that was something entirely different. Fraud and deception."

Lorrimer nodded. "That's what Pritchard said." He rubbed absently at the scar on his neck. His eyes were tired, and his face looked more drawn than usual.

"You're worried about her?"

"I am. As you said, she knew more than she was telling us. I'm hoping that she's gone into hiding rather than…well… Look, if you know where she is, tell me."

I drew back. "What makes you think *I* know where Nellie

is?"

Lorrimer raised his hand as if to placate me and looked around. We were still being observed by curious eyes. "I simply wondered if she'd told you of other friends or relatives or places she might have gone."

I shook my head. "I'm afraid I have no idea, Inspector." I must have been better at outright lying than I had thought, as he closed his eyes and rubbed his hand over his forehead. He was clearly concerned about Nellie's whereabouts, but whether it was concern for her welfare or fear of what she might know and tell, I didn't know. "Look, I'm sure she's just tucked away somewhere and will be perfectly fine." In fact, I could almost guarantee that she would be tucking into one of Ellen's fine lunches – if Ellen had overcome her chorus girl aversion, that is.

"I hope you're right, Miss Adair, I hope you're right." He turned and walked off, his limp more noticeable than usual, as if he couldn't be bothered to hide it.

I turned and continued along the corridor to my office, nose in the air as I passed curious eyes, and slammed the door as I went in. With every step I heard outside in the corridor, I fully expected a visit from Superintendent Orr, terminating my employment. However, either he had decided to toy with my nerves a little longer or his concerns over Flossie's connections outweighed his desire to be rid of me. I spent the day taking statements, the usual assortment of women whose faces were etched with a mixture of fear, sadness, rebellion and resilience. I wondered if I should spare Superintendent Orr the trouble and simply hand in my resignation. What was I doing here? What difference could I make?

When I left at the end of the day, it was with a heavy heart. I decided to try and clear my head by walking home to Blythswood Square, rather than catching the tram, despite the coldness of the evening and the beginnings of a yellowish-gray smog that lent everything a sickly sheen under the street-lamps. I picked up my pace and arrived home out of breath and longing for a hot bath, a hearty dinner and an evening of pleasant conversation and laughter, only to be greeted by an almost empty house.

Ellen was the only one to greet me. "They've driven that Nellie off to the seaside for the day, to buck up her spirits and take her mind off things."

"Oh, I see. Will they be back for dinner?"

"No. They said they won't be back until late as they're going to see that new Marion Davis film and have a late supper before driving home." Ellen, might have called her 'that Nellie' but she no longer accompanied the name with a sniff, so I assumed that she had warmed to her somewhat. I was disappointed that I would have to spend the evening on my own, but Ellen lit a cosy fire in the parlour and brought me a tray with a plate of curried pheasant and a warming Atholl brose for dessert.

The alcohol in the dessert made me sleepy and I was tucked up in the armchair in front of the fire, covered with one of Flossie's soft shawls when Ellen came in with a note for me which had just been delivered. *Miss Adair — if you wish to learn something to your advantage concerning your mother, please meet me outside the Lock Hospital at 9pm.* I sat, note in hand, and thought about it for a while. Ellen was unable to give a description of the young woman who had delivered the note, other than she seemed to be of a 'low sort'.

I had read enough mystery stories to know that girls who went out to meet strangers at night never came to a good end, but nine o'clock was not so late and there would still be plenty of people about. Rottenrow wasn't a dark country lane, and I was not some blithe fictional heroine. I may not have been allowed out of the police station on my own, but teenage years spent with Suffragettes and factory patrol during the war had prepared me for any and all eventualities.

I ran upstairs and changed into a stouter pair of boots and rifled through my bedside drawer for the small cosh Floss had given me for my patrols. It was nearly half past eight. I would walk down to Rottenrow. I bundled myself into my thickest coat and pulled on a warm woollen hat that covered my ears.

The smog, which had not seemed too bad in Blythswood Square, seemed to get thicker as I turned into Montrose Street. The top of Rottenrow was lit by the windows of the maternity hospital. A group of nurses stood chatting outside, shivering in their capes. Some enterprising soul had set up a stall selling boiled peas and hot chestnuts just across the road. The scent was delicious, designed to tempt both nurses and expectant fathers over from the hospital.

I carried on down Rottenrow, pausing for a moment outside the building that used to be the Home where my mother and Jeannie had lived. It had closed before the war and I wondered, as always, what had happened to the girls who had lived there. Floss had tried to find out where they were and where the records were kept, but she was told that everything had been burnt when the Home closed. There was no point in keeping them, she'd been told by one of the Trustees. The girls would no doubt turn up again, he'd said, in the Magdalene, or the asylum, or in Duke Street Prison.

I turned up my collar and walked on. The yellowish smog curled about me and I pulled my scarf around my nose to try and keep out the odour of freshly-struck matches that sat heavily in the air. Rottenrow was much quieter here. There was little to attract people. The grocer's shop at the corner of Weaver Street was shut now, as was Townhead Public School, although I could see a light burning in what I took to be the janitor's rooms. There were dim lights in some of the windows of the Lock Hospital too and, again, I thought of my mother and of Jeannie.

A hand clutched my upper arm. Pain spiked through my shoulder. I was propelled painfully into a dark close, my face was pressed up against the cold, damp stone and my arm twisted behind my back. I couldn't see the man behind me, but I could smell the scent of whisky and tobacco as he whispered into my ear. "You shouldn't have interfered, Miss Adair."

I could feel the hairs on my arms and at the nape of my neck bristle. Not only from the feeling of his breath so close to my ear – almost a tickle, although infinitely more unpleasant and full of menace – but also because I recognised his voice. "Pritchard?" My mouth was pressed against the wall and the word came out muffled.

"Well done, little girl. Now, where is Nellie Mellors?"

"I don't know what you mean."

"I think you do. And do you know what told me that?" I shook my head, as much as the wall would allow. "Your seeming indifference when you told Lorrimer that you were sure she would turn up. Even Lorrimer was surprised by it."

"Really, I have no idea where she is."

He rasped out a laugh and pressed me more closely into the wall. "Well, we'll just have to get you somewhere where you feel more...amenable to telling me, won't we?"

A scuffling sound at the back of the close drew his attention and caused him to release his grip on me slightly. I reached into my pocket with my free hand and grabbed hold of the cosh, at the same time twisting around to face him. My ju-jitsu training kicked in and I brought up the hand he was holding and rotated it, thrusting it down to break his grip. He swore as he was knocked off-balance, reaching out to grab hold of my coat. I cracked him on the head with my cosh and ran.

I had no idea where I was going. It was too far to run home. I was near to the police station but didn't want to go there. I was sure Pritchard could spin a tale about me being hysterical and spirit me away.

I ran up Rottenrow, turning into Balmano Street. I didn't dare look behind me. I had no idea how hard I had hit Pritchard, or whether he would still be down. I just had to get away, and there was only one place I could think of going. I risked a glance back at the corner and, in the lights coming from the Lodging House Mission back up Shuttle Street, I could make out a dim figure. I had no idea if it was Pritchard and I carried on running, turning into Candleriggs. I could feel my legs shaking and burning and I was struggling to breathe. I stumbled down the stairs, wrenched open the door and ran straight into Winnie.

"Whit the…?"

Winnie half carried me over to her room and sat me down in one of the chairs, but I struggled to try and stand up. "No! He's coming. We need to…" I didn't know what we needed to do.

"Who's coming?"

"Pritchard." Winnie shook her head, puzzled. "He's the man…" I was still struggling for breath, but I didn't need to say any more. She knew who I meant. "Is there another way out of here?" If I could get back home, I could get a message to the Chief Constable; I could trust *him* to believe me, at least.

"Naw, hen, we're underground."

"Will you lock it?"

Winnie thought for a moment, before answering slowly. "Naw, hen. I don't think that's a good idea. If he *is* efter you, then he'll know there's something wrang. I never close till eleven. Never. An' if I lock it, we'll be trapped." She glanced around. "Here, hide in here, until we can huv a think."

She unlocked the door at the opposite end of the corridor from her office. I'd never seen it open and had assumed it was a store-room. It was. Piles of fluffy towels, bars of soap, cleaning products and several crates marked Drayton Mill Prize Medal Toilet Papers. These latter she started to heave forwards and I helped her, realising what she was doing. Behind the crates, underneath the shelves full of towels, she was creating a small space where I could hide. "In there, hen. Curl up as small as you can." I did so and she pushed the crates back and around so that I was hidden behind a wall of them. Then she piled smaller boxes on top, up to the level of the shelves, topping the pile with an open box of soaps and a couple of towels. "I'll lock the cupboard back up. Are ye' awright back there?"

"Don't lock it!" I didn't think I could bear to be locked in.

She hesitated a moment. "Awright, hen." She went out, shutting the door behind her. The cupboard was pitch black and smelled of Jeyes Fluid and damp. My nose tickled and my eyes watered from the cleaning fluid and I was worried that I might sneeze. I reached up and took a bar of soap out of the open box, unwrapping it and holding it to my nose. The carbolic smell eased the tickle in my nose, although my eyes still stung.

I tensed up when I heard the outside door opening. The sound of it was muffled but still recognisable. "Polly, hen, how ye' doin'?" Winnie's voice was loud, for my benefit, I thought, but I could only hear a light mumble from the other woman. "Ah've got a wee drap stew if ye fancy?"

The other woman must have declined Winnie's offer because soon after the outside door opened and closed once more and the voices stopped. Winnie's footsteps were sure and firm as she came over to the cupboard. "Awright, hen?"

"I'm fine, just fine." I sniffed in the tarry carbolic scent once more.

"I'll jist…" she stopped as the outside door opened once again. "Bridget, hen. How's you? Do ye want a wee drap stew?" Again, I couldn't hear the response. "Naw? That's no' like ye. Well, if ye change yer mind, hen, come back later. Here's a penny fir the cludgie."

As one of the cubicle doors slammed, I heard Winnie humming as she went about her work. After Bridget left, I heard Winnie's tapping steps come over to the door of my hiding place once more. "Ah'm gonnae pop outside, hen. I'll take my pipe and have a wee smoke while I have a good look to see if I can see anyone."

"Thanks, Winnie." Surely he would have been down by now if he'd seen me come in here. He would know I'd go straight to the Chief Constable with this. The pounding in my heart was lessening and I was starting to formulate plans. I would head out to Argyle Street and hail a taxi-cab to take me back home, from where I would phone James Stevenson.

At that moment the outside door banged open, and I heard a scuffling.

"Whit the…?" Winnie's boots clacked on the tiles as she ran from her room, where she must have been filling her pipe. "Whit are ye doin' wi' that lassie? Bridget, hen, are ye alright?"

I could hear the scuffling of boots on tile, a muffled squealing and a couple of growled oaths. "Stop still, girl, or I'll slit your throat." The scuffling and squealing ceased. "Where is she?" Pritchard's voice was low and measured.

"Where's who?"

"Where is she?" It was now a roar and the scuffling started again. He must have been dragging Bridget closer, as his voice when he spoke again was louder. "Where is the little bitch? I know she's in here. I saw her come down. And this little slut…" There was a thudding sound just outside the door, "says she heard you talking when she came in."

"Sor…sorry, Winnie." It was almost too soft to hear.

"Nothin' fir ye to be sorry about, Bridget, hen. See, mister, I dinnae ken who ye are, or whit ye're doin' in here, but if ye've jist come in tae tell me ah cannae talk tae masel'…well…"

"What's behind that door?"

"It's ma supply cupboard."

"Open it."

"Open it yersel'; it's not locked."

"I said, open it."

Winnie gave a theatrical sigh and opened the door of the cupboard. I held my breath, hoping Pritchard couldn't hear the blood that was pumping around my body. I bit down on the bar of soap in my hand to stop from screaming.

"See, towels, soap, cleanin' stuff. An' over there's ma wee hidey hole. Wanna check that out too?" Winnie's voice was combative, but as she spoke, she walked away from the cupboard, drawing Pritchard's attention with her.

"Get these cubicles open."

"It'll cost ye sixpence."

I heard a hard slap, and it was Winnie's turn to curse before Pritchard growled, "Get. These. Cubicles. Open."

Winnie's boots moved away. I could tell she was at the furthest of the cubicles, but I wasn't sure on which side. I could hear her mutter loudly, keeping up an offended monologue as she opened each of the toilets on that side and then showed him into the small cubicle with the washbasin. They moved over to the cubicles on the other side, the left, I could tell now. Pritchard wouldn't be able to see me from there.

At some point he would find me, I knew. I needed to be able to fight when he did. I slid carefully out from behind the boxes. As I emerged, I saw Bridget curled up on the floor. Her face was white, and she was shaking and blank-eyed, but her eyes widened when she saw me.

I quickly raised my finger to my lips and she blinked, nodding imperceptibly. I looked around for a weapon, but there was nothing I could use. I looked down at the bar of soap in my hand and crept out past Bridget, to the corner of the short passageway. Lying on the floor, with my head well out of view, I reached forward and launched the soap around the corner and along the floor as if it was a curling stone.

When it reached the door to the outside, the soap thwacked against the frame and Pritchard swore loudly. I risked a look around the corner. Pritchard's head was turned away, towards the noise. I launched myself after the soap, keeping my body low. I twisted my right leg around Pritchard's, pushing forward with my hip. He unbalanced and fell towards the ground, flailing his arms to stop himself. I used my momentum to push him further into the cubicle and he fell, his head hitting the marble washbasin as he went down.

For a moment, everything was still. All I could hear was the sound of my own fractured breathing and a slow *drip, drip, drip* from one of the taps. The three of us – four, including Pritchard – were silent and still, posed in unnatural positions as if for a great artist. Winnie's eyes were like foglamps, staring at me unblinking. And then Pritchard moaned, stirring slightly, breaking the spell. I turned to Winnie. "Quick, let's get some cloths to tie his hands and feet."

"In the cupboard." She pointed out the pile of cloths to me and I clambered over the boxes to get them. Bridget let out a shriek such as I had never heard. She sounded like a wounded animal. This was followed by a sickening thud and the scraping of metal on tile. We rushed over to the cubicle just as Bridget raised the now empty saucepan once more and brought it down on Pritchard's head with another shriek.

Winnie's stew steamed on the floor, and over Pritchard. As Bridget turned to us, we saw her face and the front of her dress splattered with gravy and gobs of meat. The pan in her hand clanked to the floor as she let it go and started to wail. I grabbed onto her hands and pulled her to me, taking her in my arms and rocking her. "Shhhhh, shhhhh, it's fine; everything will be fine. Shhhhhhh."

Winnie pushed past me and knelt next to Pritchard. Over Bridget's shoulder I watched her, and she glanced up. She held my eye a moment before shaking her head. "He's dead."

We sat in the warmth of Winnie's cosy room, the three of us all curled up in Winnie's big, comfortable armchair, its seams oozing horsehair. Bridget, skinny and shaking, had not spoken since the effort of strength and will it had taken to heave the enormous pot of stew off the stove, into the cubicle and down onto Pritchard's head. We had carried her over to the chair and wrapped her in blankets, trying to stop her teeth chattering. It was only when Winnie climbed onto the arm of the chair on one side, and I did the same on the other, and we pressed ourselves up against her, that the shaking stilled. She now sat, unmoving and unblinking, holding tightly onto our hands. I felt safe here with Winnie like this, and I sensed Bridget did too. Her body was relaxed and the tension drained from her face, leaving a glimmer of the little girl she might once have been. But I knew we couldn't stay like this, no matter how much I wanted it, and I knew the tension would come back into Bridget's face all too soon. I wondered what would happen to her. What would happen to me? A policeman was dead. A powerful, important man, like all the other powerful, important men out there, beyond the warmth and comfort here.

Eventually, Winnie left us to summon a boy to take a message to Floss and get her to contact the Chief Constable. Then she locked the door and we sat, whispering, in the warmth of our huddle. We talked about my mother, and about Jeannie, and about some of the girls Winnie had known. Young women who were there one day and gone the next, each with stories that none of us would ever know. I told Winnie about Floss and Jo and she told me about her daughter and her six grandchildren.

"I'll bet you're a wonderful grandmother, Winnie." I smiled. "I might adopt you as my own, since I didn't know mine."

"Aye, I remember Jeannie tellt me stories your maw had told her. In an asylum, wasn't she? An' your maw grew up with her there?"

I sat up. "Tell me! Tell me some of the stories. Floss tried to find her. She tried all the asylums in and around Glasgow but couldn't find her."

"Glasgow? Oh no, hen. Near Stirling, it was. Some French name. Beautiful something it meant. Jeannie said she and your

239

maw laughed about that, I remember. Mayhap that could help you find your people."

Before I could speak, there was a loud banging on the door. "Mabel? Mabel? Are you in there, my dear?"

I breathed out: Floss was here. Things would never be the same. Not for me, or for Bridget. But, for now, Floss was here, and where there was Floss, there was kindness, comfort and hope. And with Winnie by my side, I'd never been closer to knowing my grandmother, Lillias, and my mother, Clemmie.

"I'm ready to go home, Floss," I whispered.

About the Author

Donna Moore is the author of crime fiction and historical fiction. Her first novel, a Private Eye spoof called Go To Helena Handbasket, won the Lefty Award for most humorous crime fiction novel and her second novel, Old Dogs, was shortlisted for both the Lefty and Last Laugh Awards. Her short stories have been published in various anthologies. In her day job she works as an adult literacy tutor for marginalised and vulnerable women, facilitates creative writing workshops and has a PhD in creative writing around women's history and gender-based violence. She is also co-host of the CrimeFest crime fiction convention and is a fan of film noir, 1970s punk rock and German Expressionist artists. The Unpicking is her third novel.

Acknowledgments and Thanks

The Unpicking started life as the creative element of a creative writing PhD, so huge thanks go to my supervisors Dr Liam Murray Bell at Stirling University and Professor Karen Boyle at the University of Strathclyde for their invaluable support, encouragement and advice throughout the research project, as well as to the examining committee, Dr Susan Berridge and Dr Michael Shaw at the University of Stirling, and Dr Zoë Strachan at the University of Glasgow. I also want to thank Zoë so much for her continuing support, advice and kind words.

Thanks, too, to Anna Forrest, ex-Librarian at The Royal College of Physicians and Surgeons of Glasgow, for introducing me to the horrors of the Glasgow Lock Hospital in a conversation which was the genesis of this book. Thanks go to the staff at the archives and libraries who facilitated the research, particularly the University of Stirling's Archives and Special Collections; the Mitchell Library's Glasgow City Archives; The Royal College of Physicians and Surgeons of Glasgow; and Alastair Dinsmor, Curator of the Glasgow Police Museum.

Sincere thanks and big love to everyone at Glasgow Women's Library, the best place of employment in the world, for their friendship, support and interest. Special thanks go to Wendy Kirk – GWL's lovely librarian – and to the wonderful women who attend Story Café who let me come along and talk to them on numerous occasions about my research and listened as I read from the fiction. They encouraged me, were so engaged and provided feedback and asked questions, making a lonely writing journey nurturing and full of fun.

I owe a huge debt of gratitude to Isabelle Kenyon and Fly on the Wall Press, for taking the novel on, making it better, taking such care over the whole process and for generally being fabulous.

To all those who have supported me, listened to me, commented on/liked social media posts, read the proofs, provided blurbs and reviews…I owe you all a hug.

I couldn't have written this without the support of my partner, Ewan, who provided sympathy when things didn't go well, celebrated with me when they did, and made me innumerable cups of tea. And I am forever grateful to my mum and dad, Joyce and Patrick Moore. They nurtured my love of reading from the earliest age and throughout my life. Without their crucial formative influence, I may never have arrived at the place where I even considered writing this book.

I hope that this book might in some way stand as a monument to the real women throughout history who suffered injustice and cruelty in asylums, lock hospitals and homes for wayward girls, and also to those who trailblazed as police officers. In a broader sense, I hope that the book might also stand as a testament to all women who have experienced, and still do experience, injustice and discrimination within patriarchal systems. They are the inspiration for these stories.

About Fly on the Wall Press

A publisher with a conscience.
Political, Sustainable, Ethical.
Publishing politically-engaged, international fiction, poetry and cross-genre anthologies on pressing issues. Founded in 2018 by founding editor, Isabelle Kenyon.

Some other publications:

Social Media:

@fly_press (Twitter) @flyonthewallpress (Instagram)

@flyonthewallpress (Facebook)

www.flyonthewallpress.co.uk